FIVE BOYS

MICK JACKSON

Five Boys

ff

faber and faber

First published in 2001
by Faber and Faber Limited
3 Queen Square London WC1N 3AU

Typeset by Faber and Faber Ltd
Printed in England by Clays Ltd, St Ives plc

A CIP record for this book
is available from the British Library

ISBN 0–571–20613–1 (pbk)
0–571–21401–0 (cased)

2 4 6 8 10 9 7 5 3 1

PART ONE

The Boys

Lists and String

The children all stood to attention, like an army on parade. The teachers strolled up and down the lines, counting heads and trying to keep order. Occasionally stopped, to check their lists or make some calculation. Then went striding off again.

There had been a lot of list-making lately. Every grown-up seemed to be scrawling notes on the backs of envelopes. Bobby's mother was a tireless list-maker, but all her shopping lists and things-to-do lists paled into insignificance beside the one Bobby brought home from school the Friday before.

She read it out at the table that evening:

Besides clothes/coat for journey
  1 vest
  1 shirt with collar
  1 pair pants
  1 pullover or jersey
  1 pair knickers
  handkerchiefs
  two pairs socks or stockings
  Also . . .
night attire, comb, plimsolls, towel, soap, face cloth,
toothbrush, boots or shoes.
(Blankets need not be taken.)

Then Bobby and his parents sat and ate in silence as if they'd just heard a reading from the Gospels or a speech by the King.

On the Saturday morning Bobby watched his mother pack his suitcase. She must have checked every item against that

3

list a dozen times. Then she closed the catches, strapped a belt around it and gave it to Bobby to heave downstairs, where it sat by the front door, brooding, for the rest of the weekend.

When he left on the Monday morning his mother gave him a brown-paper package and as he stood in the playground Bobby couldn't help thinking that all the bags and suitcases were more important than the children – that they were just there to lug the things around. A couple of boys next to Bobby were getting quite excited and had to be quietened down, but after twenty minutes boredom, with its own volatility, began to seep through the lines until Mr Morely finally peeped on his whistle and the teachers prepared to move them out.

The children were led off row by row, like knitting unravelling – a great chain of children rattling through the gates, out onto the pavements and picking up speed as they went along. They marched past the park and up the high street; marched by the open market and the old Town Hall. Neighbours waved. Shopkeepers stood and watched from their doorways. And when Mr Morely strode out into the road and raised his rolled-up brolly the traffic slowed to a halt, as if now that the children were finally moving, there was no easy way of stopping them.

Mr Morely led them up and down the streets in one long conga, but eventually turned into the yard of a bus depot, where the children were shuffled into rows again. The ground was black and tacky underfoot from engine oil, and across the yard five coaches waited with their doors open, as if ready to race away. But by the time there had been another round of head-counting and list-checking, and instructions had been issued, regarding running and pushing and the making of noise, any pleasure to be had from boarding a coach was lost.

Bobby managed to get a seat by a window. Miss Peebles trotted up the steps and counted everyone's heads again.

Then the driver climbed aboard, sank into his seat and fired up the engine, which turned the stomach of every girl and boy.

It seemed to take all day to cross the city. Most of the children just stared out of the window. Some talked; some quarrelled. One or two eventually fell asleep. But the boy next to Bobby seemed to fret right through the journey, and when they finally pulled up he burst into tears. Miss Peebles came down, to see what was the matter. Apparently he'd convinced himself he was going to be put on an aeroplane and flown halfway round the world, and it took Miss Peebles quite a while to convince him that they were actually parked outside a railway station and that nobody was going to be flying anywhere.

The children were led off into the station and lined up on one of the platforms, where they stood and watched the trains shunt in and out under the great wide roof. After twenty minutes some women in armbands came round, with trays of buns and mugs of tea. Then the children were led back onto the coaches and driven home again.

On the Tuesday Bobby had a much better idea what the day ahead had in store and worked out that by keeping his eyes on the heels of the boy in front could keep in step with him. The drive across the city was hot but uneventful, the bun on the station platform was much the same as the one before and when he got back home he couldn't tell whether his mother was genuinely surprised to see him or was in on the whole charade.

On the Wednesday it occurred to Bobby that the rest of his school years might consist of nothing but endless rehearsals for evacuation – year upon year of marching through the streets (which would be good practice for being, say, a postman) and sitting on coaches (which would be no use at all). But as they left the playground on that third day he spotted his mother and some other women on the other side of the road and as the children marched along behind Mr Morely's

brolly the women crept from lamp-post to lamp-post, as if
they were spying on them, or had been warned not to get too
close. Bobby tried to keep his eyes on the boy in front but
couldn't help glancing over at his mother. She didn't wave –
as if it was just a coincidence that she and Bobby were marching along the same streets – but when they reached the depot
and were herded onto the coaches, all the mothers suddenly
rushed across the yard.

The engines started up. The mothers knocked on the windows and passed little keepsakes through to their children –
sweets, handkerchiefs, anything. Bobby's mum reached up
and pressed a penny into his hand. He was going to put it in
his pocket, but she wouldn't let go. It wasn't until he was
tucked up on a stranger's sofa later that day that Bobby
realised that the penny wasn't important. What was important was her holding his hand. And when she finally let go
she just stood there crying. Crying like Bobby had never seen
her cry before.

There were no buns or mugs of tea at Paddington Station.
They were all ushered straight onto the train, and in the
crush Bobby ended up in a carriage with a group of unfamiliar children, all except for a girl who lived next door to his
auntie. The boys were big and stood on the seats to put their
cases on the luggage racks. Bobby doubted that he was
strong enough to lift his case above his head, so he just sat
with it tucked behind his legs and his brown-paper package
in his lap and was wondering whether he should try and find
a teacher to explain that he was in the wrong part of the train
when the whole carriage suddenly lurched forward, which
produced the same sickening jolt in Bobby's stomach as the
coach's engine starting up on the Monday but about a hundred times as strong.

The train tugged and struggled into motion, as if the roots
and moorings of every child on board were being ripped
away. The station cast itself off, with all its buns and mugs of
tea untouched. The city withdrew. And in that instant Bobby

understood that this was the end of all the rehearsals and that no moment ever comes around again.

Over the years there had been a whole series of evacuations. Bobby could remember children disappearing in September '39, only to turn up again a month or two later, after the bombs had failed to materialise. His mother had always been against him going – was convinced that if she sent him away she would never see him again – and he'd stayed right through the Blitz before her will was finally broken when three generations of the same family were killed in a house just down the road.

Half an hour after they left Paddington Station Miss Peebles popped her head into the carriage and asked Bobby if he'd like her to put his suitcase up on the luggage rack. He declined – liked the feeling of it tucked behind his legs – and when she offered to put his parcel up there he said that it had things in it which he'd be needing along the way.

'Is it your sandwiches?' she said, which seemed like such a good idea that Bobby agreed with her.

String seemed to be holding Bobby together. It tied his name tag to the buttonhole on his jacket, quartered the brown-paper package in his lap and cut into his shoulder, with his gas mask at the other end. He tugged at the knot in the string around the package until it was hot and squeaked in the creases of his fingers. The countryside hammered away beyond the window. Every sort of tree and field blew by. Bobby had had no idea that England had so many miles in it – would have expected to have gone hurtling into the sea by now – and despite that tight little knot, the yards kept on unwinding until all the string in the world wouldn't reach back home.

When Miss Peebles dropped in a little later to check that the children had something to eat Bobby was just as baffled as she was to find that the only thing in his parcel was a newly knitted jumper with a note pinned to it, saying, *With lots of love, Auntie May.*

7

Miss Peebles gave Bobby one of her own cheese-and-onion sandwiches and twenty minutes later he found he was having trouble staying awake. For a while he swung in and out of consciousness, then slumped into a deeper sleep, and when he next came round Miss Peebles' sandwich was burning deep in his stomach and there was lots of cheering and stamping of feet. The other children were all crammed around the window and pointing at the sea, but the water was as flat as a millpond so Bobby closed his eyes and went back to sleep.

The vast banks of begonias and peonies at Totnes station might well have gladdened the heart of Bobby's mum or any one of his aunties, but seemed so shockingly foreign that as far as Bobby was concerned he might as well have been disembarking in the foothills of Kilimanjaro or the depths of Timbuktu.

Another gang of women with armbands moved in on the children, clucking and fanning their hands by their sides. All the drills and regimentation appeared to have been abandoned and Bobby found himself herded in a crowd, until he came alongside a coach with great creamy mudguards which rolled back onto running boards. Some old lady helped him up the steep steps. He took a seat but the upholstery scratched at his bare legs, and when the bus was full a large woman popped up, glanced round at all the passengers, waved, then disappeared.

Ten minutes later the coach was hauling itself up a hillside and Bobby could see the railway station down below, as well as a church, a castle and a river glistening not far behind. Halfway up the hill they turned onto a narrow lane where the hedges scraped and squealed along the windows and whipped in through any not properly closed and they were so tall that it was only in that last moment before the coach went plummeting down another incline that Bobby managed to glimpse the countryside through which they passed. He thought the whole place looked badly rumpled, as if a boy could easily fall into one of its folds or crevices and never be heard of again.

They didn't come across a single other vehicle, but their progress was just as laborious as their journeys across London and when the coach finally pulled up it was almost dark. They were ushered into a village hall with a tin roof. There were trestle tables against one wall with meat pies and half-pint bottles of milk lined up on them. Bobby found a quiet spot, sat on his suitcase and used his gas-mask box as a table and was eating his pie when he noticed some grown-ups standing by the door. They weren't wearing armbands, seemed to be watching the children and doing a great deal of whispering, and Bobby thought perhaps the way he and his fellow-evacuees were eating their pies was coming in for some criticism, so he sat up straight, tried to catch any crumbs, and when he had finished walked to the door in what he hoped would be considered a dignified way.

He went round the side of the hut and peed into a patch of long grass. The steam enveloped him and he stared up at the sky. The stars were as sharp as stones and there seemed to be no end of them. The air seemed to find its way deeper into him. He was tucking himself back into his shorts when he thought he heard something peculiar and crossed the road to find a shallow river. And he stood beside it for a while, watching it travelling blackly beneath the trees, and dipped the tip of his shoe into it.

When he crept back into the hall the atmosphere had defi-nitely changed. The grown-ups who had been watching from the sidelines were chatting to some of the children – were helping them on with their jackets and bonnets. Were picking up their cases and heading for the door. An hour later Bobby and two girls were the only children left in the place. The younger girl was crying. An old man had offered to take her sister but hadn't wanted her along. Bobby was tired and wishing that the little girl would stop crying when Miss

Peebles came over and said that a kind lady had volunteered to take all three of them in her motor car and find a house for them in one of the villages further on.

She crouched down in front of Bobby, who was tugging at the knot on his parcel.

'Are you going to be a brave boy?' she said.

Bobby looked at the toe of his shoe, still damp from the river, and tried to give the question the sort of consideration Miss Peebles seemed to feel it deserved. But in truth he hadn't the faintest idea how brave he was going to be.

Treacle

Just about the last person Miss Minter expected to find standing on her doorstep was Mrs Willcox. Mrs Willcox in her tweeds and brogues and her Robin Hood hat with a feather sticking out of it, smiling for all she was worth.

She lived several miles away and on the few occasions the two of them had met had never been particularly friendly, so Miss Minter had good reason to wonder what she was doing smiling on her doorstep so late at night, wearing an armband which, in Miss Minter's mind, signified death and grief and funerals and therefore nothing to smile about at all.

The county had been *inundated*, Mrs Willcox was telling her . . . *simply inundated*, without even bothering to say hello, and asking if we had the right to deny a London child a breath of *decent country air*. She was making no sense and showed no sign of abating. It was a little performance all of its own and Miss Minter soon found her attention slipping and began to stare at Mrs Willcox's cape and wonder how she managed to get in it and was thinking what a staggering pair of hips the woman had, when a young child's head peeped out from behind them and stared right back at her.

'. . . and so we were *wondering* . . . ,' Mrs Willcox was saying. 'That is to say, we were *hoping* . . .' She took a breath and rolled her eyes.' . . . if you might, possibly, *save our skins* . . .'

Miss Minter looked up at the face beneath the Robin Hood hat, then back down at the boy.

'Just until we sort ourselves out,' said Mrs Willcox, smiling.

'A boy?' Miss Minter said.

Then Mrs Willcox started talking again – seemed to think that as long as she kept talking and smiling, every obstacle would fall away – and even as Miss Minter watched, slipped her hand down the boy's back and (still talking, still smiling) pushed him forward until he was forced to take a step.

Being asked to look after a boy was, for Lillian Minter, akin to being asked to juggle handkerchiefs or swallow swords. It simply wasn't in her repertoire. She watched the feather on Mrs Willcox's hat bounce down the path and bob along beyond the hedgerow and was still standing in her doorway when the motor car roared away. She turned and looked at the boy beside her. He seemed to have a great many bags and parcels attached to him and Miss Minter thought that if she removed some of them she might have more idea what sort of boy she was dealing with.

She prised Bobby's hot little hand off his suitcase handle and led the way down the hall. The case was small but surprisingly heavy and as she headed towards the parlour she wondered what on earth it might contain.

Boys' things, she told herself.

She sat the boy down on the settee by the fire and had a good look at him. His coat was buttoned right up to his throat.

'It must be windy in Mrs Willcox's motor,' she said, which seemed to Bobby to be more of a statement than a question, so he carried on looking round the room.

They sat side by side for a while in silence. Then Miss Minter turned to him and said, 'Does your daddy let you look at the newspapers?'

Bobby nodded.

Miss Minter leant over the end of the sofa, picked up a couple of old *Daily Sketches* and dropped them in his lap. Bobby looked at the newspapers as if he might have to memorise them.

'Do you like treacle toffee?' the old woman asked him.

Bobby nodded again.

That night he slept on the settee, under an eiderdown which smelt powerfully of mothballs, and rested his head on a pillow which was about as accommodating as a sack of cement. He lay on his side, with his hands tucked between his legs; kept wriggling to try and make himself comfortable, until he felt the settee's cushions begin to shift and spread beneath him and decided that he had better lie still or risk being swallowed up.

He was surprised not to have been told to brush his teeth, and when he clamped them together they still took some getting apart. He thought about the paper bag Miss Minter had offered him and the oily slabs of toffee inside. Of slipping a finger between a couple of pieces which were welded together and trying to wrench one free.

He dozed off for a few seconds, then forced his eyes open. Found that he was indeed in the parlour of a strange old lady, many miles from home. He thought about the train and the coaches. Thought about his mother not wanting to let go of his hand. He stared at the fire, to try and calm himself down. Concentrated on it – and found that it had caves, like the bag of treacle toffee, but caves that were alive and red-hot at the core.

Miss Minter had always been a light sleeper, so when she surfaced briefly around four the following morning, to plump her pillow and turn to face the wall, her dreams parted just long enough for her to recall Mrs Willcox smiling on her doorstep and the boy on the settee down below.

She stared into the dark and began to wonder. Wondered what young boys were fed on . . . how much sleep they needed . . . how to keep them occupied. If she could only stop him from starving or drowning or catching pneumonia, until someone with the proper qualifications came along, she told herself, then she would have more than done her duty and could set about trying to forget the whole sorry affair.

The only boys she had any experience of were the ones in the village, who seemed to divide their time between a sort of sleepwalking stupor and a primitive savagery, with not much in between. But even these village boys were a mystery to her. There was no telling what went on inside them and the only thing Miss Minter's encounters had taught her was to give them plenty of room, like young cattle, in case they started kicking and bucking about.

She stared at the ceiling until daylight dragged the room from its shadows, racking her brains for tips to do with boys. She must have heard *some*thing over the years, she thought, but the only thing she could come up with was the supposed benefit of getting children out of doors. It was an idea which made more sense every time she returned to it, especially a boy from London whose lungs were apparently full of soot. A lack of any other ideas did nothing but lend extra conviction to this one and though, in truth, Miss Minter could see no particular virtue in being exposed to the elements when there was a fire in the grate, she began to see the wisdom in getting a child away from the house, so that any harm which befell them might be blamed on somebody else.

As she dressed she told herself that no matter how ill-conceived her attempts at child-minding, it was essential they be carried out with unwavering authority. So, even as Bobby ate his bread and jam Lillian was fetching his jacket from the coatstand, and before he'd finished rinsing it down with a cup of tea she was feeding his arms into his jacket's sleeves. He was barely awake when he found himself being ushered out through the same doorway Mrs Willcox had been so eager to usher him through the night before. He put the brakes on long enough to ask Miss Minter what time he was expected back. Miss Minter assumed an expression of unflappable self-assurance.

'You'll need to be home before it gets dark,' she said.

Bobby looked up at the sky, which had not a trace of darkness in it. The hours of daylight seemed to stretch right over the hills. He wondered if the days down here were somehow shorter and turned to put this to the old lady, but she was already shutting the door in his face.

Dreams of Heavy Women

Bobby stood by the gate, bewildered, whilst Miss Minter watched from an upstairs window and quietly willed him on his way. Left and right both seemed to go nowhere. There was nothing to aim towards, but after some deliberation Bobby buttoned his coat, turned to his left and followed the lane down to a bridge, then on to a crossroads, and went straight on up the hill.

The night had swept away all the motor cars and coaches. Bobby had never had so much space to himself. It was a disconcerting feeling, and as he tramped up the lane the hedgerows towered around him and he entered a steep green corridor of stillness, with a ceiling of blue sky high overhead. He hiked up that lane for what felt like half an hour, with nothing but his own anxious thoughts bearing down on him, then the hedgerows finally fell away and he passed the gates to a farm, then a couple of cottages and a Post Office and more cottages, each with its own orderly garden and smoke pumping out of its chimney pot.

The whole village appeared to consist of nothing but the three lanes which met at the war memorial, where Bobby stopped and read the inscription to see if there were any dead soldiers with the same surname as his. There weren't, so he crossed the road and had a look at the big old church and the gravestones scattered around it and was studying the church noticeboard when a loud tapping sound suddenly started up.

He turned around, but the village was deserted. Not just devoid of people, but spick and span – as if someone had just been through it with a dustpan and brush. There was no natural place from which the sound could have originated and

Bobby was beginning to think he must be losing his mind when the tap-tap-tapping started up again and he spotted a figure at the window of a cottage who, seeing how his tapping had finally got Bobby's attention, began to frantically wave at him instead. Bobby glanced over his shoulder – thought the figure in the window must be waving at someone else – but the lane behind him was just as empty as the one in front and the more baffled he became, the more tapping and waving he seemed to provoke.

Bobby finally grasped that it was *he* who was being beckoned and slowly made his way over. The window panes were thick and flawed and the closer Bobby got the more the fellow behind them looked like some swimmer trapped under the ice. He was an old chap, in a threadbare jerkin, and when Bobby was near enough to make him out the fellow stopped flapping his arms and pressed a coin up against the glass. He opened his mouth but the words which came out of him were so deadened and distant that they made no sense at all.

A bout of indigestion was brewing up in Bobby to rival the one brought on by Miss Peebles' cheese-and-onion sandwich and didn't improve when the old man put his thin lips right up to the glass and proceeded to move them in a slow and deliberate manner, like a lunatic at the bars of his cell. Plenty of pointing and face-pulling followed but Bobby managed to stay put long enough to realise that the old man was actually directing him around the side of the house.

There was an old wooden porch in which Bobby stood, like a sentry, and after a while the door opened far enough for a head to pop out and look him up and down.

'Got your wits about you?' said the head. 'Eyes and ears, eh?'

Bobby was disheartened to find that even when the words were perfectly audible they were just as meaningless as the ones which came through the glass, but there was such expectation in the old man's eyes it was clear that all he was after was confirmation, which Bobby duly offered, then a hand crept out towards him, turned and opened, to reveal a couple of coppers in its palm.

'Get some cakes from old Marjory,' said the old man, 'and see what's stretching.'

The old man smiled, which cheered Bobby – he was pleased that the old man's thin lips were capable of such a thing – although he was no closer to understanding what was being asked of him.

His mystification must have been apparent for the old man suddenly became exasperated.

'The *shop*, boy,' he said. Then, 'The *Post* Office,' and nodded down the lane.

Bobby felt that he was now at least in comprehension's neighbourhood, even if he didn't have the exact address, and took the coins.

'Whatever you fancy,' said the old man. 'But no scones. And no Eccles cakes,' as if he had just recognised in Bobby the tendency to dabble in such things.

The hand retreated into the shadows, the head followed and Bobby was about to set off in search of Marjory and her cakes when the head sprang back out.

'Remember,' the old man said and narrowed his eyes. 'You're a mole.'

He looked left and right, then settled on Bobby.

'There'll be questions,' he said, then disappeared.

Within five minutes Bobby was back with his bag of cakes, knocking at the door and bracing himself for the old man's head to pop out at him like a jack-in-the-box. But from deep inside the cottage a voice called out, 'It's open,' so Bobby held down the latch, heaved against the door and eventually landed in a large, low-ceilinged room, dimly lit, with the old man in an armchair by the window, hunched over a cluttered tray.

'Nearly there,' said the old man without looking up.

All the walls were lined with bottled butterflies. The old man was nipping and tweaking at something with a pair of tweezers and had a quilted sleeping bag pulled right up to his armpits which made him look as if he was emerging from his own, rather tattered cocoon. As he waited, Bobby had a closer look at one of the bottles. A tiny ship sat in a ruffled pool of turquoise plaster. Its sails billowed stiffly and its rigging of threads was as taut as an egg-slice. A handwritten label beneath read, 'The *Bentinck*, passing Aden, 1844'. And as Bobby watched, all the other butterflies transformed themselves into miniature ships.

'So,' said the old man, setting his tray down on a table, 'what have we got for our elevenses?'

He nodded at a footstool by the window and as Bobby went over and settled himself on it his host picked the cakes out of their paper bag and explained how sultanas and raisins tended to get under his dentures and not want to come back out.

'An inconvenience I hope you'll be spared,' he said and took the iced bun, leaving the Bakewell tart for Bobby. Then the old man sat back in his armchair and slipped his free hand down into the sleeping bag where, Bobby imagined, it would be nice and warm.

'So what was Marjory up to?' said the old man.

Bobby thought for a moment. 'Nothing,' he said. 'Just getting the cakes.'

The old man winced, as if he had woefully overestimated Bobby's abilities. The iced bun hung in the air and he stared down at the rug, as if setting an example in the kind of concentration he had thought Bobby capable of.

'Anything else?' he said.

Bobby was gravely aware that he had somehow forfeited one precious chance and might not be granted many more, so he paused and thought hard about the big fat lady in her tiny little shop.

'I think,' he ventured, 'she might have been sucking on a sweet.'

The old man's face lit up. He nodded. 'That wouldn't surprise me,' he said, then chuckled, and his hand shifted in his sleeping bag. 'She's always at them jars of sweets.'

Bobby wondered briefly whether the old man's interest in the lady at the Post Office wasn't simply the appreciation of one person with a fondness for jars and bottles for another.

'And what do you reckon she was sucking on?' the old man asked. 'Did you happen to catch a whiff?'

'I'm not sure,' said Bobby and saw all the hard-won warmth drain from the old man's face. So he thought back to the woman tucking the sweet into a cheek as she leaned over the counter and asked Bobby if the old goat up the road had got him running his errands for him. 'But it might have been cinder toffee,' he said.

The old man gazed out of the window and nodded.

'Could be,' he said. 'She likes her cinder, does Marjory.'

The old man's thoughtful little interlude gave Bobby the opportunity to take a bite of his cake. He had never had Bakewell tart before and was surprised (but not entirely disappointed) to find that it tasted quite like the treacle toffee he had had for his supper the night before.

'What did you make of her?' the old man said.

Bobby continued to chew with great deliberation, as if giving the question some thought.

' . . . generally speaking,' the old man said.

By the time Bobby finally got round to swallowing he still had no idea what reaction his answer was going to get.

'I thought she was quite large,' he said and looked meaningfully out of the window, just as the old man had done a minute before.

The ship-builder beamed, recognising a fellow after his own heart. He let out a deep sigh, accompanied by further activity in his sleeping bag.

He nodded. 'She's a fair size, is she not?' he said.

Bobby was again struck by how differently things were done down here: the days were shorter, the meals were sweeter, and speaking frankly about people's size was quite acceptable. A year or two earlier he had made some quite innocent comment about a fat lady in the queue at the butcher's and got a terrible telling-off from his mother on the way home – a recollection which stirred such strong emotions in him and brought such a significant lump to his throat that his mouthful of Bakewell tart couldn't find a way past it and he began choking, which broke in on the old man's reverie and had him worrying he might have to turn the boy upside-down.

Thankfully, this proved not to be necessary and when at last the food was heading in the right direction Bobby wiped the tears from his face.

'Went down the wrong lung, that bit, didn't it?' said the old man, but the boy kept staring at the floor.

'Yes,' the old man said to himself. 'She's a fair old size, is Marjory Pye,' then looked over at his tray of tiny tools and slivers of wood and balls of thread and for a while talked abstractly about the perils of drilling a jib boom when you've got icing all over your fingertips.

Bobby had just about recovered himself when the old man suddenly turned to him.

'I don't believe you've been introduced to the Captain, have you?' he said.

Bobby wasn't sure he was up to any more introductions. He wanted to be back home, tucked up in his bed. And it was only when the old man got to his feet and held out the hand not holding up his sleeping bag that Bobby realised how the Captain and the old man with whom he was having his elevenses might be one and the same.

Miss Minter was finding that, contrary to popular wisdom, Bobby's being out of sight in no way constituted him being out of mind and the moment he disappeared down the lane she began to worry what she was going to do with him when he returned.

Considering how long it took her to come up with the idea

of giving him breakfast and getting him out of the house, the idea of bathing him came to her with comparable ease. Certainly, it came a good deal easier than the effort necessary to generate enough hot water to fill her old tin bath. The fire in the range needed stoking, then constant attention, and there were countless trips between the boiler and the pump out in the yard, as well as dragging the bath in from the out-house in order to bring it up to room temperature and avoid it instantly chilling any hot water introduced to it.

She began heating the water soon after lunchtime, convinced that Bobby would come skipping up the path at any moment, covered from head to toe in mud. Meanwhile, Bobby, mindful of her instructions regarding his return was, in all his mindfulness, having difficulty recalling whether it was meant to precede, coincide with or follow the onset of darkness. So, having had his elevenses at the Captain's and investigated the last few corners of the village soon afterwards, he climbed through a hedge halfway down the leafy lane and spent most of the afternoon throwing stones into a field.

He must have lain down and closed his eyes at some point for he dreamt of old Mr Evans (which was odd as he hadn't seen Mr Evans in years). Then he climbed a tree and kept an eye on the sun until it began to sink between the hills, and went down the lane after it.

Bobby had no trouble finding the old woman's cottage. He just followed the thick column of smoke pouring from its chimney, but it wasn't until he entered the house that he appreciated what was producing it. As soon as he opened the parlour door the heat hit him with all the force of a cricket bat and a great cloud of steam billowed out into the hall. The windows dripped with condensation. The sills were dappled with small, mercurial pools. There was so much steam that all the linen on the clothes rack, which had been bone-dry that morning, looked as if it had just been dragged out of the wash. Bobby could just make out Miss Minter, bent over the range like a fireman on the footplate of a locomotive. She looked over her shoulder, but her spectacles were so fogged up she had to tip her head forward and peer over them.

'Here he *is*,' she said, without a hint of reproach. 'I've been keeping the water hot.'

She dragged a damp tangle of hair back from her forehead and hooked it behind an ear. Stepped forward and took Bobby's hands in hers.

'Good God,' she said. 'You're freezing.'

On the contrary, Bobby thought the old lady was roasting. Miss Minter, meanwhile, was noticing how little mud Bobby had on him, but taking solace from the fact that the bath would at least heat him up.

She picked up the poker and struck the tap on the boiler. A plume of steam flew out with the jet of boiling water and Miss Minter had to wave a hand through it to make sure the water was landing in the bath. Then she stood aside as the range gushed and spluttered, like some geyser running its course, added a dash of salts from a green glass beaker and several jugs of cold water and invited Bobby to climb in.

When he was undressed and in the bath, Lillian Minter pulled up a stool and they sat silently beside one another, as if Bobby was in the sidecar of her motorbike and they were enjoying a country run. Miss Minter was tempted to ask what he had been up to, but knew that whatever he said would only give her more to worry about. Besides, the parlour was calm for the first time in hours.

'Is that nice?' she said.

Bobby nodded. The way the water cradled him, the smell of the soap, the roaring fire – all were recognisably nice. As he pulled his shoulders down under the milky water the strange Captain and his homemade ships came back to him and Bobby wondered if the old man was ever tempted to try them out before bottling them.

'Does your mummy soap your back for you?' Miss Minter asked him.

At first she thought he must not have heard her. He was so still she thought he must have drifted off. But when she looked again she saw a tear creep down his cheek – watched it drop into the bathwater and send a series of ripples sweeping back and forth across its surface.

She couldn't believe her lack of sensitivity – was sickened by it – and had to leave the room under the pretext of fetching a towel from upstairs. She opened the cupboard and buried her head in the linen. Cursed herself over and over for making the poor boy cry. But when she went back downstairs she offered no apology and made no reference to Bobby's tears, thinking that it would only embarrass him on top of everything else.

She let him soak for another few minutes, then wrapped a towel round him and dabbed him dry. Got him into his pyjamas and dressing gown and led him round the back of the settee where she spread an old newspaper out on the floor. Then she left the room and returned with a large jar of dried soup mix.

She gave the jar a shake. 'Now,' she said, 'all these peas and beans have managed to get themselves mixed up.' She made an effort to look highly vexed. 'Do you think you might sort them out for me while I have the bath?'

She unscrewed the lid and poured the jar's contents out onto the newspaper. Bobby looked at the mountain of dried beans and pulses – saw a whole evening's work ahead of him – but he knelt down beside it and told Miss Minter that he would see what he could do.

Five Boys

Considering all the trouble he took over their tiny reproduction the Captain seemed to get no end of pleasure from telling Bobby how the real ships came to be wrecked. During those first few days of his evacuation Bobby thought he must have heard about every cutter, smack, ketch and man-of-war which had had the misfortune of coming up against Devon's unforgiving coast, and when the Captain wasn't quizzing him on what sort of shape Marjory Pye was in or what sort of sweets she was eating, the old man seemed to like nothing better than to wriggle right down in his sleeping bag and talk romantically about all the wrecks littering the seabed, fathoms deep.

Devon seemed to draw them in just like a magnet, cracking them open on Prawle Point or Bolt Head and easing them back beneath the waves. But if they ever ran aground, the Captain said, the locals would race out and help their crew to safety, whatever the weather, before helping themselves to whatever was down below.

A barge packed with plum saplings was once beached not far from Dartmouth and every last twig was spirited away before the gentlemen of His Majesty's Customs and Excise had laced their boots. The Captain got to his feet and waddled over to the window. Come spring, he said, all the villages would be awash with their blossom – as if the sea had drummed up a wave of such might that its spume and spray had come crashing all this way inland.

On the day of Sylvia Crouch's wedding, he told Bobby, the plum blossom had been so thick on the ground that half the village went out and filled their baskets and the bride and groom stepped out of the church into a blizzard of the stuff.

'You know how many weddings there were that spring?' said the Captain.

Bobby shook his head.

'Five,' said the Captain and raised the fingers of one hand.

'And you know what newly-weds are like,' he said.

Bobby wasn't sure that he did.

'They have a habit of becoming mothers-to-be,' the Captain said.

He turned and stared out of the window, and it occurred to Bobby that perhaps the old man never left his cottage and that the rest of the world only existed through the buckle and sway of the glass.

The autumn after the weddings, the Captain said, the whole village seemed to be pregnant. Nothing but pregnant women bumbling about the place.

'Such stomachs,' he whispered. 'Such lovely, womanly weight.'

He'd watched them traipse down to the shop and stretch their backs at the war memorial. But one week they all disappeared. The streets were empty – they must have been indoors with their feet up – until the district nurse came cycling down the hill. She went hurrying from one cottage to another. The woman was nothing but a blur of gaberdine. Then the village was quiet again, until the young mothers finally crept out into the sharp light of February with their big black prams, to show their boys off. Just five minutes at first, but taking more time as the days grew milder. Then whole hours spent hanging round the war memorial, chatting and generally blocking up the roads.

'Which is where the Five Boys come from,' said the Captain.

He turned to Bobby. 'Have you come up against them yet?'

Bobby shook his head.

The Captain nodded and turned back to the window. 'Well, I don't doubt you will,' he said.

The faces on the Five Boys chocolate bar wrapper just about managed to encompass a child's entire emotional range, from the pitiful child at the beginning to his gleeful counterpart at the other end. All one had to do, the wrapper seemed to suggest, in order to bring about such a happy transition was give in to your boy's demands. But if the villagers first used the phrase because their own five boys were born within weeks of each other and, from the day they first toddled, toddled together (making it nigh on impossible for anyone but their own parents to tell them apart), the name stuck because the boys never lost their capacity to exhibit almost any emotion at the drop of a hat.

In time, they began to develop their own characteristics. Aldred and Lewis were never going to be as big or broad as Finn or Hector; Harvey would always walk around in a bit of a dream. But they had their own collective spirit. And whilst most of the villagers regarded them as a harmless, if occasionally hot-headed, little tribe, others felt sure they detected a certain menace whenever they were in each other's company.

Mrs Heaney once came across them huddled at the roadside. As soon as they saw her they all jumped to their feet.

'What are you up to, you Boys?' she said.

But the Boys didn't answer. They just stood and stared, until she finally left them to it and walked off, wondering what poor creature they were torturing or what sort of black magic they were attempting to conjure up.

News of the arrival of an evacuee didn't reach the Five Boys until Friday evening, but first thing Saturday they were all lined up on the bridge just down the road from Miss Minter's, hoping to catch a glimpse. Finn thought they should just walk up to the old lady's house, knock on the door and ask to have a look at him, the others wanted to do some sneaking about and the matter was still under discussion when Lewis spotted Miss Minter coming down the lane towards them and they all hid behind a hedge.

As soon as she'd passed, the Boys raced over to her cottage. They peered in through every window. Either the evacuee had slipped away straight after breakfast or was hiding under a bed upstairs, and he'd left nothing lying about to give the Boys any idea what an evacuee might actually look like in the flesh.

Given their knowledge of the local terrain and the thoroughness with which they covered it the Boys expected to flush him out during those first few days, and would have done so, no doubt, if the Captain hadn't been telling Bobby to keep his head down whenever they walked by the window, which in the end only made the Boys more determined to make the most of Bobby when they finally got hold of him.

The education of the local children was as slow and steady as if they were roasting on a spit. On their first day they were installed in the front row, under the very nose of Mrs Fog and every autumn graduated to the row behind, it being the governors' one decree that they be exposed to plenty of reading, writing and arithmetic before being flung out into the fields.

The children grew as they receded. The boys' voices dropped, the girls' bosoms swelled. So when they cleaned their slates at the end of the day and held them up for Mrs Fog's approval they formed a gently sloping roof, which she was sometimes inclined to see as the shelter their education provided them but, just as often, as an indication of how little knowledge they'd retained.

As far as the children were concerned, the years between that moment when they first entered the classroom and the moment when they finally lifted the latch on their liberty was too vast a span of time to contemplate. Their only aspirations were for a desk close enough to the stove to stretch their feet out at it or close enough to a window to seek distraction there. To Mrs Fog, however, their slow retreat was as inexorable as if they moved on driven belts, and as time passed she couldn't help but feel that the belts were turning faster and that some of the gentler children seemed to be whisked away far too soon, although admittedly one or two others seemed to take for ever to reach the door.

Mrs Fog stood at the top of the stone steps on the Monday morning swinging her brass handbell, whilst the children lined up in the playground below and the terrible clanging of her bell raced down the lanes with as much alarm as a fire engine and any child in its way instinctively broke into a trot.

Her face was full of folds and creases and framed by a mane of frizzy hair, so that her cold, grey eyes seemed to peer out at the world through something close to fogginess itself. The children took great delight in referring to her privately as 'Old Foghorn', unable to conceive that the nickname might have been in hushed circulation since their own mothers' and fathers' infancy any more than they could imagine Mrs Fog having a life beyond the school's four walls. She lived in a different village, so the possibility of there being a *Mr* Fog or even Foggy offspring never crossed their mind. She was there to meet them at the top of the steps in the morning and helped them on with their coats at the end of the day. After that she probably just turned the lights out and lay down on the bare floorboards until the sun came up.

For years Mrs Fog had striven to instil into her children an appreciation of a life governed by Routine. Routine, they were assured, laid down the tracks and handrails which would guide them through their darkest and most difficult days. So, for her to stand at the front of the class this Monday morning with her hand resting most unroutinely on the shoulder of an unfamiliar boy was bound to cause a stir. The boy was certainly new to the school but, as the children could see, was already too grown-up to be seated in the front row, and if his plan was indeed to insinuate his way among them (and he was not simply some specimen Mrs Fog had brought in to show the class) then that most sacred of all routines was threatened – namely, the interminable withdrawal from Mrs

Fog's immediate firing line towards the generals dozing at the rear.

'This boy,' said Mrs Fog, 'has run away from London to get out of the way of Hitler's bombs.'

The class looked the boy up and down, but found nothing singed or smoking.

'His name is Robert,' she said, 'and I want you to take good care of him.'

She turned to Bobby. 'Now, Robert,' she said. 'I want you to tell the other children exactly where it is you come from.'

Bobby's hands, which he had been keeping stiffly by his sides, began to creep into each other's company and before he uttered a single word his fingers were tangled in a knot.

'Bethnal Green,' he said. Then, to show that he wasn't frightened, added, 'Just down the road from Cambridge Heath.'

For a moment the room was silent. The children had never met anyone from further afield than Buckfastleigh. Bobby stood there and prayed that his ordeal might be over. Then the laughter rose up and washed him away.

Miss Minter had returned from the Post Office on the Saturday to find a note lying on her doormat which informed her, in perfect copperplate, that the billeting arrangements were taking longer to sort out than anticipated and asking if she might hold on to Bobby for a further week or two. In so doing, the note suggested, she would earn the heartfelt gratitude of several ladies of Mrs Willcox's calibre. The note finished by saying that she would receive a form regarding the necessary expenses and that the village school would be expecting Bobby on Monday, first thing.

Lillian Minter pictured Mrs Willcox hiding in the bushes, then sneaking up the path as soon as she left the house, and wondered what chance there was of Dexter Fadden or some other overenthusiastic poacher spotting the feather on her hat among the foliage and blasting the woman to kingdom come. But on the Monday she'd duly buttoned Bobby into his best clothes, sent him off up the hill, then spent the rest of the day trying to do some housework and remember what time Mrs Fog shut up shop.

She finally spotted Bobby at the gate late in the afternoon and opened the front door for him, but he just stood and stared at the ground. After his reception that morning he'd vowed to say as little as possible – a decision he more or less stuck to, except for his interrogation by the Five Boys at lunchtime and its continuation after school. As he made his way back down the hill the Boys had accompanied him and put various proposals to him, in an incomprehensible West Country accent, the main accusation being that he was, in fact, a fifth columnist. By the time they had finished with him Bobby had vowed never to open his mouth again.

He seemed unsure whether or not to enter the cottage. Miss Minter tried to encourage him in by telling him about the shepherd's pie and roly-poly pudding she'd made for supper and thought she'd finally managed to lure him in when he suddenly grabbed at the door jamb, as if struck by a fit of vertigo, dropped to his knees and proceded to vomit onto the bristles of the welcome mat.

With four or five pumps Bobby's stomach was empty. He sat back on his haunches, eyes streaming, trying to catch his breath. A fine dribble of saliva hung between his mouth and the pool of sick, like a guy-rope. Miss Minter looked at the vomit and saw something writhing in it. Whatever her weak-nesses, squeamishness was not among them. She bent down and picked it up.

'It's a worm,' she said.

Bobby nodded. He knew exactly what it was.

The Five Boys had followed him down the lane like moths around a lantern. Two were big, two were small and the other was somewhere in between. Bobby knew the two big ones were called Finn and Hector because Mrs Fog kept telling them off for talking and he sensed, quite rightly, that they were the ones most intent on causing him harm.

Hector seemed convinced that Bobby was some sort of spy or infomer, going so far as to bark a few German-sounding phrases at him to see if he might slip into his native tongue. But it was Finn who first laid a hand on Bobby, when the village was out of sight. He grabbed hold of his wrist and lifted it up. Bobby's hand was clenched with terror.

'Open,' said Finn. 'Open up.'

Bobby did as he was told and the other boys crowded round to have a look. Their disappointment seemed only to fuel the Boys' conviction that they were dealing with the craftiest sort of spy.

'Where is it?' said Hector.

Bobby hadn't a clue what he was talking about.

'Where's the swastika?' said one of the other boys.

The small boy with the bulging eyes, said, 'We're not going to hurt you,' but Bobby was not the least bit reassured. And suddenly they were all over him, lifting his shirt and pulling down his trousers and checking every inch of his skin.

When they'd finished Finn clamped a hand around Bobby's throat.

'Open,' he said.

Finn and Hector put their faces up to Bobby's and said a great many threatening things. The word 'mole' was mentioned several times and one of the boys asked Bobby if he knew what moles had for their tea. Then the worm was dangling before Bobby's eyes, with a few flecks of earth still clinging to it.

'Open up,' Hector said.

The same worm now wriggled and twisted between Miss Minter's fingers. She was beginning to appreciate how a boy from London might take some time to get used to being out in the country. She looked at the worm, then down at Bobby, still hunched over the doormat, and shook her head most sternly.

'You mustn't eat worms,' she said.

31

Gas

Bobby's first few days at Miss Minter's were thoroughly disorientating. The whole place was an absolute puzzle; nothing was where it was supposed to be.

The house had its own peculiar rules and rituals. Boots had to be removed at the front door and carried to the fireside; any scraps of food were scraped from the plate into a swill bucket under the sink. Treacle toffee only came out in the evenings, to be eaten whilst listening to the wireless. The milk was delivered every couple of days and kept in the pantry, in a can which clanked as the milk was ladled from it and with a lid so snug that Bobby always worried he was going to unleash the lot.

But he slowly began to develop some sense of which nooks and crannies he was allowed to poke his nose into and the few which were out of bounds, not least the small door in the flue over the range whose key he once turned to see a heap of soot fall into the pot of carrots below.

The more time he spent in Lillian's company the more he found her to be an unlikely combination of frailty and strength – forever turning her good ear in his direction and dozing off in her armchair, yet capable of splitting great logs with the axe by the back door and heaving huge pans up onto their hooks.

But by far the most significant discovery of Bobby's first week in Devon was that thinking about his mother or father, far from bringing him any comfort, actually stirred up in him the most dreadful misery – a homesickness of such depth and breadth, of such debilitating terror, that he was convinced that he was going insane. So he began to steer any thoughts which seemed to be headed in their direction round to something else and make his way through the day from moment to moment, and with great deliberation, as if carrying a sleeping baby to bed. It seemed to spare him any pain on top of that which was inevitable. Yet the first sip from a mug of sweet tea or the warmth of the bathwater had a way of side-stepping his resolution and bringing home to him all the good he was going without. Then he would have to rein himself in and concentrate on something cold and dead and unyielding – would have to hold on tight until the danger passed.

Bobby's second bath didn't cause half as much fuss as the first one or use up anything like as much fuel. Lillian washed his hands and face with a flannel, then let him soak for a couple of minutes. But as she sat on her stool, with the towel in her lap, looking forward to having the bath after him, it occurred to her that she couldn't very well ask him to sort out the soup mix again when all the peas and beans and lentils were still perfectly sorted from the time before.

As she buttoned up his pyjama jacket Miss Minter asked Bobby if he was allowed to use scissors. He said he thought he probably was. And once he put on his dressing gown he was led around the back of the settee, wondering what kind of things the old lady might need cutting up. He watched as she dragged open a sideboard drawer and handed him a pair of ancient scissors. He inserted his finger and thumb and tried them out and was still snipping at the air when Lillian dropped a stack of newspapers on the rug and knelt down beside them. She opened one up and began nodding and raising her eyebrows as if she found it very interesting.

'Now, I'd say that some of these pictures look like they could do to be cut out,' she said.

Bobby agreed that they did. She turned the page and pointed at one or two photographs she liked the look of and encouraged Bobby to do the same.

'I shall leave you in charge,' she said and got to her feet.

33

'But take your time. We want them nice and neat.'

By the time she stepped into the bath she could hear Bobby busily snipping away behind the sofa. He had already cut out a British soldier guarding the wreckage of a downed Me 109, a tram on its side in a tangle of overhead wires and a bearded sailor leaning on a harbour wall with a Capstan Full Strength wedged between his fingers and the same dreamy expression as the Captain when he talked about shipwrecks or Marjory Pye.

'I'll put them in a pile,' Bobby announced from behind the sofa.

'Good boy,' said Miss Minter and slipped down, so that the water came right up to her chin.

On the first Monday after the outbreak of war Mrs Fog stood at the front of the class in her gas mask. The straps clamped her hair to her head – made her look like a muzzled bear. She stood with her hands on her hips, defiant, staring at one desk then another until the only sound in the classroom was the air wheezing in and out of the filter at the end of her snout. The children were beginning to find her behaviour deeply disconcerting – were beginning to wish she would stop staring and open her mouth – although Aldred Crouch thought it quite possible that she had been talking for several minutes but they just couldn't hear what she had to say.

When she finally peeled the mask back from her face her hair sprang back to life. She pulled a handkerchief out from the sleeve of her cardigan and blew her nose. She had it on good authority, she said, that Mr Hitler had plans to drop gas on the village. And as the idea of Hitler's gas coiled around the children's ankles Mrs Fog added that if any boy or girl needed proof of the terrible damage gas could do, they need look no further than Joseph Stewart of High Cross Farm, uncle to their own Connie Barlow, who was blinded by mustard gas in France in 1917 (which came as quite a shock to young Connie, who'd always been under the impression that her Uncle Joe had been blind since he was a baby and deeply resented the poor man being paraded before the class).

When the Germans dropped their gas on South Devon, the children learnt, their only refuge would be the gas mask at their side, and the time it took them to get it out of its box and over their face would determine whether they lived or died. Mrs Fog opened her desk drawer and took out the clock she used on the annual sports day. Then, row by row, the children were directed over to the coathooks to collect their gas masks and told to find a corner for them in their desks.

Mrs Fog folded her own mask back into its box and slotted the lid back down on it. Then the children watched as her hand crept towards the clock.

'Is everybody ready?' she said.

They could hardly have been more so – could already make out the distant rumble of German bombers – but had to wait for what felt like an eternity, with Mrs Fog's hand hanging in the air, before she finally called out, 'Gas attack!' and hit the clock.

The only children not holding their breath were the ones screaming. There hadn't been this much excitement in the classroom since Hector Massie had set fire to his coat. Children were struck in the face by their neighbours' elbows, gas masks and boxes went flying and in no time the boys and girls found themselves choking on the imaginary gas.

But within a minute or so they all managed to get their masks on, and when the last child was finally sitting bolt upright Mrs Fog hit the clock again. She turned its face to her and shook her head.

'Too slow,' she said, 'and much too sloppy.'

She cast a withering glare over at Lewis who had somehow managed to get his mask on upside-down. Lewis Bream, she calmly informed his classmates, would now be gassed to death.

So, before the next wave of planes was summoned Mrs Fog

went through the four steps again: separating the straps between fingers and thumbs, tucking the chin into the ridge at the bottom, pulling the straps back over the head so that the mask was snug against the face and running one's finger around the edge of the rubber to ensure there were no gaps for the gas to get in.

The children stuffed their masks back into their boxes and the boxes back into their desks. Mrs Fog reset her clock, then raised her hand and looked around the faces, as if almost daring someone to make a sound. Her forefinger floated before her face, with all the children's eyes on it. At one point it seemed to be heading towards her lips, to try and squeeze even more silence out of an already silent class, then at the last second changed its mind and shot towards the window.

'Gas attack!' shouted Mrs Fog.

She wore an expression of bug-eyed asphyxiation – a theatrical touch which so impressed some of her pupils they almost ripped the lids off their boxes trying to get at their masks. The ensuing calamity differed from the previous one only in that it was over sooner. There was just as much shrieking and just as much clattering of desk lids, but when they were done and Mrs Fog looked out at the rows of masked, anonymous children she was heartened to find that they had at least all got them on the right way round.

As her charges would happily testify, Mrs Fog was not an easy woman to please, so when they saw her nod at them a wave of relief swept round the classroom and they began to pull their masks from their heads. But Mrs Fog raised her hand and announced in a muffled voice that they must keep them on for two whole minutes – and held up two fingers to emphasise the point – to make sure they could breathe whilst wearing them.

The children turned and peered through their visors at their neighbours. Some fiddled with the straps. Others studied their own hands and nodded at friends across the room. It made for an eerie sort of atmosphere. The only sound was the air being drawn in and out of all the gas masks and the steady ticking of Mrs Fog's clock. Then one of the Boys discovered that by exhaling with some force it was possible to produce a farting sound between his cheek and mask. This got all the other children giggling and trying to make farting sounds of their own. They couldn't help themselves. They doubled up in fits of laughter but when they came to take a breath found it impossible to fill their lungs.

Their eyes streamed, their chests dragged at the filters and if it hadn't been for Mrs Fog's formidable presence they would have pulled their masks away. The straps caught at their hair, the smell of rubber filled their heads.

'This is what it will be like when the bombs are dropped,' they thought.

For a few precious seconds the war and its ridiculous paraphernalia had been humbled, ridiculed. Then all of a sudden it wasn't funny any more.

The pull of the gas mask's strap on their shoulders and the knock of the box against their hips were soon so familiar as to be unremarkable, and the only novelty, apart from swinging it at the head of an adversary, was in using the limited space around the mask to store something precious and sufficiently small. Lewis Bream achieved brief notoriety by squeezing a fieldmouse into his, but Mrs Fog's spot-checks, instigated after the mouse had chewed a sizeable hole in Lewis's mask, put a stop to that and in the intervening years the gas-mask boxes were opened only during the practice on the first Monday of each month and soon became nothing but another appendage, like their scarves or gloves.

Bobby could see that the Boys were up to something. They had been in conspicuously high spirits all afternoon, glancing over at him, whispering to one another and knocking knees beneath the desks.

Mrs Fog had spent the last half an hour comparing the sentence on the blackboard to a goods train. Each word, she insisted, was a carriage with its own important packages and parcels and every one of those carriages must be coupled up in the right order before they could head off down the track. But all the talk of trains put Bobby in mind of his own recent journey and the many miles he was from home, and when Mrs Fog picked up her duster and swept her train of words into oblivion he couldn't help but feel that any hopes of ever finding his way out of all these hills and hedgerows were erased with it.

As he collected his coat there seemed to be even more eyes on him than usual and he crossed the playground to find the Boys already loitering in the lane. They muttered a few words to one other and when Bobby walked through the gate Hector Massie – the boy who, a couple of days earlier had been so convinced that Bobby had a swastika tattoed on him somewhere – stepped up to him.

'I reckon you'll be going back along the top road,' he said.

The other Boys were all shoulders and smiles – were flushed with excitement. Bobby looked down the lane towards Miss Minter's cottage, which seemed suddenly distant.

'I don't think there *is* another way,' he said and could hear the terrible whine in his own voice.

Hector put his mouth up to Bobby's ear.

'You know what?' he whispered. 'If I were you, I'd just start running.'

There was no appeal – no arbitration. For a second Bobby froze. Then he turned and ran – towards the Captain's cottage and the whole unknown world beyond. And as he ran some of the other children hung over the wall and watched, more excited than at any sports day they would ever attend.

Bobby ran for his life and for those first few seconds Devon was almost transcended. In his terror he almost managed to shake off the misery that had plagued his every waking hour. The village was obscured. Its sounds fell away, its faces retreated. Then suddenly Bobby felt his feet hit the ground, could hear himself puffing and panting. Could hear the Five Boys start up after him.

He didn't get far before they caught him. He surrendered as if he knew what he was guilty of. The Boys took him by the arms and led him away, like the German pilot in the photograph Bobby had cut out a few days earlier whose plane had been downed in a Wiltshire field. And he was taken round the back of the houses and down a path onto some allotments with their sheds and canes and rows of vegetables.

Barely a word was said throughout the whole proceedings. Bobby was bundled into a hutch and the door was locked behind him with an almost professional manner. The box wasn't much bigger than a coffin and was rich with the ammonial stink of poultry excrement. The Boys stood and watched Bobby kick at the door and tug at the chicken wire and after a while they turned and quietly walked away.

They couldn't have been gone for more than a couple of minutes. It was only when Bobby saw them heading back that he made a sound. More words and tears came out of him in those few moments than had come out of him the whole week before. The Boys strode towards him in their gas masks, carrying their pesticide sprayers. They crouched down at the chicken wire and peered in at him. And despite all his kicking and screaming, they pumped some pressure into their sprayers, aimed them in at Bobby and turned them on.

They sprayed him from head to toe. Soaked every twisting inch of him. Pumped long enough to drown a whole army of greenfly. But they found that wearing a gas mask and exerting themselves was altogether different from simply sitting at their desk. And long before they ceased, through sheer exhaustion, and with the thrill of tormenting the evacuee still flooding through their veins, the Boys were already beginning to speculate on the ultimate price of such terrible fun.

Half the posters on the classroom wall warned about germs bringing the nation to its knees. Perhaps they could claim that they really *were* fumigating him. 'Germs' and 'Germans' were close enough to be almost indistinguishable and if Bobby wasn't quite German he was about as foreign as they come.

When they'd finished, the Boys pushed back their gas masks and wiped the sweat from their brows. Bobby lay in his hutch, snivelling and sodden. His hair was plastered to his head. The Boys had stopped their spraying but Bobby just kept on crying – kept on chugging like an idling engine – and as they got to their feet and prepared to leave the Boys felt their guilt creep towards irritation, then anger at his refusal to acknowledge that, if they had wanted, they could have done a great deal worse to him.

Hector tapped his boot against the chicken wire. 'And don't you go *telling*,' he said.

His words didn't seem to make much of an impression. The evacuee just kept crying and shaking until, eventually, the Boys got sick of the sight of him and headed home.

When Aldred returned, five or ten minutes later, Bobby lay perfectly still. His visitor looked in at him, then sat with his back against the chicken wire and started fiddling with his shoelaces.

'It wasn't poison,' he said over his shoulder. 'It was just water from a water butt.'

Without looking Bobby could tell that it was the boy with the freckles and the bulging eyes.

'Where are the others?' he said.

'Having their tea,' said Aldred. 'Mine's not ready.'

Neither boy spoke. Aldred continued fussing with his shoelaces, until Bobby lifted his face from the dirt.

'Are you going to let me out?' he said.

Aldred looked up and down the allotments and shook his head. 'Not just yet,' he said.

Aldred turned and directed his enormous eyes at Bobby.

'You come from London, don't you?' he said.

Until these last few weeks Bobby had never thought of

himself as a Londoner, but down here everyone seemed to think he lived right round the corner from Buckingham Palace and Trafalgar Square.

Bobby nodded and the boy with the freckles and the big eyes nodded back at him.

'So,' he said. 'You reckon you can do it?'

Bobby had no idea what he was talking about.

'Do what?' he said.

'London,' said Aldred and opened his eyes even wider. 'Do London in a day.'

Aldred Crouch's over-active thyroid was never going to be treated when his father took such pride in never having missed a day's work through illness and had trouble enough making ends meet without paying doctors' bills. An old woman once stopped Aldred in Totnes High Street and told him how she used to have a husband whose eyes used to stick out of *his* head and how *he* ended up with a goitre the size of a grapefruit under his chin. Aldred did his best not to dwell on such weird encounters, but the other Boys went out of their way to remind him of his condition at every turn. As far as his father was concerned his son's eyes just stuck out of his head much the same as his grandad's. They didn't seem to cause the boy any discomfort, apart from a bit of aching just before a cold snap, which some of the allotment-keepers took as a sign to cover their vegetables.

The first time Bobby laid eyes on Aldred he thought he must have slammed his finger in a door, and had often wondered since what it must be like to be so excruciatingly open-eyed, so wildly awake. But by the time Aldred opened the hutch and Bobby went stumbling down the lane he would have been happy never to see the boy again.

Any qualms he might have had about betraying the Five Boys were effectively put aside, for even if he'd come up with a story to explain his being so late, his sodden clothes and his bleeding fingers, he would not have been able to sustain it.

'Good God,' said Miss Minter as he staggered into the parlour. 'Who did that to you?'

'The Five Boys,' Bobby said.

Only Miss Minter could say whether she recalled the worm on her doormat and suddenly came up with a more sinister way of it getting inside Bobby, but the speed with which she took up the shovel from the coal scuttle certainly had about it the conviction of someone who had discovered a grave injustice and the appropriate measures long overdue. She was out of the door and up the hill before Bobby had uttered another word and he was still peeling the wet clothes off his wretched body when she hammered at the first of the Five Boys' front doors.

Phyllis Massie opened the door. Lillian Minter could hardly contain herself, but had the sense, at least, to tuck the shovel behind her back when she asked if her son was home. Hector appeared, rather sheepishly. He had a whole set of explanations at the ready, but he wasn't given the chance to try them out. Miss Minter grabbed him by the neck. His head went down between her slippered feet. Then tremendous events were suddenly taking place around the back – a slamming and clanging which threatened to pump his body full of indigestible pain.

Grim vengeance carried the old lady from one cottage to another, so that even if one of the Boys had wanted to warn the others, he would have had to be mighty quick. Only the clang of a shovel and the occasional howl rising over the roofs might have told the Boys who had yet to have a visit that their excuses were getting them nowhere and that retribution was on its way.

By the time her shadow fell across the Crouches' doorstep Miss Minter was beginning to tire, but she was determined that Aldred's beating should be as vigorous as the first. Aldred had long since resigned himself to his punishment and when the old woman grabbed him by the scruff of his neck he wondered only how much it was going to hurt. In fact, it hurt a great deal and in time he would retire to his bedroom, pull down his pants and find shovel-shaped welts across both cheeks. But he could have taken some comfort from the fact that when the other four Boys were given a good hiding a few minutes earlier their eyes had briefly popped out of their sockets almost as much as his.

London in a Day

There was just enough room under the stairs back home in Bethnal Green for Bobby's mum to wheel the Ewbank in and out. Old tins of paint were stacked up beside rolls of lino and cardboard boxes and Bobby's old pram was folded up somewhere at the back. But when he slipped in and pulled the door to all the odds and ends ceased to matter and he disappeared into the dark.

The coats on the back of the door embraced him – smelt of his mother's scent, his father's hair oil – and Bobby imagined himself stowed away on a ship off the shore of some far-flung country with palm trees waving in the breeze. The meters ticked and turned behind him, the crew could sometimes be heard hurrying up and down the stairs and with a little effort Bobby would feel the whole ship gently pitching in the swell.

But when the bombers came that tiny room became the family refuge on the nights when it was too cold to contemplate going down the garden to the shelter and Bobby would sometimes wake in his father's arms as he was carried down the stairs or passed in to his mother, then they would take the coats down from the hooks and put them round their shoulders and huddle together to keep warm.

Bobby's mother would sometimes get claustrophobic and announce that she'd rather be bombed in her bed than stuck under the stairs and Bobby's dad would tell her that things were bad enough without that kind of talk. Then he would start up with *I have it on good authority*, or an old hymn, or *A Bridge in Donegal*. And Bobby and his mum would join in on the chorus and the songs would carry them through the dark.

Then they'd hear the awful drone of Heinkels and their Messerschmitt escorts – would hear the ack-ack bringing them in. And that drone would slowly grow – would sweep overhead like a smothering blanket, until no amount of singing could keep it out. And they would all look up, as if they could see the planes hanging high above them and might be able to tell where the bombs would fall.

But when Bobby thought about it down in Devon all he remembered was his father's voice and the sleepy smell of his mother until he thought that he was going to make himself sick with grief. And when Miss Minter tucked him up on the sofa and turned the light out she might as well have cast him adrift on a raft. The walls of the cottage fell away and the vast black night arrived around him, and if he wasn't missing his mother and father he was wondering what the Five Boys would have in store for him the following day.

There wasn't half as much space under the stairs at Miss Minter's. You couldn't stand up straight, it was full of old boots and newspapers and rusty buckets and had just a small triangular door to get in and out. But Bobby managed to make himself quite comfortable and sometimes slept for two or three hours at a time and still get back on the settee before Lillian came down.

She might have been none the wiser had she not leant out of bed one night and knocked over her glass of water as she fumbled for it in the dark. She wasn't especially thirsty but the fact that there was now a small pool on the floor was enough to prevent her getting back to sleep. So she swung her feet out of bed and into her slippers and heaved herself up into the night.

She stopped at the top of the stairs. Thought she could hear voices. She must have left the wireless on. She cocked her good ear into the dark and crept down the stairs, until she made out a solitary voice coming up beneath her feet:

> *The heavens declare Thy glory*
> *The firmament Thy power*
> *Day unto day the story*
> *Repeats from hour to hour . . .*

She opened the door to find Bobby in a heap of coats, with just his head poking out, like some animal settling itself into hibernation. He stopped singing and stared vacantly back at her.

'Hello there,' she said.

She coaxed him out and the two of them hung all the coats back on the coatstand. Then she took his hand and led him back upstairs, counting each step as they went.

Bobby just knew he wouldn't be able to sleep next to an old lady, no matter how kind and considerate she might be. The bed seemed to be several yards off the ground and took some effort to get into. Miss Minter tucked him in, went around the bed in her big white nightie and climbed in the other side. She patted the sheets into place under Bobby's chin, propped herself up on her pillow and began whispering to him. He looked up at her – at the fine down on her cheeks . . . at the smooth, shiny skin on her neck. She stroked his hair and kept on talking in a warm and careful way and Bobby found that in time the Boys and the world's terrible distances were put to one side and sleep began to find its way through to him.

'You're a good boy,' she said. 'A good boy. And Auntie Lillian is going to keep you safe.'

Listening to the wireless was the first foundation of Lillian and Bobby's routine. They would finish their supper and wash the dishes in time for Children's Hour, listen to the News and Announcements and hope that some revue would follow. Only a military band or musical recital could be guaranteed to have Miss Minter reaching for the controls.

She tuned the wireless like a safe-cracker. Put her ear right up to the speaker and inched the dial between her finger and thumb. Stared straight ahead through all the whoops and whinnies, like a ship's captain riding out a storm, and her eyebrows would rise and fall, sometimes independently of one another, as the needle slowly scythed through the cities on the glass.

Lillian sometimes knitted and Bobby would keep his newspaper cuttings up to date, but as the evening wore on the gentle clatter of knitting needles would gradually slacken and Bobby would look up to see her nodding off with her knitting collapsed in her lap. And as he sat there, with the wireless blaring, Bobby would think about the waves of sound ranging across the countryside – the fields dark and empty, but the air thick with undeciphered sound.

One evening Arthur Askey was singing one of his songs and Miss Minter was still awake and *buzz, buzz, buzzing* along, when there was a knock at the door. Lillian turned the wireless down and listened until whoever was out there finally knocked again, and as she went down the hall it occurred to her that the last time someone came calling in the evening they were handing out evacuees and she opened the door, half-expecting to find Mrs Willcox with another one hidden behind her, but the light from the hall fell instead on the red hair, many freckles and eager eyes of Aldred Crouch.

'Is the London boy in?' he said.

Miss Minter looked him up and down. This was the boy who nearly put her neck out when she gave him a spanking a couple of days before. The longer she stared at him the more his confidence seemed to wane.

'I can't remember his name,' he said.

'You mean Bobby?' said Miss Minter.

'That's the one,' said Aldred, his confidence fully restored.

Miss Minter asked if Bobby was expecting him, which seemed to rather take the wind out of his sails.

'I don't think so,' he said, thinking that it was a rum old business when someone had to be expecting you before you were allowed to call on them.

Miss Minter led him down the hall and into the parlour where Bobby sat on the sofa. Aldred waved and went and sat beside him, apparently oblivious to the fact that Bobby had turned to stone. Arthur Askey had made way for the sort of orchestra which, under normal circumstances, would have been turned off, but Miss Minter felt that perhaps Bobby and Aldred could do with something to paper over the cracks and for a while they sat there with the flutes and oboes picking their way through the opening bars of Dreyer's 'Salutations' with the prospect of great musical clatterings to come.

Miss Minter couldn't believe that Aldred had the gall to show his face, but her manners finally got the better of her.

'Would anybody like a glass of milk?' she said.

Aldred's huge eyes swivelled round onto her. 'Thank you, Mrs,' he said. 'I would.'

She turned the wireless down so that it banged and crashed a little less intrusively and, as she passed, whispered to Bobby, 'Why don't you show your guest your cuttings?'

Bobby had no intention of showing Aldred his newspaper cuttings. Bobby's only wish was to make Aldred feel so unwelcome that he would be driven out of the house. But self-consciousness seemed not to come naturally to Aldred and as soon as Miss Minter was rattling around in the pantry Aldred pulled a booklet out of a pocket, waved it in Bobby's face and dropped it in his lap.

He shuffled along the settee and before Bobby had even opened it he could feel Aldred's warm breath on his neck.

HOW TO DO
LONDON
IN A DAY

was printed on the cover, above an etching of St Paul's Cathedral, and beneath it, *A handy guide for quick sight-seeing.*

Bobby opened it up. Each page of text was accompanied by a sketch of a London landmark. But what made the biggest impression on Bobby was the age of the book – not just that it was scuffed and had a crease down its cover, like the creases in the palm of his hand, but that the sights depicted in it bore such little resemblance to any Bobby had visited with his parents or seen through the coach window a few weeks before.

The Albert Memorial was bathed in sunshine, its concourse deserted, except for a single stationary carriage and a horse which seemed to be sleeping on its feet. The Tower of London sat in its own oasis of tinted trees like a castle in a fairy tale, with all its flags flapping, the Thames blue and tranquil beside it but barely a boat or beefeater in sight.

The information on the opposite page was the kind of thing Bobby would normally not bother to read but an occasional sentence, such as 'The handsome memorial to Queen Victoria, unveiled by the ex-Kaiser, opposite Buckingham Palace', had been heavily underlined and the margins were covered with illegible scrawl.

Nelson's Column had just a handful of figures strolling beneath it, wearing the same tall hats and long, trailing dresses as the guests in a photograph Bobby had once seen of his grandparents' wedding.

'Trafalgar Square,' said Aldred and tapped one of the lions at the base of the column. 'Designed by Sir Edwin Landseer – 1867.'

Bobby had never heard of any such man, or any such year, and for a while just sat and stared at the book in silence.

'Have you ever been to London?' he said, after some consideration.

'I'm not old enough,' said Aldred. 'But my dad has.'

The only time Bobby had been to Trafalgar Square it had been packed with people. He'd bought a tub of birdseed from a man in a wooden hut and the moment he'd stepped away from it the pigeons had descended on him like a mob.

Aldred plucked the booklet from Bobby's hands and flipped through a few pages. When he passed it back it was open at its middle pages where a small street map was printed, covering an area from Tower Bridge to Buckingham Palace. The staples – one just to the east of the Temple and the other by Waterloo – had rusted, and the paper around them looked as if it had been singed by the flare of a match. Only landmarks of the stature of the British Museum or the Houses of Parliament were marked on it. The roads were empty, except for a pencil line, which wiggled along them like a discarded rubber band, and appeared to have wiggled along one or two others, then been erased.

'What's it for?' said Bobby.

'It's my route,' said Aldred.

'What route?'

'For doing London in a day.'

Bobby stared at the map. The pencilled line was hooked with arrows, to indicate the journey's direction. The city's streets had been filled in like a maze in a puzzle book.

'Test me,' said Aldred.

Bobby stared at the map then back at Aldred.

'What do you mean?' he said.

'On *London*,' Aldred insisted. 'On my *route*.'

Bobby shrugged his shoulders.

'Just say the name of a place on the map,' Aldred said.

So Bobby looked down at the booklet and read out the first words he laid eyes on. 'The Bank of England,' he said.

Aldred nodded, very slowly, and brought a hand up to his temples, like a Memory Man.

'*The Bank of England,*' he declared from behind his fingers, '*was founded in 1694. It is known affectionately as the Old Lady of Threadneedle Street and comes . . .* ' – Aldred paused and rubbed his finger across his forehead – ' *. . . right after the Monument and just before St Paul's.*'

Aldred emerged, triumphant, from his trance. Bobby was still staring down at the map. The pencil line did indeed seem to wind its way between the landmarks in the order that Aldred had listed them.

'You seem to know your way around,' he told him.

Aldred beamed. 'Better than you, you reckon?' he said.

Bobby was already regretting his generosity. 'It's hard to say,' he said.

'Why?' said Aldred.

Bobby was struggling to think straight.

'Well, the thing is,' he said, 'you're learning it from a book.'

Aldred chewed this over for a second, then rejected it. 'What difference does that make?'

'Well, until you actually *get* there,' Bobby said, 'how do you know what it's going to be like?'

Aldred pondered this.

'What I mean,' Bobby continued, 'is how are you going to get round it all in one day?'

'My *route*,' Aldred said.

The fact that he had managed to link all the landmarks with his pencil seemed to be proof that he would be able to do the same just as easily on foot, and it dawned on Bobby that perhaps he saw the city as having the same dimensions as his own village, with streets just as empty and no building more than a five-minute walk away.

For a while the two boys sat in silence, each stumped by the other's stupidity.

'Have you ever been up Cleopatra's Needle?' Aldred said eventually.

'I don't think so,' said Bobby.

Aldred shook his head and a coy smile played upon his lips. Bobby was a stranger in his own city.

'You should,' he said.

Miss Minter had poured out the milk but decided to give the boys a couple of minutes on their own before barging back in. So she stood in the hall, like an old maid, with a glass of milk warming in each hand, and listened to Aldred's incredible confidence being pitted against Bobby's modesty, as the Devonian told the Londoner all about Cleopatra's Needle, its incredible vistas and its fateful journey to the Embankment all those years ago.

Anxious Hands

Bobby stood in the lane, wondering which drainpipe to tap on. He had a map in his hand that Aldred had drawn for him. The same pencilled line that had wiggled around the streets of London wiggled up and down the village's lanes. It had led Bobby to Aldred's own terrace of cottages without any trouble, but the note at the bottom, telling him to *tap on pipe*, failed to specify which one. So Bobby stood and puzzled over the choice of drainpipes. Then stepped up to the nearest one and raised his fist when a window swung open above him and Aldred appeared.

'Wait there,' he whispered. 'I'll be down in a minute.'

He was about to close the window but stopped and looked back down at Bobby. 'You're not scared of heights, are you?' he said.

Bobby had been so scared on so many different occasions that it would have taken him hours to sift through them all.

'I don't think so,' he said.

Aldred nodded. 'I knew it,' he said and disappeared.

When he emerged he had on his head a balaclava which was so old and stretched that it gathered in folds on the collar of his coat. He adjusted it so that he could see where he was going, slipped his arm through Bobby's and led him off down the lane. He wanted to know if his map had been useful . . . told Bobby he could keep it . . . said that sometimes he would just sit and draw maps of made-up places – places that nobody else had heard about. The only time he stopped talking was when he climbed up onto a garden wall and began plucking plums from a tree and stuffing them into his jacket pockets.

'Ammo,' he whispered, then jumped back down.

The light was fading and the village was deserted but when they got to the war memorial Aldred suddenly dropped to the ground. He dragged Bobby down next to him, slowly crawled around the memorial's stone base, checked up and down the lane, then sprinted over to the church gates, bent double, as if some sniper in one of the nearby cottages had him in his sights. When he waved at Bobby to follow he put his head down and sprinted just as Aldred had done a few seconds before. Then they crouched by the gates, Aldred checked the lanes again, pushed the gate open and ushered Bobby in.

Bobby had felt no inclination to visit the graveyard in broad daylight and was trying to remember why on earth he had agreed to go creeping around it so close to dark. The church stood before him like a rock face, the graveyard was full of shadowy sumps and when Aldred left the gravel path to weave between the tombs and headstones Bobby followed only because he didn't want to be left on his own.

Aldred raced ahead. Bobby tried to take a short cut but got stuck in a gravestone cul-de-sac and by the time he found his way out and caught up with Aldred he was standing over a headstone in a billowing cloud of his own steam.

'I'll just give old Wenlock a rinse,' he said and winked at Bobby. 'It keeps the ivy off him.'

Bobby had already discovered that being out in the country meant a boy could urinate more or less at will, but to do so on the grave of a dead man seemed to be just asking for trouble. Aldred was apparently not the least bit bothered. He buttoned up his trousers, took Bobby off to a quiet corner and told him not to move, whilst he went and got the key from its hiding place – a speech delivered with such gravity that there seemed to be no guarantee of him returning alive.

So Bobby turned and stared out over the gravestones as Aldred's footsteps receded, then crouched down and read some of the inscriptions on the headstones in the dwindling light. Judging by the dates, Devon's dead had done most of their dying a long, long time ago and Bobby could see how somebody might think it was a good idea to send a boy all the way down here to get him away from all the dying going on back home. The week before he left a boy from his class had been found under the rubble, curled up in his grandad's arms. The month before, sixty people died in a shoe factory when the roof fell in on them.

But it was old Mr Wenlock and his underground neighbours who increasingly occupied Bobby's thoughts, and the longer he waited the more conscious he became of the old Devonians packed beneath his feet. The wind had begun to whistle in the trees and some creature was making the sort of hooting which can make a boy on his own in a graveyard nervous, and when Bobby felt a hand fall upon his shoulder he nearly jumped right out of his boots.

Even after he saw that it was Aldred and not Mr Wenlock complaining about all the rinsings he'd been getting, it was quite a while before Bobby's heart stopped rattling in his ribcage and a while longer for him to properly shake off the idea of Wenlock being up and about.

The key to the church was old and heavy – as Bobby discovered when Aldred let him hold it for a second or two – and a little larger than Bobby thought strictly necessary considering the size of the door. For instead of entering the church via the slab of oak in the porch, Aldred led him round to what he referred to as the 'back door' – which was, he insisted, a *special* door, to be used only by people such as the reverend and the organist and himself. The moment they were inside and the door was closed behind him, Bobby felt a deeper darkness envelop him and a silence descend which his ears had trouble fathoming. The only things he could pick out with any certainty were the smell of polished wood, rotting flowers and no end of cold, uncompromising stone.

He couldn't see a thing, but Aldred assured him that he had made this journey a hundred times, took Bobby's hand, put it on his shoulder and led him through the dark. They crept around the organ (which took so long to navigate, it must have been about as big as a bus) and between the choristers' pews until they were clear of all the railings and tables and other clutter and heading down the aisle.

Their steps rang out on the stone flags. Bobby sensed a great vault of religious air above him and when he clipped his hip on the end of a pew, pictured the bruise blossoming under the skin. But he blundered on with his hand on Aldred's shoulder, until the darkness began to ease from black to blue and he could make out the arches of the windows and a stack of collection plates glinting up ahead.

The next door was even smaller than the last one. It ground against the floor as Aldred pushed it open and a damp, earthy smell came seeping out. Aldred took Bobby's hand and guided it to a rope which was lashed to the wall just inside the doorway. But as he slipped by and headed off into the dark Bobby suddenly doubted that he had the courage to go after him.

'How long will it take?' he said.

Aldred came back down a step or two.

'All you've got to do,' he said, 'is keep hold of the rope and keep on walking, and you'll be there in no time at all.'

So Aldred set off up the tower's tight spiral and Bobby went after him, feeling as if he were entombed in stone. The only light came in through the narrow slits in the wall to his left and as he wound himself round, from one to the next, he had the peculiar sense that while his mind was all too painfully present, his body drifted in a dream.

'How many steps altogether?' he called out.

'Two hundred and sixteen,' came the reply.

Bobby gripped the rope with both hands and hauled himself deeper into the darkness. Mad thoughts rattled around inside him, like a bird trapped in a chimney, and every step did nothing but add weight to his conviction that he should turn and try to find his way back out.

They seemed to have been walking up the steps for hours

when Bobby finally stumbled out into some sort of chamber. And suddenly he could smell timber, could hear the steady knock of clockwork, which both had some humanity to them and gave him hope that he might yet live to tell the tale.

He rested his hands on his knees until he got his breath back. A little moonlight came in through the louvres and dusted the shoulders of six vast bells. They hung at head height, with great wooden wheels beside them, like the ones on firemen's ladders. The bells could have been cut from granite and Bobby got the impression that they didn't much care for their visitors and was carefully making his way round them when Aldred called out and he looked up to find him on the other side of the belfry, floating in mid-air. Neither boy was particularly troubled by Aldred's levitation. He was pinned to the wall but seemed not to be suffering. Bobby felt more asleep than awake, but he blinked and kept on blinking until he finally grasped that Aldred was on a ladder between the roof and floor.

'Mind the rungs near the top,' Aldred called down into the chamber. 'They're rotten.' Then he carried on climbing.

By the time Bobby had made his way round the bells' cradle and reached the foot of the ladder Aldred was opening the hatch in the roof and clambering out of sight, leaving a neat square of stars for Bobby to aim towards. He put his foot on the bottom rung and set off, rather warily, and was halfway up when the ladder began to bow in and out and he had to stop and wait for it to settle. Below, the six bells continued their colossal meditation. The room was their temple – their nursery. Then Bobby set off again, inching ever upwards, until Aldred popped out among the stars and held out his hand.

'Come on, London boy,' he said.

It was like stepping out onto a tiny, sky-bound courtyard. The village's roofs buckled far below and the moon lit up a landscape which was bigger and more barren than any Bobby had seen before. Perhaps it was the effect of the fresh air working on him or, despite his earlier assurances, he was just giddy from having left the ground so far behind. Either way, the moment he set foot on the roof his legs turned to lead and he waddled about on them like a sailor stepping back onto the quay.

'That's better, isn't it?' said Aldred.

Bobby nodded, and for a while they just leant against the battlements, with the wind ruffling their feathers and nudging the weathervane up on its spike. Then Aldred stepped into the middle of the roof and stretched out his right arm and pointed down the valley.

'Miss Minter's,' he said.

He swung his arm round to his right.

'Totnes,' he said.

He kept on like this, picking out houses, nearby villages, the river, the sea. He swung his arms around like a policeman directing traffic, as if whole towns and tides were queueing in the dark. Then he went back over to Bobby and leant on the ramparts and nodded at an old stone barn a mile or two outside the village, with a sloping roof which caught the moonlight, and as they looked at it Aldred asked Bobby if he ever wondered about the pyramids.

'What pyramids?' he said.

'The pyramids in Ancient Egypt,' said Aldred. 'And all the gold they buried with the dead boy king.'

Bobby had never heard of Ancient Egypt. He had a good idea what a pyramid looked like, but was not about to pit his piddling wisdom against the authority next to him.

'What's there to wonder about?' he said.

Aldred rested his chin on his hands. 'You know how many men died towing Cleopatra's Needle to London?' he said.

Bobby had to admit that he didn't.

'Six,' said Aldred. 'Drowned in the Bay of Biscay.' A faraway look came over him. 'I saw a picture once.'

This picture must have made quite an impression on him, for its very recollection seemed to carry him off into a reverie of drowned Egyptians, with whom he rolled and turned for some considerable time, leaving Bobby at a bit of a loss and a little embarrassed, but he thought it best not to interfere. And in time Aldred rolled his head on his hands and cast his thyroidal gaze up at him.

'Cursed,' he said, pausing for dramatic effect. 'And if there's one sort of curse you don't want to get mixed up in, it's an Ancient one.'

A few minutes earlier, Bobby had never heard of Ancient Egypt or been the least inclined to wonder about its pyramids, but the more Aldred kept on about it, the more he was troubled by its evil curses, and soon the church's very crenellations threatened to crumble beneath his fingertips.

'You know what's buried under Cleopatra's Needle?' said Aldred.

Bobby didn't and was tempted to say that if his finding out was likely to unlock yet more curses, he would rather things stayed that way. But Aldred was already raising a hand to his forehead and assuming the persona of the Memory Man.

His words came out of him almost automatically, as if they were being communicated to him from the other side. '*Bibles in several languages,*' he reported,' . . . *wire ropes . . . specimens of marine cables . . . a box of assorted pipes . . .*'

Bobby hadn't the faintest idea what Aldred was going on about. The only thing it reminded him of was the game they sometimes played at his Auntie May's in which a tray of household objects was brought into the parlour, then removed and you had to try and remember what you'd just seen.

'. . . *a shilling razor,*' Aldred continued, '. . . *jars of Doulton ware . . . a box of hairpins . . .*'

He surfaced briefly, winked at Bobby, then added,' . . . *photographs of pretty English girls . . .*' which seemed to Bobby to be neither particularly Ancient nor particularly Egyptian but Aldred carried on, oblivious.

'*Bradshaw's Railway Guide . . . a gentleman's walking stick . . .*'

he said, but his little recitation seemed to be running out of steam. '. . . *Whitaker's Almanac*,' he said, and screwed his eyes up. The wheels had stopped turning. '. . . *and other things of interest*,' he said.

He opened his eyes and turned blinking to Bobby to bathe in the glory of his mnemonic feat and would have bathed a little longer had Bobby not asked him what an Almanac was.

'It's a bit like whisky,' Aldred said, distracted, 'but you can rub it on, like medicine. What's important is, why was it buried under the Needle?'

Bobby shrugged.

'*So that Man may know of us*,' Aldred declared, '*when London's greatness has ebbed away.*'

Bobby stared blankly back at him.

'Like Noah's Ark,' Aldred said.

London, he said, was full of landmarks with things hidden under them. The poets' bones under Westminster Abbey . . . the bronze from captured cannon on the base of Nelson's Column . . . the torture chambers under Buckingham Palace . . .

But all this talk of bones and London's ruination was doing Bobby no good at all. And the more Aldred persisted the more panic Bobby felt stir in him, like the horror he'd felt as he trawled through Miss Minter's newspapers and come across a blasted terrace which looked just like his own.

His chest was as tight as a joint of brisket. He felt as if it had been bound with cable and wire ropes. He didn't *want* London's greatness to ebb away. Didn't want to have to grub around for hairpins or old crockery to know that his mother and father had once lived there.

The tower seemed to tighten around him. He tried to take a breath but couldn't get on top of it. And even as he said to himself, *You're panicking . . . panicking . . .* , he saw his mother and father lying side by side in the rubble . . . the house flattened . . . London razed to the ground. History raced ahead and made the world a desert. And Bobby felt the tower tighten, slowly tighten. Tighten and finally explode.

59

The first chime rattled every bone in Bobby's body and was still diminishing when the second erupted under his feet. By the third or fourth, Bobby had just about grasped what was happening and by the fifth and sixth could follow them as they swept out over the fields, dipped into the valleys and gathered there. As the last chime slowly soaked away into the landscape Bobby finally managed to take a satisfying breath and felt relief coursing through his veins. Then the other four Boys came boiling up through the trapdoor and spilled out onto the roof.

They moved so fast that Bobby had trouble keeping track of them. It was all he could do not to burst into tears.

'Has he started yet?' said one of the bigger Boys to Aldred, but Aldred just shook his head and stared out over the roofs.

The Boys seemed to be everywhere: dropping the hatch, buttoning up their jackets and wandering all about the place. A couple of them leant over the ramparts and watched their spit race towards the ground. Another was trying to locate his own chimney stack.

It was a while before Bobby realised that the Boys were actually ignoring him – a state of affairs he was more than happy with. The only boy who seemed to be paying him any particular attention was Lewis, who was not much bigger than Aldred and had sat down on the other side of the roof. Bobby could feel him watching, but did his best not to catch his eye. He kept this up until Lewis addressed him directly.

'Got your plums, boy?' he said.

The speed with which the other Boys turned and looked at Bobby suggested they had been paying him a good deal more attention than they had let on. Meanwhile, Bobby was struggling to make enough sense of the question to have a hope of answering it.

'Your *plums*,' said Lewis.

Bobby was absolutely baffled. The more he thought about plums the less sense he squeezed out of them and soon the only thought in his head was what his punishment was likely to be.

'Bobby and me are sharing,' said Aldred and stepped forward.

He crouched down and began pulling the plums from his jacket pocket. They rolled off in all directions and he was still coralling them back into each others' company when Harvey crouched down beside him, dug a hand in his pocket and began adding his own supply of plums to the pile. By the time the last of the Boys had squatted down and emptied his pockets there must have been forty or fifty, stacked up like cannonballs.

Bobby was getting more confused with every passing minute but had the good sense, at least, to keep it to himself, and when the Boys withdrew and lined up along one of the walls it was clear that if he didn't go and join them he would be left on his own. So he got to his feet and went and stood next to Aldred looking out over the ramparts. Finn was the only boy missing and when Bobby glanced over his shoulder found him sitting on the roof with his back to the others, flipping a plum from hand to hand.

'Right,' said Finn. 'Who're we going for?'

'Pearce,' said Hector.

'Which one?' said Finn.

'Drowned Pearce,' said Hector.

The Boys slotted their elbows into the corners of the parapet and rested their chins in the palms of their hands. At least, Bobby *assumed* that was what they were doing and took up the same position until Aldred nudged him, with both hands cupped around his eyes.

'*Binoculars*,' he said.

The first plum Finn lobbed over his shoulder landed in a tree at the far end of the graveyard and was greeted with unanimous derision.

'Nowhere near,' said Hector, from behind his binoculars. 'Forty degrees south, fifty degrees east.'

Bobby glanced over his shoulder and watched as Finn

shifted one buttock, then the other, so that he rotated frac-
tionally round to one side. He was still settling when Hector
gave the order to fire.

'Hang on,' said Finn, picked another plum from the pile,
quickly composed himself, then flung it up into the sky.

The boys followed its flight.

'That's better,' said Hector. 'Ten degrees north, twenty
degrees west.'

In this way the Boys occupied themselves for the next ten
minutes, singling out a gravestone, systematically bombard-
ing it, then moving on to another one. Harvey and Lewis
each took a turn at despatching the plums, but it seemed that
only Hector and Finn were qualified to give the coordinates.
The others made muffled explosions in their cheeks as each
plum landed, but of all those thrown only one definitively hit
its target, spattering the shrouded urn on one of the more
ostentatious graves and making a distinct 'clink' when the
plumstone struck the stone.

The troops were still celebrating when Harvey hissed from
behind his binoculars, 'He's coming, he's coming. Here he is.'

The Boys swung their binoculars round to the right, onto a
cottage just beyond the war memorial, and with a little effort
Bobby picked out a figure at the attic window. It was an old
man. Then Bobby realised that it was, in fact, the Captain,
who had taken the unusual step of sloughing off his sleeping
bag to stand at his window in nothing but his vest and
underpants. Bobby drew his binoculars down from his face
and looked over at Aldred but decided against disturbing
him, and when he looked back at the attic window the
Captain was setting a telescope on a stand.

The Captain made a few adjustments, then bent down and
peered through the eyepiece. When he straightened up he
had a handkerchief in each hand. Stood as stiff as a board for
a few seconds then suddenly flung his arms out – one up to
the right, the other out to the left – and froze. But just as his
handkerchiefs were settling, he flung them out into a new

position – one out to his right this time and the other straight down at the floor.

It was as if several hundred volts were being sporadically fed into him, inducing a highly mechanical PT display.

'He's like a little bloody windmill,' said Lewis and sniggered to himself, until one of the bigger Boys shushed him up.

Bobby knew that they were all meant to be keeping quiet, but after watching the Captain wave his arms around for a couple of minutes suddenly couldn't stop himself.

'What's he *doing*?' he said.

'Signalling,' said Hector.

Bobby carried on watching. 'What's he saying?' he said.

Lewis shrugged his shoulders. 'Nobody knows,' he said.

The Captain must have flapped for five or ten energetic minutes, stopping only to squint through his telescope before going back to his hanky-waving with vigour renewed – must have contorted himself into every letter of the code's alphabet until, all at once, he crossed his handkerchiefs before him and dropped his head onto his chest. A moment or two later he snapped himself out of his little trance, dismantled his telescope and disappeared from view.

'Is that it?' said Bobby.

Lewis nodded.

'Until next Tuesday it is,' he said.

As the boys made their way down the lane ten minutes later any illicit thrill Bobby had felt from spying on the Captain was easily eclipsed by the euphoria of having spent almost an hour in the Five Boys' company without them hurting him. When he was sure the others were out of earshot he turned to Aldred and told him how impressed he'd been with Finn and Hector's technical know-how, regarding the aiming and firing of the plums.

'You mean all the degrees and the easts and wests?' said Aldred.

Bobby nodded.

'Oh, they just make them up,' he said.

Sugar Beet

The speed with which the Five Boys' fathers had enlisted was either a measure of their willingness to defend the land they worked on or their eagerness to leave it far behind. For Arthur Noyce and Lester Massie, at least, any respite from the tedium of animal husbandry and the trudge around the seasons was worth a look. Both men liked nothing better than to sit in the Malsters' Arms and bemoan the loss of their wives' figures to the ravages of motherhood. At best, they thought, they might encounter something young and slim and exotic on their travels; at worst, might learn to appreciate their wives a little more.

Two days after they'd gone, Jem Hathersage followed, pedalling out along the Totnes road on a borrowed bicycle. He was in serious danger of missing his train after a hurried few minutes' intimacy with Mrs Hathersage and had his suitcase strapped to his back so tightly that on the uphills it almost throttled him and on the downhills threatened to throw him over the handlebars.

Of all five fathers Alec Bream was the only man to pack his bag with any real sense of purpose. He had been predicting the war for years and thought it a war worth fighting, but his only objective was to get back in one piece, unlike his father, killed twenty years earlier, whose name was one of those carved on the base of the village's memorial.

Last to leave had been Bernard Crouch, Aldred's father, for whom the whole undertaking was an unutterable shock. He had no idea how much store he set by his home and family and felt grief-stricken, as if he had left his very soul behind. He began writing home on the first day of his training – letters written in such haste and with such desperation that his wife, Sylvia, found them almost illegible. They arrived in twos and threes, quickly grew into bundles and were tucked behind his pipe-rack until they nudged it off the mantelpiece, then were stuffed in Sylvia's sewing basket, from which they erupted whenever she went near the thing.

Only Howard Kent, a bachelor, believed he served his country better out in the fields than in a uniform – an opinion, as it happened, shared by the army doctor who, after the most cursory of examinations, concluded that he was a danger not just to himself but his fellow-soldiers, though whether there was something wrong with his feet or his eyes or, as his neighbours suspected, his head was never established and Howard always insisted it was his indispensable qualities as a farm labourer that prevented him joining up.

In the years since, Howard had undergone a process of intense self-modification. He had always found women to be strange and intimidating but the lack of other young men in the village did wonders for his confidence, and he began to stride up and down as if he owned the place. The new Howard Kent was, he felt, a hearty soul, worldly-wise and always willing to stop and chat with the local women – a character, needless to say, the local women found just as revolting as the original one.

Bobby first came across him when he accompanied Lillian to the Post Office. Howard stood among three or four women and rubbed his chin as if grand ideas were bubbling up inside him. But even as he spoke, Bobby couldn't help noticing how Howard kept sneaking a peek at Mrs Crouch's bosom, as well as any other bosoms in his range, and when he finally departed, in a blaze of laughter, the women let out a collective sigh and adjusted their coats and cardigans as if Howard's hands had been fumbling about inside.

Bobby and Aldred had spent the morning going through Bobby's cuttings. Despite Bobby's best efforts, Aldred remained unshakeable in his perception of London as a barren and peopleless place, finding nothing to contradict it in all the pictures of blasted buildings and brick-strewn streets. The sandbags stacked up against the walls of Whitehall looked to him like a pyramid's foundations, and with all its toppled columns and derelict churches London seemed to grow more Ancient by the day.

There was never any real doubt who was in charge of the archive. Bobby selected the pictures, cut them out and categorised them. Aldred's role was that of a visiting curator, albeit one with plenty of opinions of his own. The two boys would discuss at length the merits of recent acquisitions or how the collection might be filed anew, and Bobby always knew that he could easily put things in the order he wanted just as soon as Aldred was out of the door.

Two photographs were examined far more than all the others. In the first, titled *A London store damaged by H.E.*, a dozen bicycles dangled from the joists of a gutted building, with a mound of mangled bicycles on the floor below. It provoked a profound sense of melancholy in the boys which they attempted to rekindle each time they returned to it.

In the other photograph, a group of men stood round the edge of a twenty-foot crater. Two were servicemen, resting on crutches with one leg missing and staring morbidly into the pit. A couple of civilians in flat caps stood beside them and pointed up at the sky. The roof of the hospital ward in the background was completely stripped of its slates. The men in the flat caps seemed to follow the plane as it retreated, yet the servicemen seemed to be looking at the very spot where they had lost their legs. It never occurred to the boys that the men might have been injured elsewhere, or that the two civilians might be pointing at the sky several hours or even days after the attack. It barely mattered. Bobby and Aldred's principal pleasure in studying the photograph was to try and imagine the enormity of a blast which could make such a hole in the ground and to contemplate a life with only one leg.

They were wondering, not for the first time, what might

have happened to any bicycles which survived the fire in the shop in London and whether a one-legged man might still be capable of riding a bicycle when Miss Minter, who had been reading the newspaper in an armchair nearby, decided that they should get out of the house for a while.

'Take him up the hill,' she told Aldred, 'and show him the view.'

It was in Aldred's nature to require his own motivation for an assignment before being able to direct his formidable enthusiasm towards it, and they had crossed the bridge and were halfway up the lane before he worked out how a hike up the hill might easily incorporate a trip down to the river and a visit to the boathouse and Old Tom, its resident drunk. The moment the trip fell under his jurisdiction his spirits lifted. He took hold of Bobby's arm and hurried on, telling him all about the time Old Tom was famously woken when the prow of a trawler, high on a flood tide, crashed through his bedroom window and pinned him to the wall.

They marched through the village and carried on up the lane and Aldred pointed out various plants in the hedgerow capable of sustaining a man if he ever found himself out in the wilderness. Bobby lost interest when he waved at a clump of nettles and talked about how much good they'd do you if you made them into a soup and his words were nothing but a babble when they reached a five-barred gate.

A great mound of earth-caked vegetables was piled up in the field beyond it. They looked to Bobby like a heap of old boots. Aldred climbed onto the top bar of the gate and nodded at them.

'You know what that is?' he said.

Bobby had another look. Thought it looked more like elephant dung – was the right sort of colour and the right sort of quantity. What had originally put him in mind of bootlaces, he now saw, were hundreds of stringy roots.

'Sugar beet,' said Aldred proudly. 'There's enough sugar there to sweeten your mother-in-law.'

He gave Bobby a wink and Bobby nodded as if he had the faintest idea what he was talking about. In fact, Aldred's understanding of the phrase was probably just as dim as Bobby's, having overheard it only the summer before. But he had recognised at the time how the wink was as big a part of the joke as the actual mother-in-law.

'How do you get the sugar out?' said Bobby.

Aldred grew suddenly solemn and for a moment Bobby thought he was going to bring his hand up to his temples and do his Memory Man routine.

'Well, first of all,' he said, 'you've got to boil it up . . .' He paused. '. . . then you keep on boiling it. And when it's been boiling and boiling and boiling . . .' He paused again. '. . . you just sort of squash it out.'

Bobby stared at the heap of beet, wondering how any amount of boiling and squashing might cause white sugar to pour from it, when a head popped up out of the vegetables. Bobby jumped. Aldred almost fell right off the gate.

Howard Kent must have been woken by all the talk of boiling and squashing. As he came blinking towards the boys in his muddy overalls Bobby thought that it was probably much more likely that Mr Kent had been relaxing *against* the far side of the heap of beet rather than deep within it – but it still seemed like an uncomfortable place to take a nap.

Howard leant over the gate and looked up and down the track to see if the boys had any young mothers with them.

'What are you two up to?' he said.

Aldred was anxious to recover his authority. 'I'm taking Bobby down to see Old Tom,' he said.

Howard turned and headed back towards the sugar beet. 'Well, you'd better be getting along,' he said.

When they reached the top of the hill they filled their lungs, then sat and looked down into the valley. The river was flat and silver far below them and wound its way across the valley floor so benignly that Aldred decided to save all his stories of currents and drownings until they were along-side it, when things would hopefully look a little more dangerous.

He pointed out a clump of trees, packed as tight as broccoli, on a small peninsula where Old Tom's boathouse was tucked away and, on the other side of the valley, a derelict building which had once been a cider house, run by an old woman who used to put curses on any customers who got behind with their bills.

They got to their feet and Aldred was getting ready to go charging down the hillside and already planning a little trip and tumble towards the end. He turned to Bobby to say 'Ready, steady . . . ', but Bobby was miles away.

'What?' said Aldred.

Bobby was gazing down the river, beyond the trees with the boathouse buried beneath them, to where the water glinted between the interlocking hills.

Aldred squinted but couldn't see anything.

'What?' he said again.

Then he saw a smudge just above the water, like an insect caught in the sun. And a gust of wind brought a short blast of sound up the valley – the same drone of an engine that Bobby had picked up a few seconds before.

'It's a Spitfire,' said Aldred.

Bobby shook his head and kept staring down the river. 'It's too rough for a Merlin,' he said. And they both stood and watched as the plane kept on towards them – real now and its engine constant – until Bobby suddenly laughed out loud.

'It's a One-Ninety,' he said. 'It's a Focke Wulf.'

Bobby waited and for a while Aldred stood firm beside him. Bobby's eyes never left the approaching plane, which had now ceased to be a mere fraction in the valley and become the only important thing in it.

The closer it came the more speed it gathered about it, until suddenly it was tearing a great hole right through the day. Then it was over the woods below. Then dipping a wing to pull out of the bend in the river. Then heading straight towards the boys.

Bobby wasn't aware of Aldred's departure. But seeing the fields and hills so easily breached threatened to overwhelm him. And something in the dull shudder of the aeroplane's engine had him back home, tucked away under the stairs.

'*The heavens declare Thy glory,*' he heard his father singing, '*the firmament Thy power . . .*'

The plane levelled its wings and swept up the hillside – the same hillside Bobby and Aldred had just been contemplating running down – and Bobby stood and welcomed it and the confirmation that it brought with it that the war and his mother and father were all alive and well.

It took the brow of the hill thirty yards to his right and in that blink of an eye, he saw the pilot – the face with the mask clamped over it, the hunched shoulders, the hands on the controls – saw him glance out of the cockpit as he went over and take Bobby in. Then he was gone and there was nothing but the great roar of its engine and the flash of its undercarriage as it went tearing on its way.

Aldred was still getting to his feet as Bobby ran past him.

'Did you see that?' Aldred shouted after him. 'Did you *see* that?"

Then they were both running back towards the village. Chasing the plane, as if they had a hope of catching it, with its engine still roaring in their ears and the rattle of gunfire up ahead.

Ecclesiastical Insurance

There was only the one good lung in Mr Mercer – the other had gone bad many years before – and the only time the other villagers tended to see him was when he went up and down the lane in his Bath chair, with his little wife struggling behind. His jackets always looked a bit too roomy, his shirt collar always had an inch or two to spare, so that when he heaved himself up out of his Bath chair there was often a moment or two when his clothes seemed to be considering staying where they were.

The Reverend Bentley's constitution was not much better than Mr Mercer's. When he arrived in the village he was already so ridden with arthritis that even a handshake could bring tears to his eyes. The villagers thought it odd that their new vicar, when introducing himself, should keep his hands tucked deep in his pockets and nod wanly at them, as if the spiritual grace which came with the dog collar would reach out and do the job for him. Marjory Pye reckoned he must have been warned about the dangers of getting his hands caught in agricultural machinery. In fact, the reverend would have liked nothing better than to step out as first batsman for the village cricket team (if they had had one) or stay up half the night reading the latest Dorothy Sayers, but turning the pages of any book with those knotted clumps of knuckle was just about impossible, let alone the church Bible, which sat on the lectern like a block of stone, its pages blunted by the thumbs of all the vicars that had gone before.

So within hours of landing in the village the Reverend Bentley had resolved to find an able-bodied boy to mark the passages in the pulpit Bible and assist Mr Mercer on his slow shuffle from Bath chair to organ-seat. And when he opened his front door an hour or two later who should he see striding down the lane but Aldred Crouch, his glands pumping at their usual phenomenal rate, which the reverend mistook for a look of steely determination and it seemed to him that here was a boy of application and rock-steady reliability, who could probably pump out a hymn or two along the way.

Aldred took the job on the spot. He had never been so flattered – had never felt so proud. The reverend's assurance that he would be rewarded not only in the next life but might find a few coppers in his pocket on Easter Sunday and Christmas Day was neither here nor there. And so it was that Mr Mercer's shortness of breath, the reverend's arthritis and Aldred's own overactive thyroid came together in a trinity of affliction and rewarded him with his own key to the church.

On his first day, Aldred was so fearful of overlooking one of his jobs or attending to them out of turn that he wrote them out,

1. *Pick up key*
2. *Do the Bible*
3. *Do the numbers*
4. *Pick up Mr Mercer*
5. *Pump the organ*
6. *Drop Mr Mercer off*

and on those first few Sundays he must have pulled out that scrap of paper and consulted it a dozen times or more. These days he could carry out his duties with his eyes closed, but the list had become a sort of talisman. His own handwriting was barely legible, the paper had split along the folds, but if he ever happened to leave home without it he would feel so nervous that he would have to go back and pick it up.

As he stood on the bench in the porch the day after the Focke Wulf went over, with his hand deep in the wall, Aldred felt his usual Sunday morning sense of purpose come upon

72

him. He closed his fist around the key and could feel the church, the village, the whole wide morning being levered into life. Before the war, the bells would already have been ringing high above him as he followed the gravel path around the solid walls of the church. The Reverend Bentley once told him that when the bells came to rest just before the service started and all that was left was that single, mournful toll, it called out, *Come . . . Come . . .* to its congregation, and Aldred could easily imagine how all the ropes and wheels in the belfry might somehow winch them in. But the bells hadn't moved since the day the war broke out – hung like six dead lungs in the chest of the church – and if they tolled at all these days it would be to warn the villagers that the country was being invaded. The bellringers were far away, fighting the war, and the rest of the village was still indoors, knotting ties and shining shoes. All the same, Aldred couldn't help but feel that his little routine helped bring about a bit of winching of its own.

When the Reverend Bentley first went through Aldred's duties and mentioned his difficulty in turning the pages of the Bible, Aldred not unreasonably envisaged himself up in the pulpit beside the vicar, with his own upholstered stool. Saw himself silently rise, to pinch the corner of the page between his fingers and sweep it over when the reverend gave him a nod – even tasted the bitter catarrh of apprehension at the back of his throat as he saw himself going down the aisle, kitted out in his own little surplice and big-buckled boots, when the reverend explained that all he wanted was the Bible open at the appropriate place before the service started and, if the passage went on to a second page, a wooden ruler marking it, so that he could turn to it without too much fuss.

Upholstered stool, sombre surplice and fancy boots all went up in a puff of smoke. Other boys might have been disappointed, but disappointment did not come naturally to Aldred Crouch. He experienced instead what felt like a

73

peculiar interlude in which his thoughts were reordered and his interpretation of the facts rearranged and by the time he got home twenty minutes later, his interview with the Reverend Bentley had been revised to such a degree that his grandma Crouch was soon clapping her hands with glee at the news that her only grandson had apparently just been invested with about as much church clout and clerical say-so as a bishop.

Aldred stopped at the door and lifted the key on its string necklace. He could have tucked it inside his jumper but preferred to wear it out, like a crucifix, even though it tended to bounce around when he was in a hurry and leave small bruises on his chest. He slotted it into the door and felt the old mechanism turn deep inside it. Stepped in and took a breath of holy air. Then he made his way round the organ, climbed the stairs up to the pulpit, pulled out the note from under the bible and studied the reverend's arthritic scrawl.

'Romans 10: 6 ,' it said, and beneath it was a list of numbers: '19, 392, 47, 106, 198.'

Aldred couldn't remember which bit of the Bible the Romans inhabited, but had an inkling they might be somewhere near the end. So he heaved it open, hoping, as always, that it might miraculously part at the right chapter and, as always, it did not.

Once they started moving, the Bible's pages soon found their own momentum, buckling and rolling in great papery waves, and as he looked for Romans hiding out among them, with the church all hushed and empty, Aldred thought, not for the first time, that he would quite like to do a little preaching of his own. He imagined the whole village staring up at him, enraptured, with the Reverend Bentley and Mrs Fog right down at the front as he enlightened them on ancient curses and the drownings in the Bay of Biscay.

Generally speaking, Aldred thought the church was far too wordy. Not just the ones weighing down the Bible and pouring out of the Reverend Bentley. Hymn books and prayer books were stacked shoulder-high by the main door, words were carved into stone tablets along both walls, there was Latin script in the stained-glass windows and framed notices and embroidered quotations at every turn. The moment you set foot in the place you found yourself playing hopscotch on the epitaphs of dead men. And most of the words were too old or worn away to make any sense. If he ever started up his own church Aldred would certainly make a few changes. Films about London's famous landmarks and Ancient Egypt would be projected onto bare walls and from time to time Aldred would play a couple of tunes on the organ. But people would be free to come and go as they pleased – could sit and nod off without fear of reprisal. It would be the world's one and only wordless church.

The Romans finally turned up between the Corinthians and Mary anointing Jesus' feet, and as the passage continued onto the following page Aldred tucked the ruler right up to the binding, and pulled the first page back over it. He let the hymn board down on its pulley, gently laid it on the pulpit floor and fished out the box of numbers from its hideaway at the back of the pulpit and began picking out the ones he needed for that morning's hymns.

The blocks slid easily along the board's beaded grooves, chinking against one another like dominoes. But Aldred took care. One tile out of place would have the congregation racing off in one direction and the Reverend Bentley in the other. Some hymns came up with such frequency that Aldred recognised them straightaway and could be halfway through the first verse before he slid the last block into place. Dirges such as 'O God, our help in ages past' (279) and 'Raise up thine heart' (563) were particularly popular with the reverend, whereas Aldred preferred the stirring 'Onward Christian Soldiers' (432) or 'Eternal Father, strong to save' (138), which always gave him the willies as the chords shifted under, 'Oh hear us when we cry to thee . . .' before being resolved with' . . . for those in peril on the sea'.

By the time he'd checked all the numbers and hoisted the hymn board back up the wall, Aldred's monopoly of the church was usually broken. Mrs Heaney would be fussing over one of her flower arrangements and the ushers would be restacking the hymn books for want of something useful to do. But, as Aldred often reminded himself, only *he* had a key on a string necklace and only *he* was allowed to climb the pulpit stairs, and no amount of strutting about on the part of the ushers or evil glances from Mrs Heaney from the cover of her chrysanthemums would alter the fact that their business was down among the groundlings, whilst he was practically the junior manager and had the run of the place.

He crept back down the stairs, out through the side door, and made his way through the graveyard. Then leant against the little gate and picked at its paintwork until Mr Mercer's Bath chair came creaking into view. From a distance the Mercers could look a little ramshackle, but as soon as Mrs Mercer had steered the Bath chair into its berth beside the step, they launched into a routine of the kind of complexity rarely seen outside the Edinburgh Tattoo. Mr Mercer flipped back his blanket, took up his walking stick and swung both legs out. Mrs Mercer jammed her foot against a wheel to steady the chair. Then her husband clamped his free hand down on Aldred's shoulder, took a lungful of air and heaved himself up, with his jacket not far behind.

If Aldred sometimes felt as if he was helping a dead man out of a wicker coffin then it was a resurrection they managed between them every week. Yet in all those Sunday mornings Mrs Mercer never said a single word to Aldred. It wasn't something which particularly bothered him. He didn't imagine the two of them would have had much to say. What bothered him more, as he headed back towards the church with Mr Mercer's powerful hand on his shoulder, was the fact that most boys his age were considerably taller than he was and he couldn't help wondering if having Mr Mercer press down on him every Sunday morning wasn't somehow squashing out of him any growing he'd done in the previous week.

Aldred had learnt to adjust his steps to those of the man behind him. The slightest tightening of Mr Mercer's fingers on his collar-bone told him he was struggling; the merest pressure of his thumb on the muscles above his shoulder-blade told him he had a little breath to spare. There were days when Aldred felt sure Mr Mercer's hand had smoothed into existence its own shallow cavity. He would be sitting at his desk on a Tuesday or a Wednesday and suddenly feel his hand resting heavily on his shoulder, with Mr Mercer nowhere to be seen.

The walk to the church was certainly not getting any faster, but Aldred always took great pride in being able to gauge Mr Mercer's general well-being by keeping an ear on the rattle in his chest, so when he felt the old man dig his fingers into his clavicle on this particular morning Aldred was first sur-prised, then disappointed in his own lack of sensitivity.

'Careful,' wheezed Mr Mercer. 'Mind the plums.'

They stopped for a cough by Mr Wenlock and paused again just before the door. But as soon as they were inside they fairly raced for the organ – a burst of energy, Aldred assumed, intended to show those worshippers already seat-ed just how hale and hearty their organist was. That last dash took its toll, and Mr Mercer would sometimes slump on his bench for several minutes before sitting up and begin pulling out the stops.

With all the organ's pipes racked up around him, Mr Mercer looked like a man at the gates of a fort. The pipes were the same blue, Aldred often noted, as the robes of Jesus, with enough firepower to sink a battleship. He had thought about taking up organ-playing himself, just to get his hands on all those stops and keys – liked the idea of doing that little quickstep over the pedals. What put him off was the prospect of having to learn how to take all the squiggles on the pages of Mr Mercer's hymn book and convert them into something his hands could comprehend – a technique Aldred suspected involved the deadly numbering favoured by Mrs Fog.

Aldred left Mr Mercer and made his way round to his own station at the back of the organ. It was a good deal more dusty and dingy, with none of the polish of the front. He would have quite liked an audience for his pumping and felt that the congregation would have found much to admire. On the other hand, he had his own little den in which to do his thinking and anything else which didn't make too much noise.

The pump handle stuck out of the back of the organ as if someone had buried an axe in it. Aldred undid its clip, cranked it up and down, heard the bellows shift deep in the woodwork, then sat on his stool to wait for the hanky to dance on its string.

A notice was pinned to the back of the organ, about two feet from his face.

DESTRUCTION OF CHURCHES
BY FIRES ORIGINATING IN
THE ORGANS

1. *The organ is damp, a lamp or stove is placed in it and left to burn all night, with the result of setting it on fire.*
2. *The organist, the blower, the tuner, or a workman making repairs, strikes a match, or lights a spirit taper, or candle, which he leaves burning, with the result of setting the organ on fire.*
3. *The music desk lights are movable brackets which can be placed so that the flames touch woodwork; this is done once, and the whole is set on fire.*

ECCLESIASTICAL INSURANCE OFFICE
Lim. 11, Norfolk Street, Strand, London wc

Aldred could recite whole chunks of it verbatim, but despite the fact that it had been pinned up long before his investiture and that the paper on which it was printed was now as dry as old parchment, he couldn't help but take its dire warnings personally.

'Originating' and 'Ecclesiastical' were far beyond the realms of his vocabulary and, no matter how many times he turned them over in his head, 'spirit taper' and 'movable brackets' failed to make any dependable sense. The implication, however, was clear. The organ was primed for conflagration – was a fireman's nightmare, a tinderbox – and, hearing that Aldred was going to be in its vicinity, a committee had been convened in London and a list of directives drawn up.

So the moment Mr Mercer tugged on his end of the string and Aldred saw the hanky jump, he began pumping – to fire the opening chords across the bows of the congregation . . . to keep the airless Mr Mercer inflated . . . to keep that great wooden palace of an organ afloat and dragging the audience a beat and a half behind . . . to build up his muscles and make himself as big as the other boys. But he pumped hardest of all because of those flames which threatened to flicker into existence in the vast, dry wastes of the organ's insides. Pumped until he was puffing and panting almost as badly as Mr Mercer to keep those flames from coming about. *The dampness . . . the spirit taper . . . the movable bracket* – three easy ways for an absent-minded boy to let an organ catch fire. Three blazing organs, side by side, and every one of them his own fault.

The only bit of the notice which offered him any consolation was the Ecclesiastical Insurance Office's address. Aldred knew very well that the Strand was right next to the Embankment. From their window the people whose job it was to warn organ-pumpers about setting fire to organs would be able to see Cleopatra's Needle – be able to relax in its shadow on a hot summer's day. So as Aldred pumped and felt the sweat trickle down his back he kept his eyes fixed on the Strand until Mr Mercer held down the last chord and he heard the reassuring clunk and clatter of the congregation returning to their seats.

Aldred had pumped out 'Let us with a gladsome mind' and 'Lord of mercy and of might', and the Romans had marched in and back out again, when the Reverend Bentley's voice dropped by the best part of an octave and he whispered, 'Let us pray.' Aldred put his hands together, closed his eyes and rested his forehead on his fingertips. He had often wondered why children prayed with such devotion whilst their parents just linked a few indifferent fingers and stared at the floor. He wondered also how the Reverend Bentley prayed at all with such swollen fingers, but the man obviously managed, for his prayers would sometimes last upwards of five minutes and cover a whole host of things.

On this particular Sunday they included a reference to a leaking roof (which might have been real or metaphorical), a fallen tree (likewise) and some ginger biscuits which had arrived in the post from a sister in Salisbury. The reverend's meditations could last so long and meander so wildly that Aldred would sometimes be tempted to steal an illicit peek of light, but when he heard the reverend mention the Focke Wulf's attack on the village he felt the powerful beam of celebrity swing onto him and squeezed his eyes even tighter shut.

Thanks were given that no one in the parish had been seriously injured. One could only guess, the reverend said, whether the pilot had been despatched with orders to terrorise the citizens of the South Hams or had simply added it to his itinerary. The Reverend Bentley then informed the congregation that he had been out that morning, following the path of bullet-holes up and down the lane and made a rather startling discovery. The reverend paused. Aldred stared into his own deep well of darkness and tried to imagine what it might be and when the reverend finally continued his voice was so quiet that when Lillian Minter turned her good ear towards the pulpit the rest of the congregation did the same.

There were bullet-holes in the war memorial, the reverend told them. Bullets in the monument to the Great War's dead. What kind of man, he asked, would show such contempt for the fallen? What kind of man, he demanded, would strafe a village street? And, in an uncustomary fit of fire and brimstone, he suggested that for those who regarded themselves as being above the law of God, Judgement Day would prove a rude awakening.

But his pronouncements were wasted on Aldred, whose eyes had popped open at the first mention of bullet-holes in the war memorial and when the reverend moved on to other prayerful considerations his organ-pumper was left far behind. The congregation said their amens without him, the reverend announced the next hymn and Mr Mercer plucked at the string and the hanky twitched behind the organ but Aldred Crouch just stared into space. Time and again, Mr Mercer held down the opening chord of 'The Saviour's head was crowned with thorns', without a whisper coming up from the organ's great arsenal of pipes. The only sound was the light clatter of his fingernails tapping the keys, and the whole service had lost its way when either the hanky or the congregation's embarrassed silence finally managed to get between Aldred and the war memorial. He leapt to his feet, grabbed the lever and started pumping. Pumped harder than he had ever pumped before. And, like a gramophone cranked back up to speed, the organ groaned into life, the bones of a tune were thrown to the congregation and the great cogs of Sunday morning turned again.

The journey back through the graveyard seemed to take for ever and along the way Aldred had to weather a terrible, if wheezy, tirade. But the moment the organist let go of his shoulder and gravity was pulling the old man back into his chair, Aldred was off like a shot towards the war memorial with his key flailing about his ears.

A small crowd had already gathered around it. Some old fellow was pointing his walking stick up at the bullet-holes, as if he might take some credit for picking them out. Aldred forced his way through to the front until he could see the holes himself, then stood and stared at them with what he hoped was the same sort of expression as the one-legged

81

servicemen looking into the hole in the ground, and the harder he stared at the spidery cracks in the stone the more convinced he became that they spelt out some strange message of their own.

England Expects

Considering the incredible commotion when the Focke Wulf went over, the only wonder was that it didn't leave more carnage in its wake. The few people who actually saw the plane fly down the high street were unanimous in their opinion that if it had been any lower it would have trimmed off all the chimney pots.

The Post Office had been in full session, with Miss Pye telling her customers in the strictest confidence about a suspicious pregnancy out in Tuckenhay, and Mrs Mercer was crossing the road to join them when she heard what she thought, at first, was a lorry hurtling down the hill – a lorry which must have taken the brow above the church at such a lick that its wheels had left the ground. Then suddenly the lorry had wings and was heading straight for her. And was nothing like a lorry at all. She saw the road erupting towards her. Heard the rattle of gunfire. Then she was scrambling over her own garden wall and throwing herself headfirst into her own lupins to get out of the way.

Naturally, the Boys were delighted that their village had been singled out for such malevolent attention, but couldn't help but feel that the occasion would have been better distinguished by a fatality or two. If the pilot had only swung by when the pow-wow at the Post Office was dispersing he would have had plenty of old folk hobbling about the place. Then there would have been stretchers and blankets and bandages, and ambulances racing up and down the lanes.

They gathered by the war memorial late on the Sunday afternoon to gaze at the runes of the bullet-holes. Someone suggested getting a ladder so that they could run their fingers along the tiny cracks and crevices, but no one could be bothered to go and look for one. Then they set off down the lane, from one bullet-hole to another, like a tour around old Pompeii, with Bobby and Aldred newly promoted to second-lieutenants alongside Finn and Hector, and Harvey and Lewis bringing up the rear.

They came to a halt outside the Mercers' cottage. A few bits of the drystone wall were still scattered in the lane and Hector turned one over with his boot and wondered aloud how things might have turned out if Mrs Mercer had failed to find a foothold or been pushing her one-lunged husband in his Bath chair and had had to abandon him.

Lewis was pointing to the broken lupins, indicating the area where Mrs Mercer had landed among them and the likely path of her flight, when there was a violent rapping at one of the windows and the boys looked up to see Mrs Mercer herself shaking a bandaged fist at them. For a couple of seconds they stood their ground, as if they had been doing nothing wrong and were determined that they had every right to be there. Then they turned and, engaging one another in rather self-conscious conversation, shuffled off down the lane.

On the whole, the village tended to tolerate the Captain's odd little habits. If he wanted to lock himself away all day with his boats and bottles then that was his business. Harvey's mother reckoned she was about as much of a captain as he was and the one time Hector's father tried to coax some nautical anecdote out of him he swore you could see him piecing the story together as he went along. But if sitting hunched over a tray all day was considered quite harmless during peacetime, doing so on a Sunday when the country was at war was something else again. Some of the Boys had heard their mothers use the word 'unpatriotic' to describe such behaviour and as their own attitude towards the man alternated between ridicule and suspicion it wasn't long before they managed to link the Focke Wulf's visit with the Captain's semaphore.

Bobby and the Five Boys met one night round the back of the graveyard to discuss the possibility that they had a Nazi sympathiser in their midst. Establishing the Captain's guilt took only a matter of seconds. What took a little longer was agreeing a suitable response. Lewis proposed setting fire to the Captain's cottage, and for a while they all sat around and imagined the flames spewing from the windows and the old man trapped inside. Finn and Hector were in no hurry to oppose the idea, knowing that sooner or later one of the other boys would voice their concerns, and it was Lewis who eventually pointed out that any incriminating charts or codebooks would go up with the Captain and the proposal was put to one side.

Other offensives were bandied about – there was much talk of tunnels and rope with hooks attached to the end of it – but all the Boys wanted to do was break into the Captain's cottage and have a snoop around. It was generally accepted that the attic room from which he sent his semaphore was probably the heart of his operations, where all his files and papers would be stored, and from that point on the discussion concentrated on how they might make their way up to it and what they might be likely to find.

Aldred was all for forging a letter from Miss Pye, full of hints and promises, with a map and directions to some far-flung tryst. Finn suggested luring him out into the garden and hitting him over the head with a brick. The longer they waited, they knew, the more chance there was of common sense prevailing, so they resolved there and then to break into the Captain's house on the night of his next semaphore, which would enable them to find out who he was sending messages to. Hector proposed that Bobby should be the one to do it. It would, he said, be a sort of initiation, although the word meant nothing to Bobby or any of the other Boys.

Bobby was so relieved to be on the same side as the Five Boys that any misgivings he had about creeping up on the Captain were swept away. If the old man was stupid enough to draw attention to himself, he thought, then he would just have to face the consequences.

Bobby was a bag of nerves all day Tuesday and hardly touched his supper, which got Miss Minter worrying that the Five Boys had been at him again, and as he crouched in the alley by the Captain's cottage at eight o'clock what little food he'd managed to get down him threatened to come back up.

Aldred was on the roof of the church tower with his imaginary binoculars directed at the Captain's cottage. The moment the light went on in the attic he dropped to his knees, crept over to the far wall and put his head through the parapet.

'He's there,' he whispered down into the darkness. 'He's *there.*'

Lewis saluted and set off across the graveyard. He'd been standing among the gravestones for the last five minutes and was glad to be leaving them behind. He marched down the path but covered the last few yards on all fours, as agreed in the briefing, and popped his head above the gate. He waved at Harvey who was crouched beside the war memorial and when he waved a second time Harvey spotted him and waved back.

Finn leant against the corner of the Captain's cottage and Harvey was aware that he could easily have strolled right over to him, but dutifully crawled round the base of the war memorial and waved in Finn's direction until he disappeared down the side of the house.

Bobby was wearing Aldred's balaclava. It was meant to help him sneak about the place without being seen, but seemed to be doing nothing but generate a great deal of heat and make his ears itch and he was still debating whether to take if off and put it in his pocket when Finn came jogging down the alleyway.

Hector was right beside Bobby and patted him on the shoulder.

'You ready?' he said.

86

Bobby nodded, took a breath and headed towards the Captain's porch.

He must have got to his feet a bit too fast after so much crouching. All the blood which should have been in his head seemed to be slopping around in his boots. But he kept his eyes on his destination and tacked his way towards it like a drunk. And once he was inside the wooden porch he paused and hung off the door handle for a few seconds to try and recover himself.

He must have opened that door half a dozen times during his first few days as an evacuee and when he thought of all the cakes and peculiar conversation he'd shared with the Captain a wave of shame threatened to wash him away, but he threw his weight into the door, the door popped open. Then he was in the Captain's parlour, with the Captain nowhere to be seen.

As he closed the door behind him Bobby felt as though he was shutting the door on his own prison cell. He tip-toed into the room, stood and looked around for a moment before crawling into a corner and hiding behind an armchair. He drew his knees up to his chin and studied the weave of the material a few inches from his face to try and calm himself, but his head felt as if it was boiling and Aldred's balaclava was now damp and heavy with sweat.

'What if he smells me?' Bobby thought. 'What if he smells me hiding in his house?'

It had been agreed that Hector and Finn would count to a hundred before knocking, so that Bobby would have enough time to hide away, and as he sat there he was sure he could hear them slowly reeling off the numbers out in the alleyway. The bottled ships were stacked all around him and Bobby thought of all the work that had gone into them. Then he imagined the tiny ships lying wrecked on the floor in a sea of shattered glass and the Captain standing among them, heart-broken. He reached a hand out and lifted down the nearest bottle, and was still looking in at all the flags and the tiny cannon hatches when Finn and Hector began to hammer at the door.

They must have got themselves all fired up because they hammered a second time before the Captain was even halfway down the stairs. Bobby saw him go by, pulling his dressing gown around him and as soon as he heard the door open and Hector and Finn start talking, Bobby crept out and headed for the cover of a table, with the neck of the bottle still gripped in his hand. He got to his feet and set off up the stairs, watching each plimsolled footstep, expecting a loud creak with every one and was so preoccupied with the stairs that when he reached the attic he thought he must have entered the wrong room.

There were no radios, no charts, no Nazi banners. Just the telescope balancing on its tripod and a couple of boxes up against a wall. He crept forward; could still hear Heck and Finn blathering away far below him. He bent over, put his eye up to the eyepiece and squinted into it. A second later he recoiled, blinking. Stared at the floor, bewildered, before putting his eye back to the telescope.

Whatever subject Finn and Hector had decided to bring to the Captain's attention could not have been half as engrossing as they had hoped, and Bobby was still peering through the telescope when he heard the door slam shut and, a moment or two later, the Captain's feet on the stairs. All the briefings were suddenly redundant. He was meant to gather some evidence, hide in the back bedroom and make his escape when the Captain returned to his semaphore. But there *was* no other bedroom and if he ran down the stairs now he would only meet the Captain coming up.

Bobby looked frantically round the room, still gripping the bottle. Felt as if his balaclava was about to burst into flames. The Captain had taken off his dressing gown before he'd got to the top of the stairs. He strode into the room, threw it to one side and went straight over to the telescope. Put his eye up to it, then pulled away. Looked again, shifted the barrel an inch or two to the left. And when he was satisfied that it was back where it should be, he turned to shut the door.

Lewis and Harvey had joined Aldred on the church tower the moment their signals had been passed down the line and with a little effort could just make out Heck and Finn chattering away to the Captain. They saw Bobby appear behind the attic's net curtain. Saw him peering through the telescope. Then the door to the Captain's cottage slammed shut.

Lewis turned to Aldred. 'That's not long enough,' he said.

Bobby stuck his head out between the net curtains and stared helplessly into the night and the three Boys abandoned their binoculars and began waving and hissing to him across the great divide. When the Captain swept back into the attic the curtains were still settling. The Boys watched him go straight over to the telescope, look through it, adjust it. Saw him turn and shut the door, then slowly return to his handkerchief-waving, with Bobby spreadeagled against the slates just a yard or two to his right.

The Boys ducked back behind the parapets.

'What's he got in his hand?' said Lewis.

'A bottle,' said Aldred.

Lewis tried digesting this information. 'Why a bottle?' he said.

Bobby didn't dare move for two or three minutes. He lay there with his feet in the gutter, convinced he'd be spending the rest of his life stuck up on that roof. Then he got the idea that if he could only climb up to the chimney stack he might find a less precipitous way back down and twice set off for it only to slide back down to the gutter with his fingers clutching at the slates.

He rested his cheek against the cold roof and brought the dimple bottle up to his face. Looked in at the ship. He thought of all the strong men on a boat like that. Then he went down on all fours and, with his left knee dredging the gutter, began to crawl away from the window until he reached the corner of the house.

The ground was a good forty feet below him. In a couple of minutes, he told himself, it would all be over. He saw himself being congratulated by the other Boys. Then he turned, swung his legs out over the gutter and began to ease himself down into the dark.

He fished around for the drainpipe with his foot. The gutter dug into his stomach, and he had to lift himself out and away from it before being able to drop down and get his arms around the pipe – a manoeuvre he thought he'd successfully completed when his descent was suddenly halted, something pulled at his hair and he realised that Aldred's balaclava had snagged on one of the gutter's brackets. He hung there, as quietly as possible. Didn't have the strength to pull himself back up and was not about to let go of the drainpipe. He began to slip. The balaclava began to throttle him. He could feel the power in his arms and legs begin to fail. He felt a blackness slowly flood his vision and the blood in his head go cold. Then his neck slackened, his head dropped back, slid free and he left the balaclava hanging from the gutter, with a hank of his hair in it.

The Boys watched in awe as he climbed down the side of the cottage. The only thing which would have impressed them more would have been if he'd slipped, fallen and broken his neck. But as soon as he was on the ground they charged down the steps of the church tower and once they'd reconvened in the graveyard any inclination to praise him for his heroism had been superceded by their eagerness to hear what he'd spied through the Captain's telescope.

Bobby seemed reluctant to share his findings and the more cagey he became the more the Five Boys pressed him.

'*Ladies*,' he said, at last.

The Boys looked at one another.

'What sort of ladies?' said Hector.

Bobby rubbed the back of his neck. 'Ladies,' he said, 'like your mums.'

The Boys were dumbfounded. They had never imagined

that their mothers might be caught up in a spy ring. It was almost inconceivable.

'At the keep-fit class,' said Bobby, 'at the village hall.'

The Boys still didn't understand.

Bobby reached out his arms and mimed some of the spins and twirls he'd seen through the telescope. Without the Indian clubs, they looked remarkably like the Captain's semaphore.

The Boys sat in silence and considered the implications.

Aldred was staring at Bobby. 'Where's my balaclava?' he said.

If the Invader Comes

The people of south Devon had always taken great pride in their coastline and had a particular affection for their beaches. But when the war came that affection suddenly soured and they became the place where the enemy was most likely to come sweeping in.

Lorryloads of soldiers turned up and spent all week sinking great lumps of concrete into the sand. Laid thousands of mines and rolled out great coils of barbed wire, so that by the time they left, the beaches looked less like a place anticipating a battle and more like a place where one had just passed through.

In the years since, France had fallen. Now German E-boats patrolled the Channel, and morale among the villagers had never been lower when they woke one morning to find a leaflet on their doormat, headed

If the

INVADER

comes

—

WHAT TO DO AND HOW TO DO IT

The text was laid out below in four narrow columns, like a political manifesto with all the optimism trimmed away. Instead, the dead hand of the War Office prevailed, cheerlessly listing the steps each civilian should take if the enemy ever landed on their shore. One's primary concern, it said, should be to hamper the invading army's progress and accommodate the British forces' response, but whilst the pamphlet went to great lengths to emphasise the need to keep one's head, its very existence did nothing but convince the villagers that the enemy was at the door and might come bursting in at any time.

Vigilance, the leaflet insisted, was paramount. Rumours should be given no credence, and in the unlikely event of an invasion the British troops would be served best by people staying put, rather than blocking the roads in flight. In fact, if necessary, they should consider putting their vehicles out of action to avoid them being commandeered by the enemy – a recommendation a local police constable was said to have inflicted unstintingly (and somewhat prematurely) on his bicycle, hiding its various parts all around the house and flower beds. A few days later, when his need for his bicycle outweighed the likelihood of an invasion, he set about reassembling it, but it was never quite the same. He couldn't remember where he'd hidden the saddle. The bicycle could still be ridden for shorter journeys, with him standing on the pedals – an inconvenience he sought to conceal by looking intently over the hedgerows as if suspecting nefarious activity there.

Certainly, the threat of invasion was real enough for every villager to lie in bed at night and imagine the invading army – stormtroopers marching past the Post Office or gangs of men, blacked up, creeping along the ditches with their bayonets drawn. But if everyone had their own idea what the invaders might look like, they all came up from the coast, still gritty from their landing, and talking in the same strange Germanic tongue – so when the South Hams finally fell it was doubly confounding for the locals that the invasion should come from the north, rather than the sea, and consist not of Germans but of gum-chewing Americans.

They came in twos and threes at first – high-ranking military men who stepped out of chauffered cars in their trench coats, to point their batons across the fields or stare through binoculars along Slapton Sands. And, since all the signposts had been uprooted as a precaution against a possible invasion, they were often obliged to stop their cars and ask the locals where they were.

These occasional sightings encouraged precisely the sort of rumour the War Office disapproved of – of German battle-ships massing out in the Channel, of extra armaments being shipped in to keep them at bay. Of fifth columnists arrested at Blackawton in possession of a map of Buckfastleigh. All sorts of rumours did the rounds that autumn, but the ones con-cerning American servicemen coming to south Devon to pre-pare for landing on continental Europe came up with such frequency that the others eventually fell by the wayside to be replaced by variations on this single theme.

An additional and more worrying rumour was that, in order to accommodate these manoeuvres, a great swathe of the county was to be requisitioned and all its inhabitants cleared from the site – a bit of gossip only the gloomiest Jeremiah could have taken any pleasure recounting, since no one knew where this commandeered territory was meant to begin and end. So when posters went up announcing impor-tant meetings in village halls, everyone had an idea what they might be about, even if they could never quite conceive such an evacuation coming to pass.

In the event, three thousand people were given their notice that November – were given just six weeks to pack their things and go. And as Mr Steere told anyone who cared to lis-ten, it wasn't just the pots and pans you had to take with you, but every last possession you didn't want to risk being blown to bits.

The Reverend Bentley thought his parish got off rather lightly. The thirty thousand acres to be evacuated stopped just short of the village, with the lane around the bottom of the hill acting as its perimeter, and of all the farms and hous-es which bought their groceries at the Post Office only Miss Minter's cottage and Steere's farm fell within its bounds.

The village would ultimately have a ringside seat for the arrival of the Americans, but only after witnessing the depar-ture of all the Devonians who had been ousted from their homes. By late November two or three families were passing through the village each day, their trailers packed under tarpaulin and drawn by a borrowed tractor or a horse. But as December's deadline approached, more and more of Devon's refugees crept by with their world in tow, until the last few days when they seemed to be going by every half an hour.

The children sat up on top of the trailers, waving and smiling as if they were running away with the circus whilst their parents travelled up front, barely managing a nod or a wink as they went by. But it was *their* parents, the old folk sitting stiffly beside them, who seemed unable to comprehend what they were living through and had the same bewildered expressions on their faces as the next of kin at a funeral.

Many of them had never set foot outside the same few hills and valleys. Some refused to go. Doctors were called out, sedatives were dispensed. The WVS arrived and brewed up great urns of tea. But all the tea in China couldn't explain to the elders of south Devon why they were being cleared from the land they had spent their lives nurturing to see it turned into a bombing range.

Henry Fowler was two days short of his seventieth birthday when the evacuation was confirmed. His son called in on his way home from the meeting, sat beside him and told him what he had just been told himself. Over the following weeks, whilst every other farmer was rounding up his livestock and boarding up his windows, Henry Fowler didn't pack a single box. His only interruption was his son and daughter-in-law who dropped in every few days with news of a nephew up near Dartmoor who'd be happy to have him, or old friends out near Exeter who could do with the company.

When the car finally came to collect him the driver knocked on the front door for a couple of minutes then went round the back and found him sitting among the vegetables. He sat cross-legged in his best suit, with his elbows resting on his knees – had underestimated how much blood he had in him and the enamel bowl in his lap had overflowed onto the soil.

It could be said that Henry Fowler was just the first of many casualties, and that by finding his way into the graveyard before the area was sealed off he finally managed to have his own way. Half an hour after the funeral the vicar was fixing chicken wire over the stained-glass windows and packing the last of the church's valuables into straw, and by December 20th every last man, woman and child was cleared from their houses, with no idea how long it would be before they'd be allowed back in.

Bobby was getting used to being evacuated. Lillian had given him the option of moving into a house in the village but he chose to accompany her out to her sister's farm near Dittisham. Before leaving, Miss Minter gave Howard Kent strict instructions about looking in on her cottage and making sure that everything was secure before the roadblocks finally went up. So, on that last afternoon, with the light already fading, Howard crossed the bridge, marched up the path and went right round the cottage, rattling the doors and checking the latches and generally wondering what kind of state it was going to be in in six months' time. He cupped his eyes at the parlour window and pictured GIs getting up to all sorts of mischief inside. There's not a lock or bolt yet invented, he told himself, which will stop a man breaking into a house if he puts his mind to it.

He stood at the gate, looked up and down the empty lane and decided to take a more circuitous route home, via Duncannon and back along the riverside. As he went along he thought how there was something quietly sinister in the air – as if some terrible calamity had been visited on the place. Half a mile down the road, Steere's farm looked oddly empty – all battened down, as if expecting a hurricane. There were no rusting ploughs or piles of timber, no chickens scratching at the dirt, and Howard strolled up the track and had a good look through the windows there as well.

As he walked on, something about all the deserted houses began to arouse him. He imagined himself going silently from room to room in another man's property, free to do whatever he liked. To relieve himself against the stone sink where the owner's wife stood to do her washing. To kick in the door to where their precious children slept.

His thoughts blossomed and bloomed and carried him along with them, until he could hear his heart thumping in his ears and had to stop at the side of the road and unbutton his trousers. And the moment he got hold of himself he went back to prowling round the houses and kicking down the doors.

Half an hour later he was walking down Duncannon's steep high street, with all the front doors locked and every window stripped of its curtains. There was no lamplight, no fires burning. There was a deadliness at work, as if the breath had been sucked right out of the place.

He quickened his step and hurried on between the rows of dumb houses, but when he got to the bottom of the hill he turned, to try to establish what had been bothering him. A large grey rat sat in the middle of the street, washing its whiskers. It looked as happy as a king. Howard had seen plenty of rats in his time, but this one was especially repellent. When it finished cleaning itself it just sat there looking at him – seemed to be waiting for him to go.

The first GI steered his jeep around the war memorial soon after eight o'clock the following morning and raised an almost apologetic hand to Mrs Heaney, but within the hour the trucks were rolling by, bumper to bumper, and the soldiers were waving and throwing sweets to the children as if they were liberating the place.

By mid-morning the lanes brimmed with the sweet blue mist of diesel exhaust. It seeped through the hedgerows and spilled across the winter fields. The villagers lined the streets and covered their mouths with their handkerchiefs. They were accustomed to recognising every person who came down the high street, and as Miss Pye leant against her window sill and rattled a humbug around her mouth she couldn't help but look at each face as if it might suddenly become familiar – which made her first giddy, then a little sick.

The lanes around the village had barely changed in centuries – the same sluggish circulation sustaining the same cottages and farms. At half past seven there was hardly a soul out on them. Then the whole world seemed to come crashing in.

The Boys were the village's first ambassadors. Reports had reached them that the soldiers at the checkpoint on the bridge down by Miss Minter's were brandishing rifles and had a wind-up telephone and that there were jeeps sweeping up and down the lanes, so on the last Saturday before Christmas they formed a delegation and set off down the hill.

They got as far as the crossroads, with the soldiers clearly visible a few hundred yards away, before their nerve suddenly failed them. Harvey Noyce had been working himself up into a lather. The soldiers would be jumpy, he said. They were in a foreign country. Five strange boys suddenly turning up could easily startle them and who was to say they wouldn't open fire?

It was hard to tell how nervous a soldier was from such a distance. Aldred suggested sneaking down the ditch and having a closer look, but Harvey was insisting that they should give them a couple of days to settle in and come back later, when a jeep came speeding round the corner of the boundary road. The Five Boys scattered, convinced that they were about to be gunned down. Heck and Finn ran back up the lane. Harvey and Aldred clambered through a hedge. Lewis leapt into the ditch – had high hopes of vaulting the fence on the other side but the ditch was so deep and its contents so thick that it gripped him by the ankles. The other Boys could hear his cries for help echoing across the fields but kept on running and when they eventually stopped and looked back, fully

98

expected to see him being handcuffed and bundled into the jeep but instead saw the jeep's driver and Lewis engaged in apparently amiable conversation and, after hastily reviewing the situation, began to creep back down the hill.

It was their first opportunity to look at an American jeep at close quarters. It had a white, five-pronged star stencilled on the bonnet and a complicated sequence of numbers over the arch of each wheel. The driver was in the wrong seat, along with his steering wheel. By the time Aldred climbed back through the hedge and joined the others the conversation was well under way, and as the soldier talked he noticed that one of his front teeth was solid gold. It glittered in the sunlight and Aldred wondered what it must taste like. He was, frankly, impressed that someone with such an obvious physical shortcoming could have risen through the ranks to the point where he had his own jeep. The soldier scratched his neck between the rim of his helmet and the collar of his jacket and seemed about as relaxed as a grown man could be. He looked like the kind of fellow, Aldred thought, who, if he was your father, might still have enough spirit in him to have a little wrestle with you at the end of the day.

The Boys did their best to keep the conversation going and give themselves more time to take in the great tread of the jeep's tyres and all the dashboard's buttons and dials, but after a couple of minutes the driver sat himself up, revved the engine and began winding the steering wheel and seemed ready to go when he paused, turned back to the Boys and flashed that gold tooth of his. He gave them a wink and his eyes dropped down their bodies. The Boys had no idea what he was going to do and it wasn't until he leant over and placed his hand on theirs that they realised what a tight hold they had on the side of his jeep.

They stepped back, the soldier revved the engine again and saluted them. The wheels ripped at the dirt and the jeep sped off down the lane. The Boys stood and watched it disappear. Then stood there a little while longer. If they waited long enough, Aldred thought, the jeep would come round again.

Lewis hopped back to the ditch where he'd left one of his boots and the others watched as he retrieved it, then they headed back towards the village, and as they hiked up the hill Hector asked if anyone had noticed the jeep's windshield and how it was hinged so that it could fold down onto the bonnet, and somebody else mentioned the soldier's gold tooth. And first one, then all the others admitted that they hadn't understood a single word the soldier had said.

Americans

The village would frequently wake, confounded. Would find itself steeped in a meteorological condition somewhere between mist and drizzle, capable of lasting days, sometimes weeks at a time. No rain ever fell, no mist materialised. But each cottage was cast adrift. Lamps were extinguished late in the morning and relit early in the afternoon and anyone stepping out, even to fill the coal scuttle, stepped back in to find their hair and coat shrouded with dew.

One such stupor descended soon after the Americans and hung about for the best part of a month. Christmas '43 was muted by it; 1944 crept blindly in. All the lanes into the evacuated area now had a checkpoint on them and every request to enter, whether it was old Raybe wanting to pick up a bedstead or Steere wanting to check on his roof, was politely refused. Patrols drove up and down the perimeter road, like druids in their hooded waterproofs, and a motorcycle messenger would sometimes blunder through the village, but there was no sign of all the lorries that had roared by a few weeks earlier, as if the land had simply opened up and swallowed them.

It was assumed that the Americans were busy preparing for, or already participating in, manoeuvres too distant or too clandestine to be heard. The locals liked to talk about the ease with which a fellow could slip through a hedge and stroll straight into the commandeered area, but the fact that none of them knew what sort of reception would be waiting for them was enough to keep them out.

There were occasional sightings of Americans beyond the area's boundaries. In early January a retired butcher bumped into a couple of GIs having a stroll down by the old paper mill and was asked how many more days of such deadly weather they might have to endure. The ex-butcher peered into the murk and sniffed the air with great authority before informing them that he hadn't the faintest idea. The three of them sheltered under a tree and smoked a cigarette and when they parted one of the GIs gave the ex-butcher a full pack of Lucky Strike which he placed on the bar beside his pint in the Malsters' Arms that evening and kept him in conversation until closing time.

A week or two later a young mother returned from the shops in Dartmouth to find her daughter perched on the wall beside a large black man. The girl had been showing the off-duty soldier her embroidery and the soldier had shown her a cross-stitch of his own. When he saw the young girl's mother approaching he rose and introduced himself – said his name was William Johnson but that his friends all called him BJ. He was invited in and in the time it took the kettle to boil he drew a map of America on a paper bag to show where he came from, but all the woman saw was a crumpled rug of a country and the soldier's home somewhere lonely in the middle which, by his own admission, was nowhere near New York or Hollywood.

In late January the Reverend Bentley stepped off the train at Totnes, having spent the day with a colleague in Dawlish, to be greeted by the stationmaster who informed him that the town's only taxi had come off the road at Boreston Foot, flattened an outhouse and ended up in the poultry pen. This came as a mighty blow to the reverend and even as the news was being relayed to him he could feel twinges of anticipatory pain in his hips and knees, and the only thing to distract him from them was trying to gauge how much of the stationmaster's evident pleasure was due to the taxi's accident and how much came from the inconvenience it was causing the likes of him.

There were no buses and no prospect of them. They rarely ventured out much after noon and when they did, steered a course around some of the villages as if they were the last strongholds of the bubonic plague. The reverend felt a rueful attitude come upon him. He set his case down. It was getting dark and he pictured his warm coat hanging up in the hallway of the vicarage and was chewing over the stationmaster's lack of humanity when a lorry pulled up, the driver wound down the window and, in a thick American drawl, asked if he might offer him a lift.

It took a couple of attempts for the reverend to get up the steps, but soon the lorry was grinding up the Kingsbridge Road, with him up in the cab beside the driver, feeling as though he was being carried home, triumphant, on a tank. The two men talked until they were halfway up the hill and turned off into the wooded lanes, then they both hunched forward and focused on the few yards of illuminated road ahead of them.

It may have been his own personal counterblast against the stationmaster or a simple act of gratitude, but as they crawled through the darkness towards the village it occurred to the reverend that he should arrange a social for his good Samaritan and his fellow-servicemen and give them the welcome they deserved.

The next day, straight after breakfast, he checked the village hall diary, which was completely blank apart from Ladies' Keep Fit every Tuesday and the bring-and-buy on the Easter weekend. He dictated a letter to Mrs Heaney for the attention of the soldier's commanding officer and was on the phone to him the following day, arranging a date and how many servicemen might practically be invited. He put it in the diary, but when he asked Mrs Heaney to knock up a couple of posters for some of the neighbouring villages on the Tuesday she seemed to drag her heels. What the reverend didn't know was that by then every able-bodied woman in a ten-mile radius knew all about it and was already wondering what clothes to wear.

With half an hour before the doors were due to open the

queue stretched right back down past the Post Office and on towards Platt's farm. The women who had made their way in from nearby villages leant against the wall and slipped their feet from their boots into their best shoes. The rest tucked their chins into their coat collars and stamped their feet, as if trying to jog in them some memory of dance steps from years before. Sylvia Crouch had her arm linked through Phyllis Massie's. The other mothers were in the queue not far behind. Two hundred women stood out in the cold, waiting for the door to open. Howard Kent was about the only man among them. As he'd told Miss Pye the day before, he thought he'd better go along, 'just to keep an eye on the girls'.

In the hall, the older ladies were still furiously inflating balloons and passing them up to the reverend, who stood on his stepladder and stuffed them into the net suspended beneath the ceiling. And by quarter to eight Mrs Heaney was still putting out the cups and saucers when Miss Pye, seeing no sense in half the women in the county catching cold, told the reverend to get down off his ladder as she was about to open the doors.

The queue lurched forward and a wave of excitement surged back into the darkness. The conversation quickened and as the women shuffled towards the light in the doorway they felt that the evening was finally getting under way. As soon as they were inside Sylvia and Phyllis squeezed into the Ladies to check their grips and curls and apply another coat of lipstick. Women pressed in from all sides to get a look in the mirror. Sylvia was inclined to wonder where the hell they had all sprung from, and when she and Phyllis were finally out on the dance floor she saw just how young some of them were. She remembered one or two when they were babies – girls who only a couple of years earlier had seemed cripplingly self-conscious, but were now straightening their stockings and smoking cigarettes. If I was a soldier, thought Sylvia, who would I go for? Some eighteen-year-old who'd never had her tits touched or some sad old hag like me?

By five past eight the place was heaving, before a single American had even walked through the door, the air so thick with hair lacquer that the Reverend Bentley had trouble breathing and had to stick his head out of the window to clear his lungs. A couple of feet below him two women were taking a slug from a small bottle and, without necessarily intending to, the reverend caught a bit of their conversation. One was saying how she'd been almost beside herself with excitement for the best part of a fortnight, but now that she was here all she wanted was to have some GI walk up and ask her for a dance. He didn't have to look like Clark Gable or Cary Grant, she said. Someone clean and smart would do. Her friend nodded and said that surely, after all the drudgery of the last few years, there was no shame in getting powdered up and having a little drink and a dance for an hour or two?

Mrs Heaney wrestled gamely with the gramophone but most of her audience had their backs to her, smoothing their skirts and chatting to their neighbours, with their eyes all fixed on the door. The minutes flicked by on the clock on the proscenium arch and the conversation slowly ebbed away, until only Lena May's voice filled the air, singing about the delights of 'Running out to gather lilies' to a hall filled with women who might as well have been cast in stone.

At quarter past, Phyllis Massie turned to Sylvia with tears in her eyes. 'What if something's come up?' she said.

It was a quite reasonable proposition. Things had a habit of coming up. Something had come up in '39, just as it had done a generation earlier. Something which had led almost all of the village's men away. *And when they go*, thought Sylvia, *something goes with them. Some part of life is put on hold. War never fails to get the men's attention. You've only got to rattle a drum and they come running. You only have to peep on a whistle and they fall into line.*

'They've had to cancel,' said the woman next to Phyllis.

And in that second all their hopes were broken. All the hours of bathing and powdering seemed suddenly foolish;

the weeks of anticipation went to waste. There was nothing but the prospect of a night spent dancing with a best friend, bickering over who was going to take the lead. And Howard Kent strutting up and down the place, like the cat who got the cream.

As the word went round, some of the younger girls started crying. Most of them had never been to a dance before. Lena May exhausted the pleasures of lily-gathering and Mrs Heaney had her head tucked under the table, flicking through her box of 78s. The gramophone needle slid into the play-out groove and swept towards the shore of the label. And only then, above that gritty crackle, did the distant rumble of lorries become audible. The women held their breath; listened. Listened as the trucks' engines became distinct, then steadily grew. And they drew them in, yard by interminable yard, until the walls of the village hall began to judder. And they could hear the squeak of brakes out in the lane. The clank of tailgates falling open; the clatter of boots landing on the ground. Laughter, conversation. Living, breathing American men.

When they first walked in the soldiers must have wondered what kind of place they'd tripped over. The women just stood and stared at them, open-mouthed. A gramophone needle hissed and clicked repeatedly over the speaker, and for a moment the hall and everyone in it seemed to be caught in its own little loop.

It would have been hard to say where the applause had its origins. It seemed to spring up spontaneously in several places all at once. But it quickly spread and was accompanied by a cheer of such unbridled lust that the Reverend Bentley could only wonder what primeval urges he had let loose upon the world.

As Miss Pye told her customers the following morning, 'They wouldn't waltz and they wouldn't foxtrot. All the Americans wanted to do was *jitterbug*.'

The GIs had had the foresight to bring along their own box of records and, within minutes, had commandeered the gramophone. The noise which proceeded to pump out of the speaker sounded to the local women like nothing but a mad, chaotic clatter. They hadn't a clue how they were meant to dance to it and were a little embarrassed by the utter abandonment with which their dance partners began to hurl themselves about. After a life long governed by the dead reckoning of the ration-book this expenditure of energy alone seemed rash, extravagant. But as the evening settled into its own tempo it became apparent that whatever was loose in the room, far from dissipating, was positively multiplying itself.

The women slowly gave in to the push and pull of their partners, began to swing from hand to hand; found the lurch and smack in the music and forgot to worry what they must look like or where their feet should be. To be turned and handled so ably rekindled in them all sorts of warmth and kindnesses. The American men seemed amazingly at home in their bodies. *No Englishman*, thought Sylvia Crouch, *could ever dance like that*. There was nothing pinched or sour about them and the longer the night went on the more it seemed that everything about these men – their eyes, their hair, their skin – was shining, as if they had been warmed by a brighter sun.

In those few moments when one record was replaced with another and the dancers exchanged a word or two, the women first noticed how strangely the soldiers spoke, as well as the strong smell of apples that came rolling out of them. Not a bad thing to smell of, thought Phyllis. Sort of homely. She was dancing with a big bear of a man and thought it must be the smell of all those American apples seeping through the pores of his skin. It wasn't until the next day that she learnt how the soldiers had called in at the Malsters' and, having been warned against drinking the locals out of their precious beer, had asked the landlord to suggest an alternative and that the cider had tasted just like apple juice.

Only two people conspicuously failed to share the sense of intoxication. Watching the mass of bodies writhing around the dance floor, the Reverend Bentley had a vision of himself as a whoremaster, herding the village's womenfolk into the arms of a clearly libidinous gang of men. More profound was the bitterness at work in Howard Kent, whose heart had been the only one to sink among the hundreds soaring when the GIs finally walked through the door. In that instant he was toppled, and any remaining self-esteem was soon jostled out of him. Howard couldn't jitterbug – had no desire to jitterbug – and when he approached the drunken GI at the gramophone, to first *insist* that he play a barn dance and, twenty minutes later, *demand* the same, the soldier took him to one side and told him, in a whisper, how close he was to being taken outside and having his teeth kicked down his throat.

Howard leant against a wall and tried to look as if he was overseeing the proceedings, like a contented social secretary, whilst all his rage and pain gnawed away inside of him. He tried clapping his hands in time with the music as the women shrieked and wiggled their backsides, but by half past nine he had had enough, picked up his coat and made his way home.

From his bed he could hear the music wafting up through the village and when, a couple of hours later, he heard the opening chords of the hokey-cokey he was still wide awake. He imagined the great ring of people holding hands, the mad rush into the middle and the women laughing as they were squeezed in the crush. The singing stopped, a cheer went up and, a few moments later, there was the first of a hundred bursting balloons, and Howard comforted himself by imagining each one as a shell waiting to meet the Americans when they were finally shipped out to France.

A Pig Memorial

Whether any indiscretions on the night of the social amounted to anything quite as sordid as Howard Kent imagined nobody was saying, but by the time the sun rose the following morning the Americans' brief sortie into the civilising company of women was over and they were back in the confines of their camp.

It is just about possible that a romance founded on the village hall dance floor could have secretly been sustained over the weeks which followed, and Howard regularly speculated on the clandestine gropings and couplings this might entail, but as February fell to March and the sound of artillery began to roll in from the commandeered zone, the women could only imagine how their dance partners were presently occupied.

There were rumours of naval exercises out in Start Bay. There was talk of manoeuvres between Blackawton and Slapton Ley. A story did the rounds of a dog, left behind in the evacuation, slipping under the barbed wire, tripping every mine on the beach and taking the Royal Sands Hotel up with it. But other animals were said to be loose in the no-go area, aside from the wildlife which had so stubbornly ignored the orders to evacuate and the vermin busy making the place their own. A sizeable pig was said to be out and about beyond the roadblocks and its very existence was threatening to push at least one local man beyond the bounds of sanity.

Fred Raybe, the story goes, had packed every last case and trunk onto his trailer and was about to climb aboard himself when he suddenly remembered the Landrace sow he'd spent the best part of eighteen months fattening up. Some owners of pigs keep them in a pen and feed them leftovers. Others, Mr Raybe among them, like to let them wander, gather their own sustenance where they find it and pack on a bit of muscle as they go. So in 1943 it was not uncommon to see the Raybe pig trotting up and down the lane, poking its snout into some unlikely corner or lying fast asleep by the gate, except, of course, on that one afternoon in mid-December when Raybe was about to leave.

If he hadn't had such an arduous journey ahead of him he might have wasted more time trying to track the animal down, but in the end all he could do was heartily curse it and leave it to its fate. It was Harold Snape who claimed to have spotted the pig in Raybe's orchard as he and his own sad little retinue went by later that same day, and *his* friend, Eric Huntley, who happened to mention this to Dexter Fadden in a public house a couple of months later on. Ever since, Dexter had devoted every spare moment to thinking how he might intervene in the pig's destiny, increasingly fearful that someone else might get there first.

Dexter considered himself a man of some intelligence and at the very outset resolved that, rather than go sneaking around the place and getting yourself shot at, the thing to do was think of a way of strolling in, bagging the pig, strolling back out again and having the US Army salute you as you go. It took many hours of exhausting brainwork before he came up with an idea which met such strict criteria – an idea which would ultimately require the participation of what felt like half the town, and was the reason why such an odd collection of people came to be heading towards the checkpoint on a crisp Saturday morning in early spring.

Dexter's lifelong friend, Jackie Taylor, and two of Jackie's workmates, Will and Cyril, helped Dexter carry the coffin, on the understanding that it would be back in the workshop before bedtime with plenty of chops and bacon to follow, just as soon as the animal was divvied up. Will and Cyril had several decades' undertaking experience between them and it was their professional gravity as much as their morning suits that merited their inclusion and encouraged Dexter in his belief that he had the remotest chance of pulling off such an audacious stunt. The Captain went ahead of the coffin, with Aldred Crouch beside him, whose ecclesiastical connection was how the Reverend Bentley's black surplice came to be billowing around the Captain's shoulders as he led them down the lane. Sylvia Crouch and Maureen Tucker followed the pall-bearers, having convinced Dexter only the previous Wednesday, when he was at his lowest ebb, that a gang of men never looked quite so suspicious when they had a couple of women with them, especially when one of them was pushing a pram.

The only member of the cortège whose attendence took some justification was Howard Kent, the simple fact being that he had a knack for inveigling his way into other people's conversations and happened to own a spare dark suit, which had belonged to his father, and now hung off Dexter Fadden much like Mr Mercer's hung off him.

The other mourners weren't used to seeing the Captain out in the open. Like his ships, he tended to be viewed almost exclusively through glass. But Dexter had decided that the Captain's was the only face with sufficient wrinkles and resignation to belong to a clergyman (except for the Reverend Bentley himself), and once the role had been offered to him the Captain felt some long-forgotten theatrical ambition spark up in him and took to standing before his bedroom mirror like a Shakespearian actor and assuming what he considered to be vicarial attitudes. On this Saturday morning he had his best white collar and black pullover on back to front, but despite the others repeatedly assuring him how very clerical he looked he was halfway down the hill before the collar finally succeeded in throttling a convincing expression of devoutness out of him.

Sylvia and Maureen had dyed a couple of old doilies and stitched them to the front of their bonnets, creating veils behind which, they reasoned, any number of tears might be being shed, and the pram in which Maureen's baby slept was so vast and black that the only thing conceivably bigger and blacker would have been a hearse itself. The rest of the party compensated with solemnity what they lacked in suitable attire, but of all his home-made religious regalia only the tablecloth wrapped round Aldred's shoulders gave Dexter any real cause for concern, along with the pole (normally used to open the vestry windows) which he held out before him, with a Christmas decoration glued to the top.

The villagers marched down the hill with their minds on the task before them. In the last few days that hapless pig had been cured and butchered by every one of its mourners a hundred times. The demands on the pig were many, but the creature had loomed largest in Dexter's mind. So, just as the Captain liked to think about Miss Pye sucking on a toffee and Howard Kent chose to torment himself with the thought of local women fornicating with American servicemen, Dexter Fadden closed his eyes to see a Landrace sow, immobilised with obesity, reclining in a dappled light.

'A pig in an orchard,' he told himself before slipping beneath sleep's heavy curtain. 'No need for apple sauce.'

When they were a quarter of a mile from the checkpoint Dexter turned to issue his final instructions. His cheek squeaked against the coffin's polished wood.

'Just remember,' he said. 'We're all very upset.'

Aldred held his window-opening pole out before him like a fishing rod and watched the star on the end of it sail through a cloudless sky. He had wanted to bring the big Bible along, for extra religion, and might have had the hymn board under the other arm had Dexter not insisted that too much churchy luggage would only tire him out.

They crossed the boundary road and slowed their pace on the last bend, with Cyril, the senior undertaker, calling out, 'Left . . . left . . . left, right, left,' in a voice so rich and deep that the coffin acted as its sounding box and soon all four pall-bearers were perfectly, sedately in step. The last hundred yards were as straight as an arrow, which gave the soldiers plenty of time to behold the approaching parade, but judging by the look on their faces when the mourners finally reached them it was nowhere near long enough.

The soldiers and the mourners faced each other through the barbed wire. The only thing to breach the divide was Aldred's religious pole. The villagers all looked to the Captain. But the theatrical ambition Dexter had recently reawakened in him had been extinguished by a paralysing dose of stage fright. The same was true for most of his fellow-mourners, the only exceptions being Aldred Crouch, who had simply adopted his usual Sunday morning persona and Maureen Tucker, who had taken to heart Dexter's earlier instructions and upset herself so successfully with memories of her own grandfather's funeral that real emotion now shook her by her shoulders and real tears crept beneath her veil.

The Americans were finding the whole thing deeply disconcerting. None of their briefings had warned them of the possible appearance of a band of locals bearing one of their dead. The way they all just stood and stared was particularly unsettling and, if for no better reason than to try and break the deadlock, one of the soldiers finally opened his mouth.

'You don't plan to bring that coffin in here, do you?' he said.

The Captain stared moronically back at him. Would have stared at him a good deal longer had Dexter not prompted him from behind.

'*Show him the papers,*' he hissed.

The Captain suddenly seemed to find his place in the script.

'It's been arranged,' he said and his hand disappeared into his surplice and came out clutching a great wad of folded notes, which he passed through the wire.

The first soldier began to leaf through them and his comrade shuffled over to take a look. It appeared that they had just been given a batch of very important documents, including a letter of introduction from the Archdeacon of Exeter, a letter of transit from the Bishop of Budleigh Salterton, notes of condolence from the mayors of Totnes and Newton Abbot and a sheet of notepaper headed 'PORTER'S UNDERTAKERS LTD', with the words 'Death Certificate' written across it and 'PAID IN FULL' stamped below.

The soldier holding the papers seemed to be straining under the weight of all this information.

'Am I right in thinking,' he said, looking up from the papers, 'that you're intending to have a burial?'

'Oh no,' said the Captain. 'Just a memorial service.' He smiled, to show how much comfort such a service can bring. 'A few hymns . . . a few words of remembrance . . . a prayer or two. That sort of thing.'

'So, you intend to bring the coffin back out again?' the soldier said.

'Oh yes,' the Captain told him, most insistent. 'The coffin's got to come back out.'

The soldier looked as if he'd just received a blow to the back of the head. He passed the documents back through the barbed wire. Stood and thought for a moment. Opened his mouth as if he was about to say something. Then shook his head and closed it again.

He went over to the barrier and began to drag it back across the road. As the lane opened up before them a wave of relief swept through the mourners and they were about to move off when the second soldier, who had been doing some thinking of his own, stepped out in front of them.

'I thought the churches were are all locked up,' he said.

The Captain felt suddenly faint. He tugged at his dog collar and stared at the horizon, trying to recall the rehearsal in which this eventuality had come up. But Dexter Fadden, who stood a few feet behind him, knew all too well there had been no such rehearsal and saw his precious pig diminish – saw it shrink and all but disappear.

The whole pig-chase foundered right there on the barricade, and Dexter's many accomplices saw their dreams of ham and home-cured bacon dashed before their eyes. The cortège had finally assumed an air of genuine mournfulness – their heads hung heavy, their feet had turned to stone – when Aldred slipped a hand inside his jacket and pulled out his string necklace with his own church key dangling from it.

'I've got the key,' he said.

The GI shrugged, stepped out of the way and the mourners surged forward. Their pig flickered back to life. The pallbearers got a firm grip of the coffin, Cyril called out *left, right, left* and in no time they had got up a decent head of funereal steam.

Sylvia Crouch glanced back over her shoulder. One of the soldiers was standing and staring after them; the other was winding a telephone. She turned back to the others.

'Let's just find this bloody pig and get out of here,' she said.

There had been all sorts of stories – of barns being smashed to pieces for firewood and houses being razed to the ground – but most of the places the villagers passed seemed to be in much the same condition as when they last laid eyes on them. Once they were out of sight of the checkpoint everyone relaxed a little. The Captain undid his collar, felt the sunshine on him and told himself that he should try and get out and about like this a little more.

It took longer than anticipated to get to the orchard. The path they'd intended taking over the fields had been blocked off which meant they had to go round all the lanes. They stayed in formation in case they met any more Americans, but increased their pace to something a bit more practical and, apart from a wrong turning out by High End which obliged them to make a tight U-turn a few hundred yards further on, the star on Aldred's pole fairly flew between the hedges and in less than an hour Raybe's orchard swung into view.

As soon as they were under the trees the older members of the party slumped to the ground and Will and Cyril directed Sylvia and Maureen in the removal of the coffin lid. Over the weeks Dexter's pig had become so inflated in his imagination he had convinced himself that only a coffin of exceptional dimensions could contain it, and when Jackie Taylor had brought it round the previous evening had insisted on loading it with sandbags so that it wouldn't look any heavier when it left the evacuated area than it had done going in.

Maureen and Sylvia were still heaving the sandbags out and dumping them under the hedge when Dexter, Jackie, Howard and Aldred set off in search of the pig. They all crept forward in a tight little scrum, until Dexter said that this was bloody ridiculous and ordered the others to fan out between the trees.

Dexter went off on his own. After a couple of minutes he thought he heard something rustle and suddenly stopped, to try and establish where it had come from, only for Aldred to go crashing into him and almost lop his ear off with his staff.

Dexter turned, ready to give Aldred a roasting, but hesitated when he saw just how anxious he looked.

'Are you all right?' said Dexter.

Aldred nodded, but seemed to be in no hurry to get back to the pig-hunt.

'What's the matter?' Dexter said.

Aldred's eyes were practically popping out of his head. He leant towards Dexter, as if he was about to share the gravest confidence.

'I keep thinking about its piggy little eyes,' he said.

Dexter patted him on the shoulder and sent him off towards the part of the orchard which seemed least likely to have a pig in it. Then he turned, took a breath and went back to tip-toeing through the undergrowth.

The apples on the ground were brown with rot and flattened themselves under Dexter's boots like boiled potatoes – must have been lying there for the best part of six months.

And if Harry Snape really had seen the pig here way back in December, thought Dexter, there was no earthly reason why the animal should have hung around. It could have holed itself up somewhere. Could have swum across the river. The Americans could have caught it and roasted it on a spit.

Dexter's speculations were interrupted when a pigeon went clattering up into the trees and he turned to find Aldred running hell-for-leather back towards him with his tablecloth-cape flapping behind as if he was about to take flight himself. He was almost home when he caught his pole in a tree's lower branches. His feet flew out from under him and he landed on his back with a thump.

After a moment or two Aldred sat up in the long grass.

'I found him,' he said. 'I found the pig.'

'A horrible big brute he is,' said Aldred, as Dexter galloped past him. 'I reckon he's dead.'

Dexter ran through the orchard like a primitive. Saw himself running in a leopard-skin loincloth, like that trapeze artist he'd seen at a circus a couple of years before.

He finally found the pig in a clearing – not, by any means, the biggest pig Dexter had ever set eyes on but it was pink and had a fair bit of meat on it and lay on its side, with its eyes shut and all its teats exposed. Dexter was still standing and gawping at it when Will Henderson joined him.

Will had seen a few dead things in his time. 'She's not dead,' he said. 'She's just having herself a little kip.'

Within two minutes the other mourners had gathered around them – all except for Maureen. Maureen was creeping back to her pram. When she got to it she checked to make sure her little girl was still sleeping. Then slid a hand down the side of the blankets.

'Gently,' she said to herself. 'Gently.'

She managed to pull out the carving knife, had her hand on the Indian club and was telling herself what a grand job she was doing when she must have knocked the pram or let a cold draught in. Her baby's eyes suddenly whipped open.

There was a second or two's silence, as she filled her little lungs. Then she let out a terrible scream which carried through the orchard like a rifle-shot.

The pig, who hadn't seen a soul in months, came round to find its own small audience peering at it. It blinked twice to make sure it wasn't still dreaming.

Dexter turned and called out over his shoulder, 'Come on, Mo. She's waking up.'

Maureen plucked her baby from the pram with one hand, grabbed the knife and Indian club in the other and started running. Meanwhile, the pig was getting to its feet – very slowly, as if doing its best not to startle anybody.

Maureen ran towards the other mourners but the closer her bawling baby got the more agitated the pig became. It was on its feet now, looking around, and Dexter, seeing a gap in the bushes behind it, spread his hands wide and low and began edging in that direction before the pig had the chance to make a dash for it.

Man and pig slowly circled each other, like boxers. Only the wailing baby racing towards them threatened to intervene. But as they slowly swung on their axis the pig caught sight of the gap in the bushes and at the very moment when Maureen and her baby arrived it feinted left, wrongfooting its assailant, and made a bolt for the undergrowth.

Dexter Fadden had spent too many hours daydreaming of this meeting – was not about to surrender all that living meat without a fight – and as the pig bundled past him he threw himself at it.

My pig, he said to himself as he caught hold of it. *Mine*.

He managed to get one arm round its neck and the other round its middle which started it squealing. He held on and tried to get his legs around it and there was a hopeful moment or two when he genuinely believed he might win the day. But it bucked and thrashed with such ferocity that its torso slowly slipped from his grasp and when it finally broke free and its back trotters caught him in the face Dexter's last conscious thought was how surprisingly warm its flesh had felt in their brief embrace.

It ran at its audience, who, despite their love of pork chops and streaky bacon, were only too keen to get out of the way. But the pig seemed a little weary – was not moving quite as freely as its mourners might have expected – and Dexter lifted his face from the ground to see Howard Kent grab the Indian club from Maureen, run alongside the lumbering pig and bring the club down on its head. The second blow seemed to convince the pig that it had done running and the next brought the pig to its knees. Howard tossed the Indian club aside and turned to Maureen.

'Give me the knife,' he said.

He inserted the blade up under its chin and yanked the handle backwards and forwards. From where Dexter lay it looked as if he was cranking a car. Then Howard stepped back, the pig slowly toppled and from the hole in its throat a great spout of blood pumped out onto the orchard floor.

If the pig had not been existing almost solely on a diet of fermenting apples for the last four months and accumulated the most colossal hangover it might have been a little quicker on its feet. Oblivious, the villagers carried it home in its coffin fairly bursting with pride and would have slung it from Aldred's pole like a hunting trophy if they'd thought they could have got it past the Americans.

Howard Kent was already rehearsing his story of the day he wrestled a wild pig. Dexter Fadden, though bruised and beaten, was happy. The others had brushed him down and tried to make him presentable but by the time they passed Miss Minter's he was limping so badly that the coffin was rocking from side to side. There was such a sense of well-being among the mourners that Dexter thought he should remind the others not to look too cheery, but just then the checkpoint appeared through the hedgerow and the job was done for him.

A jeep was parked by the bridge and a third soldier had joined the other two. From the way he stood it was clear that this new fellow was a man of authority.

'Whoa,' said Dexter and drew the cortège to a halt.

When the coffin came round the corner the American soldiers could barely conceal their relief – seemed ready to welcome them with open arms.

The Captain decided to take the bull by the horns. 'Thank you so much,' he told the soldiers. 'I think we all feel a great deal better after that.'

The officer cast a withering glance over the whole ramshackle gang.

'My boys tell me,' he said with great deliberation, 'that you've been having some sort of service.'

'That's right,' the Captain said. 'A few hymns . . . a few prayers . . . a few words of remembrance.' He'd once heard how Americans like a bit of history. 'It's an old tradition, you know,' he said.

He was still wondering what other aspects of this tradition he might be called upon to invent when the officer fixed him in his sights.

'There's not a church down that road for five miles,' he said.

A terrible chill swept through the mourners. In the circumstances, Dexter was impressed by the speed with which the Captain came up with what seemed like quite a plausible explanation.

'It was an outdoor service,' he said

But the American officer was nowhere near as impressed as Dexter. He looked at Aldred and saw nothing but a bug-eyed boy with an old tablecloth wrapped round him. Aldred, feeling deeply uncomfortable, looked to his religious pole for strength, only to find that he had lost the star off the top.

'Open the coffin,' the officer said.

Suddenly every mourner had their own idea why the coffin should not be opened. The commotion woke Maureen's baby but the American officer stood his ground.

'Nobody leaves until it's opened up,' he said.

The pall-bearers carefully lowered the coffin. Will and Cyril undid the screws and lifted the lid away. All three soldiers crowded around and peered inside. The eyes of the corpse were closed, his hands folded across his chest, but he looked far from peaceful. In fact, he looked as if he had suffered a violent, bloody death.

When the officer looked up his face was ashen. In Sylvia Crouch he now saw a bereaved sister, in Mo Tucker, a widow with babe-in-arms.

'Christ Almighty,' he said. 'Forgive me. I don't know what I was thinking of.'

They were over the bridge and halfway up the hill before Dexter gave the order to stop and open up the coffin, by which time Howard was hammering at the lid. When they helped him out his teeth were chattering and his whole body was shaking like a leaf.

'That was horrible,' he said and stood in the lane, rubbing his shoulders. 'Just horrible.'

Back at the checkpoint the Americans were absolutely sickened. The officer leant against the wall of the bridge and stared into the water below. How could so much blood come to be inside a coffin, he asked the others. What terrible death must the poor man have met? A dozen different questions demanded to be answered, but the two he significantly failed to ask were why a dead man's boots would be so muddy and why a pram without a baby in it should ride so close to the ground.

Ballistics Reports

All the Boys wanted to do was to make a little whizz-bang. Something to liven up a Sunday afternoon. The idea that this might have somehow helped conjure up the Bee King would not occur to them until much later on.

They had done their rounds, winding up at the allotments around four o'clock with no obvious means of entertainment until Aldred found the remains of a bonfire, with its embers still glowing under the ash. A boy on his own might have warmed his hands at it. Two might have tried stoking the fire back into life. But it took all five to create the conditions necessary for them to organise a party to look for something combustible which might be introduced to it.

The first shed Finn and Lewis forced their way into was full of old rakes and spades and piles of potting trays, which might have made a nice little bonfire of their own and brought a good deal of misery to their owner, but lacked the explosive element they were after, so they went on to the next shed along.

The other boys were breaking up beanpoles and adding them to the embers and managing to fan some flames into being when Finn and Lewis reappeared, looking mightily pleased with themselves.

Finn held up a tin. 'This'll do it,' he said.

In the face of such overwhelming smugness Hector felt compelled to offer some resistance.

'It's just a syrup tin,' he said.

'Smell it,' said Finn.

Hector took the tin, popped the lid open and peered in at the black liquid swilling around inside. Inserted his nose and took a deep sniff. A muddy sweetness filled his head. Both lungs locked up. He was transported to a dim and dangerous place. And when he finally returned, blinking, to the allotments and his lungs finally spluttered back to life, he found his thoughts swam in the same peculiar fashion as that time he'd fallen out of a tree and landed on his head.

He passed the tin to Aldred and Harvey, who both sniffed, recoiled and nodded their approval, as if they were connoisseurs of the stuff. Then they handed it back to Finn, who stamped the lid down on it and carried it over to the fire. He held it above the flames for a while, like an offering, with the others watching. But the moment he let go of it they all scattered – dived behind sheds and compost heaps and covered their heads with their arms.

For a while the sky seemed to threaten to buckle – to rupture. There was a period of almost unbearable anticipation. Then the growing realisation that the Golden Syrup tin had, in fact, neither the potential nor the least inclination to explode.

One by one, the Boys raised their heads above the parapet. The fire still smouldered. A trail of smoke went straight up into the winter sky. Hector got to his feet and stood with his hands on his hips, squinting.

'You didn't put the bloody lid on tight enough,' he said.

The tin exploded. Exploded with such infernal anger it was as if the laws of physics had been tampered with, shaking the windows in all the nearby houses and almost knocking the Boys off their feet. But in those few seconds before they started running they quite clearly saw the tin take off. Saw it fly up and head towards the river. And as they ran, with the embers showering down on them, the Boys saw no sign of that tin can flagging. And whenever they recalled their little experiment imagined it continuing through its trajectory.

Back in 1941, when the wind was in the right direction, the villagers could sometimes hear the distant drumroll of

Plymouth taking another pounding. But by '44 the only bombardments to be heard were the ones from the evacuated area – bombardments which steadily grew in frequency and ferocity until reaching their peak in April of that year.

One night, Miss Pye stood at her bedroom window in her dressing gown, having been shaken from her dreams. Each flash of light on the horizon turned the sky into a mottled sea of red and amber, and a rumble of thunder rolled through the fields and shook the floorboards under Marjory Pye's slippered feet. She pinned the curtain back in her hand, peered out into the darkness and smoothed a sarsaparilla lozenge against the roof of her mouth. Wondered what it must be like to be caught up in all those explosions and what chance there was of one of those shells straying off course.

In the morning the villagers agreed that the firepower of the previous night's exercise easily outweighed any that had gone before and the days which followed were rife with rumours of botched landings, of American troops caught by their own artillery and even ships going down in the bay. The LST which limped into Dartmouth with its stern bent out of shape was there for all to see, and there were so many stories – of makeshift hospitals, of lorries piled with bodies and even the digging of mass graves – that it was hard not to believe that some monumental, bloody disaster had come to pass.

The culmination of the Captain's table-top labours was that moment when the ship's hinged masts were temporarily flattened and the model was eased down the neck of the bottle before the sails were hoisted back into shape.

Such moments came about very rarely – no more than eight or ten times a year – and were the closest thing each ship had to an actual launch. One Wednesday lunchtime the Captain found himself at such a juncture – had the little finger of his right hand down the neck of the dimple bottle on the tip of the bowsprit of an Elizabethan man-of-war, the lines all taut in his other hand and the yards just about squared off – when an unfamiliar fellow went past the window.

He could tell straightaway that he was an out-of-towner. A young soldier, if not quite young enough to be given a couple of coppers and sent out to buy some cakes, then perhaps willing to be lured in by a little ham and chutney. But for all his hopes of a conversation which might slowly be brought around to the subject of women on the heavier side, the old Captain watched in vain, with the little finger of one hand down the neck of the bottle and the fingers of the other clinging to the reins.

The Reverend Bentley had been clucking under the hood of Maureen Tucker's pram by the church gates for what felt like long enough to satisfy even the proudest young mother and emerged just in time to see the young soldier coming up the lane. There were so many Americans in the county it took him a while to see that this particular serviceman was actually British – was wearing a lighter-coloured khaki, cut from a rougher kind of cloth – and by the time the soldier was near enough for the reverend to make such a distinction he was also able to see just how badly his uniform hung off him. His collar and cuffs were flailing open; his tunic and trousers were soaking wet. The soldier stopped and slumped against the war memorial, as if he had just run a marathon.

'Everything all right?' the Reverend Bentley called out to him.

The soldier shook his head but kept on staring at the ground, which rather unsettled the reverend, and he was still wondering how best to handle the situation when the soldier lifted his head. His face was plastered with tears.

'What's the matter?' said the reverend.

The young man seemed incapable of doing anything but quietly sob to himself. He wiped his nose on his sleeve and shook his head again.

'Where's your tin hat?' said the reverend.

Whatever was weighing so heavily on the young man

125

briefly lifted. He looked over his shoulder, as if he might have dropped it just a second before. But the lane was empty and he turned back to the reverend, utterly puzzled.

'I don't know,' he said.

The reverend had reason to feel that the situation was generally improving and had just given Maureen a reassuring smile when the soldier slipped his rifle off his shoulder and pulled the bolt back. And in those few seconds it seemed to the reverend that the village and his presence in it were critically weakened. He watched the soldier climb onto the base of the war memorial, watched him lean against the obelisk for support. Saw him tuck the butt of the rifle up against his shoulder and flatten his face against the stock.

The first shot went clean over the church tower. The second hit the weathervane. Both shots were still rattling down the valley when the soldier pulled his rifle away from his shoulder.

'I can *shoot*,' he said, emphatically. 'I can *shoot* all right.'

It seemed that the more he tried to put his thoughts in order, the more they slipped away from him. Then suddenly he was gulping for air again and weeping and shaking his sorry head. He had one arm around the war memorial, as if propped-up by a fellow-reveller after a night on the town. He hung there for a second, then clambered down and took a step towards the reverend and Maureen, who both instinctively took a step away from him. Maureen had one hand on the pram handle and she found herself gently rocking it.

'Don't cry,' she thought. 'Please God, don't cry just now.'

The soldier opened his mouth to speak, but after a couple of moments gave up and shook his head again. Then he turned and limped off down the lane from which he'd just appeared.

Maureen Tucker would later claim that the strange lull between the soldier's departure and anyone actually opening their door was due to the villagers making sure that all the shooting was over before coming out to count the dead.

The reverend more charitably attributed the apparent delay to the peculiar clock-stopping trance he and Maureen had entered. Either way, there certainly seemed to be a moment's grace before the doors flew open and everyone came streaming out into the street – an interval in which the only sounds were the soldier's boots as he retreated and the squeak of the weathervane still spinning on its spike.

The next morning an army officer knocked on the reverend's door wearing a uniform much the same as any other army officer's but with a few more whistles and bells. He had a clipboard under one arm on which he took down the reverend's account of the previous day's events. The reverend spoke and the officer nodded, to keep him going, but barely a flicker of warmth threatened to cross his face. And when the reverend had said about as much as he could remember the officer asked how many shots had been fired.

'It's a funny thing,' said the reverend. 'Yesterday I'd have said *two*, but today it seems entirely possible it may have been *three*. Isn't that odd?'

The army officer agreed that it was and made another note. The Reverend Bentley asked if it was important.

'Going AWOL will get you into one sort of trouble,' the officer told him. 'Discharging a weapon is a different kettle of fish.'

Then he screwed the top back on his fountain pen and hooked it into his pocket.

'In his defence,' said the reverend, 'the boy didn't seem especially dangerous. He just seemed upset.'

The officer nodded. 'And he's going to be even more upset by the time we get through with him,' he said.

Health and Efficiency

The ostentation of the Americans' arrival was outdone only by the modesty with which they slipped away. For weeks the lanes had been packed with traffic, as extra troops and transportation headed for the commandeered zone. A baker, with a special dispensation to enter the area, talked about whole cities of tents further down the valleys, and Dexter Fadden reckoned that some stretches of the river were so clogged with barges that you could hop from one bank to the other without getting your feet wet. But just when it seemed inconceivable that the land beyond the roadblocks could absorb another jeep or motorcycle the villagers woke one morning to discover that the entire army had upped and gone.

The following day they were on the beaches of Normandy – had left the fields down the road to land on the newspapers' front pages. And, though few people were inclined to admit it, their withdrawal left a certain sense of vulnerability in its wake.

Much to the frustration of the farmers who had been lodging with relatives or leasing other, far inferior land, the Americans' departure failed to signal an immediate return to their property. In fact, it would be months before they were even allowed to see what sort of state their homes were in. In the meantime, a small unit of Allied servicemen assessed the damage and engineered the clearance of unexploded ordnance, but as time passed and the number of soldiers slowly dwindled the Five Boys found the prospect of burned-out farms and bombed cottages too much of a temptation and about a month after D-Day, when it seemed safe to assume that the Americans weren't about to come flooding back, they climbed over the gate on the road to Duncannon and launched their own small offensive into the overgrown fields.

Apart from the odd slipped slate or broken window the first few houses they came across were disappointingly intact. There was nothing smoking, nothing smouldering – no sign of annihilation at all. In fact, the land appeared to be flourishing. The crops came right up to the Boys' shoulders, the hedgerows billowed out into the lanes and instead of the wasteland they'd set their hearts on the Boys found themselves in a burgeoning wilderness – a world almost healed of humanity.

They hacked their way through the undergrowth like explorers, with no idea where they were headed. They reached a lane and followed it for a mile or so, weaving between the corn marigolds and burdock which had sprung up everywhere. Their only discovery during their first hour was a small crater which Lewis insisted was the result of a shell or bomb, and he made a great show of crouching down and placing the palm of his hand inside it, as if he might still pick up some trace of an explosion's warmth.

As they pressed on their sense of adventure steadily diminished. They began to tire of working so hard for such scant reward and Aldred was already contemplating the difficulties of the journey home when they stumbled upon a cottage in its own dark gully with a back door hanging off its frame.

A drift of leaves spilled right into the kitchen. The remains of what looked like a small bonfire were scattered around the range. The chimney breast and the ceiling were blackened, the floor was peppered with cigarette butts and one corner of the room was piled high with old tin cans.

Finn went over, gingerly picked up one of the cans and read the label. 'Chicken soup,' he said.

The Boys slowly worked their way through the kitchen like detectives. Imagined American soldiers sitting round the fire, smoking cigarettes and eating chicken soup. The others went through to the parlour but Lewis lagged behind, picked up a couple of flattened fag ends and put them in a pocket. When he got back home, he told himself, he might try lighting one up.

He joined the other four Boys – Finn had found a stick and was prodding some rags with it, and Harvey was kicking at the skirting board. If they'd brought some matches, Aldred was saying, they could have made a fire, but he was interrupted when Finn suddenly raised his hand.

'What?' said Hector

'Upstairs,' whispered Finn. 'I heard something.'

The Boys all stared at the ceiling.

'There's nothing there,' said Harvey.

'No,' said Finn. 'I heard something.'

Hector, seeing the chance to boost his own stock at the expense of Finn's, ambled over to the staircase, listened, then set off up it. The others gathered around the foot of the stairs and slowly clomped up after him. There were two rooms upstairs, but neither had anybody in them, which was greeted with disappointment and a good deal of private relief.

The Boys resumed their meticulous examination of the house. Of the two rooms, the one at the front had been more comprehensively ransacked. The skirting boards had been levered off the walls and some of the floorboards were missing, so that half the joists were bare. The window panes were either cracked or shattered and Hector went over, had a look at them, then squeezed himself into the sill.

'They must have sat here while they kept watch,' he announced from his cubby-hole.

The fields rolled and turned in the breeze and Hector glowered out at them, thinking what a fine spectacle of vigilance he must make, but his little performance was spoilt by a squabble breaking out behind him and he turned to find Aldred in the middle of a tight little ruck.

'Get 'em off, Heck,' he was screaming. 'They're going to *rip* it.'

Hector climbed down, waded in and dragged Harvey and Lewis off him. Aldred managed to slip from Finn's grasp and leapt across the missing floorboards. He stood in the corner, clutching a magazine to his chest.

'What've you got?' said Hector.

A coy smile played upon Aldred's lips. His eyes widened and he slowly slid his fingers down the cover of the magazine to reveal a woman waving from the top of a sand dune, with both bosoms out. The Boys made another lunge towards him and Hector had to hold them back.

This teasing and lunging continued until, under Hector's supervision and through Finn's negotiation, Aldred was eventually talked into returning, and taking his magazine over to the window where it could be seen by everyone. It was agreed that, as he'd found it, Aldred should be allowed to turn the pages and he placed the magazine on the floor and the others huddled around him, until he was almost collapsing under their weight.

The magazine was a little bigger than his mother's Be-Ro recipe book and had the same chocolatey print. In fact, some of the women were about the same age as the Boys' mothers and had similar hairstyles, the difference being that the women on the magazine's pages had not a stitch of clothing on.

They danced naked, hand in hand with other women ('*The Three Graces*'), stood naked in a field among the ricks of corn ('*Summer Idyll*') and admired the view from a ferny hillside ('*The Sun Goddess*'), apparently oblivious to their predicament. Such a hearty lack of inhibition was having a dramatic effect on the Five Boys. They felt their blood being distributed in new and unusual ways. All sorts of ungovernable thoughts and emotions began to stampede through them. Harvey felt sick. Hector felt like fighting. Lewis was stricken with what felt like a feverish infirmity.

On one page, naked men and children gambolled alongside the women. Whole naked families erected tents, played cricket and paddled in the sea. A row of naked gardeners stood by their shovels on an allotment ('*The Leeds Sun and Air Society dig for victory*'), under the watchful eye of an older man who was also naked apart from his spectacles and the pipe clenched between his teeth. But most unsettling for the Boys was the outdoor PT class in which a dozen naked women gaily swung Indian clubs about their ears.

As soon as they reached the end Aldred was inundated with demands to return to particular pictures so he turned back to the first page and began working through them again. Lewis, whilst being enthralled, had a growing conviction they were committing a crime heinous enough to have them thrown behind bars. Harvey had no such qualms and at one point tried to kiss the picture of an especially ample-breasted woman, only to be dragged off like a dog by Hector. Meanwhile, Finn managed to thread his stick through the Boys' arms and elbows and tap her on her bare behind.

But each time they returned to a photograph the Boys found that some of the potency of the breasts and buttocks had dimmed a little. The lady beside the rick of corn began to grow familiar; the Three Graces failed to jiggle as they danced. And the Boys turned instead to some of the advertisements and articles between the photographs, hoping to find further revelations there. Like any other magazine, there were adverts for Hovis and Tate and Lyle's Treacle. There were also public announcements regarding Mind Power, Vigour and Vitality and newly patented cures for Stammering and Under-confidence. But it was the news that 'Eight Glands control your Destiny' that stopped the Five Boys in their tracks. None of them was entirely sure what a gland actually did or looked like, preferring to nod sagely as Aldred read aloud that 'a man is as old as his glands'. Something profoundly glandular had been happening in the confines of their underpants. The idea that there were another seven, equally powerful glands secreted about their persons (which could be boosted by sending off for a jar of 'British Gland Pills') was almost too much to bear.

Lewis got to his feet, unbuttoned his trousers and was about to urinate against a wall when he noticed a tuft of fur poking out from a gap in the skirting board.

'Dead rat,' he said.

The others looked over at him.

'You sure it's dead?' said Aldred.

'It's not moving,' said Lewis.

Harvey suggested Lewis give it a poke with the stick by his foot.

'Give it a smack,' said Hector, 'and see if there's any more in there.'

Lewis was not particularly keen on the idea, but was not about to surrender the stick to one of the other boys. So he moved them back to give himself some room for a little run-up, drew his stick back, summoned every ounce of vigour and vitality, then leapt forward, swinging the stick down into the rat as if he was hitting a cricket ball for six.

Rats came flooding out from every corner. Went scuttling over the Boys' feet, brushing up against their ankles and leaping at the walls. The whole house was suddenly full of them. And the Boys ran screaming down the stairs, with rats under their feet and tumbling around them as they fought to get to the door.

They ran out into the sunlight and kept on running, crashing through the branches that blocked their way. Ran until the cottage was far behind them and, even then, checked over their shoulders to make sure the rats weren't after them, before daring to slow down and catch their breath.

They made their way home, snivelling and shuddering, and had been walking for almost a mile before Aldred realised he'd left his magazine behind and that his newfound intimacy with the naked ladies was at an end. A couple of steps behind him Lewis followed, convinced that the rats were some sort of retribution for their lecherous behaviour and, in a bid to purge himself, threw his cigarette butts over a hedge. Only Hector Massie contrived to find the whole thing funny, although, as Harvey pointed out, he had been the first one out of the door, and Finn marched ahead without saying a word to the others, hoping against hope that he might get home without anyone noticing that he'd wet his pants.

As they passed the woods just outside Duncannon, Lewis had the peculiar feeling that someone was watching him, and when he glanced over to his right thought he saw a man stretched out in the branches of a nearby tree. If things hadn't been so strange already he might have said something to the others but all he wanted to do was get back home and put the whole day behind him. And within a matter of seconds he wasn't sure whether he'd actually seen the man in the tree or not.

Victory

If any of the villagers happened to notice Aldred's balaclava hanging from the gutter they never drew attention to it. Only the Boys knew what it was, how it had got there and the punishment Aldred had suffered when his mother learned that he'd lost it and realised she was going to have to knit him another one.

By the time Hector and Finn gave up trying to talk Aldred into retrieving it, it had become a knitted flag, raised in honour of Bobby's bravery. The rain drenched it, the four winds blew through it and its wool slowly turned to string. But in the gutter a few feet away, HMS *Victory* sat in its dimple bottle as dry as a bone, and the only danger was that the sun might heat the air around it to such a degree that it might fire the cork across the roofs.

It didn't move until one dismal Tuesday when black clouds rolled in from the south-west. The temperature dropped. A curtain of rain swept up the valley. Its tiny outriders spat and scratched at the windows, then suddenly the rain was hammering at the slates. The water swept across the roof like riptides, flooding the gutter, then followed its gradient to the same drainpipe Bobby had clambered down.

For a while the bottle held its ground and forced the rainwater to bilge and roil around it, but such quantities of rainwater backed up behind it that eventually the bottle began to shift. Then it was afloat and moving in a manner it had never dared dream of – was sailing beneath the rolling clouds – until, almost immediately, the abyss opened up before it and it was teetering at the end of the world. It fell forty feet, cork-first. Had its fall broken by the bend at the bottom of the drainpipe, which smashed the bottle, and the ship was delivered into the gutter in full sail.

Miss Pye had just made a delivery to an aged customer at the top of the village. Had borrowed an umbrella and was trotting back down the high street and looking forward to a bit of butterscotch, when she spotted something in the gutter – something unusually intricate in its design – snagged between a couple of crossed twigs. She stopped, picked it up and had a good look at it. Peered through the Captain's window, but there was no one there. She stood with the rain drumming on her umbrella for a few baffled moments, then put the model ship on the sill of the window and hurried on her way.

There was no better diuretic for the Captain than heavy rainfall. The sound of the skies opening up and the smell of the earth taking a soaking was guaranteed to fire his bladder into life and once he was out of his chair he tended to put the kettle on. On this particular Tuesday he'd climbed back into his sleeping bag and was sitting with a cup of tea in one hand and the saucer under it in the other, when some intensity of colour caught his eye. He turned and saw, beyond the window, what looked like the billowing sails of a ship. The black and yellow hull was instantly recognisable as that of the HMS *Victory* – the ship on which he had devoted countless hours' drilling and tapering and which had inexplicably vanished several weeks before. The ship had somehow got free of its bottle. As if it had blasted its way out. The Captain froze with his cup of tea halfway to his mouth, and for that single haunting moment the ship seemed to be looking in at him rather than the other way around.

It didn't take him long to kick off his sleeping bag and charge out into the rain, but it was long enough for three or four raindrops which had been slowly racing each other down the window to unite and, with their combined momentum, finally nudge the *Victory* off the window sill.

The ship turned twice in mid-air and landed in the flooded

gutter. The bow swung around, the current took hold and carried it forward over the cobbles. And the Captain came round the corner just in time to see his precious ship cover the last few feet and disappear down the grate, off on its way to the sea.

The Stay-behind

He had no shortage of buildings in which to shelter, the Americans had left plenty of supplies behind and as long as he kept moving and went from one vantage point to another he could see his pursuers coming and have time to hide away.

He began to understand how the landscape fitted together. The hills and streams made their own natural sense. But if he ever found himself following the same circuit of paths and ditches he immediately abandoned it, knowing that sooner or later they would be waiting for him.

He went to ground several times and watched the soldiers passing – could have picked them off with no trouble at all. He managed to evade them so successfully that he began to doubt his own existence and had to whisper a few words out loud, just to reassure himself that he was still there.

It was early summer but always seemed to be raining and the nights could still be bitterly cold. And when it was dark and wet the drowned men were much more likely to surface and then the panic would get hold of him and he'd feel the desperate need to run all over again.

The isolation could sometimes bother him. Sometimes he felt that this was how the world was meant to be. There were even times when it seemed as if the world might be kind, and that there might be a place for him in it, after all.

On a couple of occasions he'd strayed into civilisation – just found himself walking along newly turned furrows or come across a cottage with washing flapping in the breeze. One day he spotted a boy in the next field with half a dozen bullocks crowding round him, like a child Messiah. The boy was pouring the contents of a large brown bottle into a tablespoon and chatting to the bullocks as he fed them. The soldier crept up to the wall and watched for a while – could have happily watched all day, but decided that he should let the boy know that he was there.

'What's the medicine?' he said.

The words came rattling out of him like broken crockery. The boy almost jumped clean out of his skin, which got all the bullocks jumping and kicking, and for a moment the soldier worried that the boy might get hurt. But after a few seconds they settled down. Then the bullocks and the boy all stood and stared at him.

The soldier pointed to the bottle. 'The medicine,' he said.

The boy looked down at the bottle as if it had just appeared in his hand.

'Linseed oil,' he said at last.

The soldier nodded.

'The cattle get redwater,' the boy said, 'being so close to the river. The linseed clears them out.'

For those first few minutes the conversation had an embarrassed hesitancy to it but once it found its stride the boy seemed only too happy to talk. He explained how he lived in the cottage in the distance and that looking after the bullocks was one of his jobs. As he spoke he slowly made his way over, and each time he took a step towards the soldier the bullocks followed nervously behind.

He was soon close enough to see what a wretched state the soldier was in. His hands and face were covered in cuts and scratches and his uniform was caked in mud.

'You hurt your head,' said the boy and pointed to a bloody wound above one eye.

The soldier absent-mindedly raised a hand to it.

'I must have caught it on something,' he said.

'You want to put some ointment on it,' the boy told him, 'or it'll go septic.'

The soldier nodded and the two of them stood in silence. Then he asked the boy his name.

139

'Bobby,' he said.

The soldier said it out loud a couple of times, to see if it suited him and as he did so Bobby took the opportunity to look him up and down.

'How come you're not in France?' said Bobby.

The soldier stared at the ground as he struggled to come up with an answer.

'I stayed behind,' he said.

Lillian and Meredith seemed to take for ever to eat their supper and it was dusk before they took their seats by the fire. The moment they started dozing Bobby crept out of the room, let himself out of the back door and headed up the hill, in case he was being followed, then cut down to the woods where he and the stay-behind had arranged to meet.

The dusk had softened the trees and drawn the colour from the land. Every sound was dampened down and as he ran down to the woods Bobby was suddenly certain that the stay-behind had been captured or frightened away. He called out, sure that the woods were empty. Stood in the failing light, more alone than he had felt in months. Then there was a rustling and the stay-behind stepped out of the bushes and Bobby hurried down to him.

He led Bobby through the trees until they came to a clearing. Bobby unbuttoned his jacket and lifted his jumper up. He had a package tucked into his shorts which he pulled out and handed to the stay-behind.

'I almost got you an apple,' Bobby said, 'but they know I don't like them.'

The stay-behind pulled the brown paper open. Found some buttered bread and a slice of cake wrapped up in greaseproof paper, and an old pair of Meredith's thick socks folded up in one of Lillian's vests.

He thanked Bobby, then sat and ate. And for a while Bobby just stood and watched him. Then he told the stay-behind about the two old ladies he lived with and their habit of falling asleep by the wireless. He talked about the Five Boys . . . the Focke Wulf . . . his scrapbook of newspaper cuttings and how he had come to be evacuated a second time. But as he talked his eyes never left the soldier. He stared at the stubble on his face and the holes in his boots. Watched him bring the bread up to his mouth. And when the stay-behind finally took a break from his eating Bobby reached into his jacket pocket.

'I got you some Germolene,' he said.

He unscrewed the lid and dipped a finger in. Then took a step towards the soldier, who sat there like a scalded child. Bobby reached out his hand with the ointment on it. Thought the stay-behind might flinch, but he didn't. He just looked at the ground and let Bobby gently rub the ointment in until the dried mud and blood was smoothed away and Bobby could see the clean skin underneath.

As he ate his supper an hour earlier Bobby had imagined the stay-behind out in the wilderness and all the adventures he must have had. But seeing him sitting there, all hunched and silent, it was clear that any adventures must have been few and far between.

'Why did you stay behind?' said Bobby.

The soldier stared at the ground for a little while longer. Then he asked Bobby if he'd heard of the Royal Observers. Bobby shook his head. The stay-behind said that he used to work in a print shop and just liked the sound of the Observers. But that in the end it didn't involve much more than him being holed-up in a bunker, with a pair of binoculars, looking out for enemy planes.

By the time he was posted, he said, there wasn't much to see. But when the Americans moved in and started doing their exercises he'd watch the ships manoeuvring out in the bay. Every now and again they'd fire off a few shells and on a couple of occasions they'd open up for hours at a time. But something went wrong on one of the exercises. A couple of LSTs got hit. Just sat ablaze out in the middle of the bay. He could see men jumping overboard, but none of the other ships moving in to help.

The stay-behind winced and stared at his boots. Raked his hair with his fingers. And when he started talking again his voice was tight, as if someone was choking him.

He went down to the water the next day to wash his pots and pans. Saw something bobbing about between the rocks. Couldn't make any sense of it at first. Then suddenly he understood and jumped in, up to his chest. Tried to turn them over. Some of their uniforms were burnt right off them. Their faces black with oil.

The stay-behind stopped and his hand went up to his forehead – just like Aldred's did when he was doing his Memory Man. But instead of drawing things out he held his head as if he was trying to keep some terrible pain at bay.

Lillian's sister, Meredith, could sometimes be a bit grumpy, and was as deaf as a post, but living on a farm out in the middle of nowhere didn't bother Bobby half as much as he might have expected and once he'd got used to the livestock and their particular smells and noises he found them to be very good company.

The geese had a pen around the back of the outhouses and their welfare, along with that of the bullocks, became Bobby's responsibility. Within a matter of days the geese had developed an intense attachment to him. So much so that Meredith would sometimes feel obliged to remind Bobby of all the wringing and drawing and trussing which was their fate. Perhaps the geese somehow sensed Bobby's revulsion – saw in him a potential liberator. Perhaps they just liked having someone around who was closer to their own height and wasn't shouting all the time. Either way, if they ever caught sight of him they would raise their beaks and call out to him, and whenever he entered their pen or took them for a walk down to the river would flank him like his own gang of feathered thugs.

The stay-behind was Bobby's first visitor. Aldred was the only one he knew about in advance. One of the Pearces' sons had a couple of things to do down in Dartmouth and Aldred arranged to hitch a ride. Bobby got a letter on the Thursday telling him when to expect him, along with a map of the route he proposed to take, and by ten o'clock on the Saturday morning he was standing on the doorstep, beaming, as if expecting hosannas and hats to be thrown in the air.

The two Miss Minters and the boys had tea and biscuits at the table, where Aldred brought everyone up to date with all the village's gossip. And after he'd downed three cupfuls and smacked his lips after each one Lillian suggested Bobby show him round the farm.

Aldred wasn't keen on the geese, didn't much like the chickens and seemed to think that the bullocks were going to bite him, which delighted Bobby no end, having always assumed that anybody raised in the country would have a natural affinity with the animal world. He showed Aldred the vegetable garden, then took him round the boundary of Meredith's few dozen acres, ending up at the wood where he'd fed the stay-behind.

From the moment he'd received Aldred's letter he knew that he would tell him about the deserter – couldn't see how he could avoid it – but as soon as he led Aldred through to the clearing and described how he'd met this bedraggled soldier and sneaked some food out to him he regretted it. And the more animated Aldred became the more Bobby felt he'd made a dreadful betrayal, until he refused to answer any more questions and made Aldred swear not to tell another living soul.

Bobby got to his feet and turned to go but Aldred grabbed him by the sleeve of his jacket.

'Wait,' he said.

He pulled something out of a pocket which Bobby assumed was another one of his booklets or home-made maps, but took it and found that it was, in fact, an envelope, with Aldred's mother's name and address written on the front.

'Read it,' said Aldred.

Bobby wasn't sure.

'Go on,' Aldred said.

So Bobby pulled out the folded notepaper and started reading. But when he'd got past the date and the 'Dear Sylvia' in the top left-hand corner he couldn't make head or tail of it. The words were in such a hurry to get to the end of the line most of the pages looked like nothing more than indecipherable dots and dashes.

'Is it from your dad?' said Bobby.

Aldred nodded.

'What's it say?' said Bobby.

Aldred shrugged his shoulders and laughed out loud. 'I can't crack it,' he said.

Bobby looked at the envelope.

'There's a big pile of them in my mum's sewing basket,' Aldred said and took the letter from Bobby. 'Some haven't even been opened.'

He leafed through the pages, put his finger on a particular phrase and turned it round to show Bobby.

'What's that say?' he said.

There were two words in capital letters. The first meant nothing to Bobby but he thought he recognised the other.

'"Infirmary",' he said.

Aldred nodded and looked back down at the letter.

'What's an infirmary?' he said.

'I think it's like a hospital,' Bobby told him.

'That's what I thought,' Aldred said. Then he folded up the sheets of paper, tucked it back in its envelope and put it away.

Bobby was carrying a pan of feed round to the geese the following Wednesday and had almost reached the gate to their pen when he spotted someone coming down the path through the field. He stopped in his tracks, which got the geese gabbling, and the longer Bobby stood with his back to them the more they gabbled and began to rock from foot to foot.

The first thought to enter Bobby's head was that the woman in the field must be another of Miss Minter's sisters and he pictured himself in the parlour, surrounded by deaf old ladies dozing in their chairs. But something strange and painful was unravelling in him – something which ran ahead of him – and he was still wondering what to make of it when the woman in the field raised her hand to him.

Bobby dropped the pan and the seed scattered across the cobbles. He stared out over the field. Then suddenly he was climbing the wall and jumping down and running towards her, with the geese all keening madly behind him and his shins whipping through the grass.

As he ran he saw her kneel and spread her arms wide for him. And the rest of the world fell away. And he ran until he reached her and she took him in and locked her arms around him. And he could feel the collar of her coat against his face.

'My boy,' she said. 'My lovely boy.'

PART TWO

The Bees

Almonds

By the time the checkpoints had finally been dismantled and the exiled farmers were allowed back home it was late autumn and the evacuated area was even more of a wilderness than when the Five Boys had stolen in. The gardens and fields tumbled into one another. Blocked ditches diverted the streams along the lanes. The crops had gone to seed, the sprawling hedgerows made half the roads impassable and down by the coast the trees were so packed with shrapnel that no one would risk ruining their saws by trimming them back.

A special unit was meant to have cleared away any explosives but such quantities kept turning up that in the end the farmers just drove their cattle back out onto the fields and let them graze, like unwitting mineclearers, for a couple of days.

By rights, the further inland a house was the less likely it was to have suffered any damage, but this was no comfort to Miss Minter, who returned home to find every last hinge and coat-hook missing. All that was left were the tufts in the timber where the screws had been prised away – as if a huge magnet had swept down the valley and pulled up every last pennyweight.

It was the same in half the neighbouring cottages – anything remotely valuable had been removed – but down the road, Mr Steere had his own problems and, despite having written to the Admiralty on the day he discovered it and getting on the telephone to the council half a dozen times since, it was almost a month before help arrived.

Steere was in his caravan washing the dishes when a moped came spluttering down the lane – a peculiar-looking piece of machinery with an oval windscreen, a suspension which squeaked in and out of every puddle-hole and a wicker trailer the size of an appling basket strapped to a set of old pram wheels rattling along behind.

The moped lurched to a halt in front of the caravan and its rider kicked the stand down with the heel of his boot. He wore an old dispatch rider's leather coat, buttoned behind the knees, and when he dismounted it stuck out from his thighs like a pair of jodhpurs. By the time Steere got to the caravan door his visitor had removed his crash helmet and was combing his hair in the moped's wing mirror. The fellow must have had exceptional hearing, for he spun around and was ready for conversation before Steere had put a foot on the steps.

'Mr Steere,' he said, smiling. 'I hear you have an infestation.'

Steere had never much cared for people who smiled for no good reason and he certainly didn't consider his current predicament as constituting one.

'See for yourself,' he said and turned to go.

But his visitor went over to his wicker trailer and began to unbuckle its leather straps. He lifted the lid, whispered a few words into it, then ducked his head in after them. When he came out he had in his arms the leanest, keenest terrier Steere had ever set eyes on. The dog looked around, blinking in the sunlight, and twitching its nostrils. But just when Steere was hoping they might finally get on with the job, the moped-rider ducked back into the basket, pulled out what looked like an old rag and started slipping it over the terrier's head and paws.

'What the hell is that?' said Steere.

'It's her little uniform,' said the dog's owner. 'It gets her in the mood.'

The dog had been sniffing and twisting from the moment it came out of its basket and in Mr Steere's opinion needed no help getting in the mood at all, and when the dog came up alongside him, straining at its lead, Steere couldn't help but notice that its little waistcoat was actually made out of a patchwork of rat-skins.

The dog seemed to know where it was going and to be even more anxious to get there than Steere himself. Its head rocked along the ground, picking up all sorts of information, which started its tail rocking from side to side at the other end, and by the time they got to the gate the dog was choking on its collar.

'Now, let's see what we've got, shall we?' said its master, then bent down and unhooked the lead. 'You go and stir them up, my girl.'

The dog shot off across the field like a cannon and what had appeared to be just another few acres of overgrown pasture suddenly erupted into life. The field was boiling with rat-heads and rat-tails and rats' scuffling bodies, which parted in a great 'V' as the terrier tore into them. The dog was a solid, thundering mass of forward motion, broken only by the occasional dip of its head as it picked a rat off along the way, and for a minute the field was a cauldron of rat activity. But just as it had been suddenly brought to the boil, so it suddenly abated and the rats drained back into their holes. Then the rat-catcher tucked a finger and thumb into his mouth and let out a piercing whistle which brought the dog to a dramatic halt. It looked mightily baffled at first – as if it had just been snapped out of a trance and was having trouble orientating itself – but when its master whistled again, the dog looked over its shoulder, saw him and seemed to come to its senses.

'Come, Sally,' he shouted. 'Come on, girl.'

Mr Steere was absolutely incredulous. 'You're surely not bringing her in already?' he said.

The rat-catcher turned and smiled at Steere. 'I'd say we're going to have to call in the heavy artillery, wouldn't you?' he said.

When the rat-catcher came down the track the next morning he had an old fellow riding pillion and the two of them bounced in and out of all the pot-holes in perfect unison. News of a mass poisoning had reached the village and the

Five Boys had been waiting on the wall for half an hour. None of them were much impressed by the rat-catchers. Only their leather coats, jet-black oilskins and matching crash helmets caught their eye.

'They look like human cannonballs,' said Harvey under his breath.

It could have been nothing more than coincidence, but as soon as the words were out of his mouth Harvey noticed a change in the rat-catcher's attitude. He turned, fixed his eyes on the Boys and inserted a forefinger deep into his mouth. He pulled it out and extended it towards them.

'I wouldn't sit there,' he said. 'Not unless you want snuffing out.'

Lewis had a sudden and powerful urge to go to the toilet. 'What's he mean?' he said to the others, who were now all doing their best to avoid the rat-catcher's eye.

'What I *mean*,' he called out, 'is that if you stay there my powder'll see to you.'

A cloud of incomprehension settled over the Five Boys but the rat-catcher waved his hand at them and kept on waving until they got down from the wall. His assistant, meanwhile, was busy with a penknife, cutting foot-long pieces from a ball of twine – a job inducing such brooding concentration in him that he might have been separating rats from their tails. The rat-catcher ambled over to his wheeled basket and brought out a stirrup pump and several coils of rubber pipe. He slung them over his shoulder and filled his lungs, like a mountaineer contemplating some fierce ascent.

By now various tins, tools and other clutter were spread out on the ground, but there was still no sign of the terrier the Boys had heard so much about. Their own recent rat encounter was still fresh in their minds and the prospect of a few hundred being eaten by a vicious dog had been the prime motivation in them coming along. Hector raised his hand. He had to hold it there for quite some time – long enough for him to think that whilst the rat-catcher might be able to pick up a whisper at fifty paces, his eyesight wasn't up to much – and in the end it was his oilskinned assistant who noticed him and tapped the rat-catcher on the arm.

'Where's the dog with the fancy jacket?' Hector asked him.

The rat-catcher shook his head, as if Hector had made an improper suggestion. 'Sally doesn't come out when we're using the gas,' he said.

The Boys didn't say another word. Didn't dare. They just watched the men doing the last of the unpacking. Once they'd finished they both went down on one knee and wound the lengths of twine around their trousers at the ankle, as if saying a prayer before entering the battlefield. Then they gathered up their equipment and the chief rat-catcher turned to the Boys.

'If you want to make yourself useful,' he said, 'you can bring along Punch and Judy,' and nodded at the wicker trailer. Then he and his assistant went on their way.

Lewis was the first to get to the basket – had high hopes of Punch and Judy being a couple of ferrets or other bad-tempered animals. Certainly something more sinister than the pair of ancient cricket bats lolling in the corner, with the string hanging off the handles. And yet, once they were lifted out and more closely inspected they were found to have considerable qualities of their own, not least the ragged bandages which bound their shafts and the fact that these bandages were caked with blood.

Lewis and Hector set off after the rat-catcher, holding the cricket bats out before them like duellists' pistols and with Finn and Harvey running alongside. Aldred had been the last man to get to the basket and was reluctant to leave it, but all that was left inside were the rat-catchers' crash helmets, their goggles and a can of oil.

He fished one of the helmets out and held it by its strap. Watched it slowly twisting. Knocked it with his knuckles to hear what sort of sound it made. He peered inside. The manufacturer's name, embroidered on a cotton hexagon in the middle of the lining, had been worn away, but a whiff of scalp-grease came up from it – a tallowy warmth which stirred up in Aldred some vague memory of his own father, even though he hadn't seen him in years.

Mr Steere and the rat-catcher had spent the previous afternoon filling in every last rat-hole, and when the rat-catcher came striding round the side of the house with his retinue of assistants and bat-carriers Steere was still out there, turning over great clods of earth with his shovel and stamping them down.

'They all tucked up, Mr Steere?' the rat-catcher called out from the gate.

Steere looked distractedly around the meadow. 'The little fuckers keep burrowing out,' he said.

The rat-catcher pulled back the latch and kicked the gate open. 'Mr Soames and me shall put a stop to that,' he said.

The two men strode out into the field with their cricket bats tucked under their arms. The rat-catcher had a cylindrical tank over one shoulder about the same size as a milk churn. Mr Soames carried the stirrup pump.

'We'll see to them from here,' the rat-catcher said.

Steere no longer knew when the weaselly little man was mocking him. He was past caring. The rats, their urinous stench and their boundless love of destruction had sapped all his spirit. The day he'd got back home after the evacuation he'd put a box of groceries down on the kitchen table and stepped back out into the yard to pick up a couple of cases. When he'd opened the door again the whole table was thrashing with them. It was the most disgusting thing he had ever seen. He hadn't had a decent cup of tea in weeks. The rats had eaten his tea, had eaten half his kettle. Had chewed through the roof, the walls, the water pipes. Even the putty in the window panes wasn't beyond their appetites. As the rat-catcher had told Steere the day before, with that irritating grin of his, some putty has got fish oil in it and the rats can't leave the stuff alone.

154

Like Miss Minter's, Steere's house had been stripped of every brass fitting. What was left the rats had done their damnedest to destroy. For weeks he'd been holed up in a leaking caravan whilst the rats worked his house over, and with such resolve that on the couple of occasions he'd dared set foot back in it, the place had the hot stench of silage to it – was warm from their relentless effort at bringing him down.

Steere limped back to the gate. Dragged his spade behind him. The Boys on the wall leant to one side, to get a better view of the rat-catchers as they laid out their strange little arsenal – a ritual which seemed to bestow upon them a degree of levity, for as soon as he'd finished the chief rat-catcher got to his feet and began tip-toeing around the field with his hands stretched out before him, as if he was sleep-walking. It was not the kind of thing the Boys were accustomed to seeing. The only thing Lewis could think of which was anything like it was watching his mother trying to find the towel after she washed her hair.

The rat-catcher's formidable hearing appeared to be directed solely towards the earth. The soles of his feet glided over it as if seeking out some underground activity – a halting little two-step which, in time, led him to a spot only ten yards or so from where he had set off.

'Pike please, Mr Soames,' he said.

Mr Soames slipped his hand between the buttons of his oil-skin and drew out a long wooden pole – a pole which was so long and emerged so slowly that the Boys began to wonder how much more was still to come. It might have been nothing more than an old broom handle with a metal spike at one end, but once it was in the rat-catcher's hands it seemed to sweep him straight back into his sleepwalk. He held it vertically in his fists, with the spike just a couple of inches above the ground. It seemed to guide him at first, then began to shift more intricately, as if tracing some arcane symbol. Paused in its deliberations, rose up, then dived into the

155

ground with such force it seemed to send a shudder right through the field.

This all made for a highly entertaining spectacle but it occurred to Finn, at least, that spearing a whole field full of rats in this manner could easily take up the best part of a week. Yet that single incision seemed to be enough for the rat-catcher and the moment his spike was in the ground he seemed to recover himself.

'Carry on, Mr Soames,' he said.

As the rat-catcher headed back to the gate Mr Soames rolled out the coils of rubber pipe. He fitted one length between the metal cylinder and the stirrup pump and the other to a nozzle at the base of the metal cylinder. Then he took the loose end over to where the pole stuck out of the ground and knelt beside it. Paused for a couple of seconds, whipped the spike out with one hand and jammed the pipe into the hole with the other. Fed another few feet in after it, then got to his feet, trod the earth down around it and brushed the dirt from his knees.

When the rat-catcher got to the gate he stopped and bowed to his audience and Aldred, for one, was all set to give him the applause he so richly deserved. But the rat-catcher plucked a clutch of grass from the ground, straightened up and threw it in the air. The breeze sent it scattering back towards Steere's cottage.

'You'd better move down the wall a bit,' he said as he picked up the two big tins. 'And if you smell almonds you'd better move again.'

This was the first time almonds had been mentioned and since his fate seemed to be inextricably linked with them Hector thought he should establish what an almond actually smelt of.

'Sort of sweet,' said the rat-catcher, 'and sort of nutty.' Then he turned and set off back across the field.

By the time the Boys had moved down the wall, the rat-catchers were pulling out great white handkerchiefs from their pockets, folding them from corner to corner and knotting them so that they covered their faces, which gave them an air of lawlessness that had the Boys wishing they'd had the foresight to bring along handkerchiefs of their own. The rat-catcher prised the lid off one of the tins, Mr Soames flipped back the top of the cylinder and the rat-catcher began carefully spooning the tin's contents in. From a distance it looked like icing sugar, but when a gust of wind threatened to get a hold of it both men averted their faces and as soon as the tops were clamped back down on the cylinder and the big can the men seemed to go about their business a good deal more easily.

The rat-catcher stood over his stirrup pump and started working the handle, whilst Mr Soames took up his cricket bat and began his own hesitant dance around the field. The rat-catcher pumped his poison into one hole, yanked the pipe out, stamped it shut, then he took up his pike and went divining again. Once or twice the Boys thought they could indeed detect a trace of something sweet and nutty and Harvey pulled his jumper discreetly up over his nose. But eventually another sound joined the creak of the rat-catcher's pump handle and the subterranean hiss of gas. It was a while before the Boys picked it out, but once they'd done so there was no ignoring it. It was a high-pitched screech – a sort of screaming – somewhat muted at first but steadily growing as more and more gas was pumped into the ground.

The Boys found the noise increasingly unsettling, but for Mr Steere the rats' slaughter could not be painful enough. He would have liked to see every last one of them writhing out in the open. The whole exercise seemed far too clinical and bloodless, and when the rat-catcher was feeding his rubber pipe into the ground yet again and treading the earth down around it Aldred heard Steere muttering, 'Is he going to pump every hole in the bloody field?'

Fifty yards away the rat-catcher straightened his back and pulled his handkerchief aside.

'Mr Steere,' he called out. 'There's only one thing a gentle-man rat likes as much as eating, and that's the company of a lady rat.' He scratched the back of his neck. 'Every rat-hole leads to another. You pump enough gas in and you see to them all.'

He pulled his handkerchief back down over his mouth and returned to his pumping. In a matter of seconds he was oblivious. He pumped up and down as if there could be no better way to spend the morning. He pumped as if he'd like to fill the whole world with cyanide.

The day settled into its own steady progress, with Mr Soames using his cricket bat to see to those few rats who managed to get above ground whilst his partner gassed the many thousands locked below. In all the time that the Boys sat and watched them they saw only one rat escape both gas and bat. It came out of the ground at quite a lick, very wisely gave Mr Soames a wide berth, then leapt over the wall, no more than twenty feet from the Boys and went tearing off across the fields, which left the Five Boys rueing their lack of long trousers and lengths of twine.

Over the next few days the rat-catcher baited Steere's house, then pumped the other meadows whilst Steere him-self ploughed up the rats he left behind. It was a gruesome harvest which he heaped at the side of the house. Later in the week Aldred and Lewis made a social call and stood in awe before what they estimated to be at least ten thousand rats – bigger, certainly, than any pile of beet they had come across.

They were still standing there when the rat-catcher came round the corner with another barrow-load. He had his hand-kerchief over his face and when he lifted the barrow's handles turned his head away. The rats slid forward, and as they hit the ground that same sweet smell came up off them.

The rat-catcher rested his hands on his hips. 'Have you ever seen so many rats?' he asked the two boys.

They shook their heads.

'Me neither,' he said.

Lewis thought there must have been enough rats there to make a jacket for every dog in the country.

'What are you going to do with them all?' he asked the rat-catcher.

The rat-catcher smiled. 'I'm going to set the buggers afire,' he said.

Keeping Watch

Howard liked to keep an eye on the ladies. Liked to sit up on the hill and watch them doing their errands and slip into the trees behind Far Bank on a Monday morning and watch Lizzie Hathersage peg her sheets on the line. But it was nothing but good fortune that had him taking a nap in one of the fields just below the village when Sylvia Crouch happened to go by.

Maureen Tucker's pram woke him up. Its wheels had squeaked ever since the pig memorial, but when Howard rolled over and peeped out through the hedgerow he saw Sylvia Crouch's lovely legs go swishing by rather than Mo Tucker's great hams, and in no time he was on his feet and cantering after them.

He couldn't think what Sylvia was doing pushing other people's babies around the place when, as far as he knew, Mo wasn't poorly and had nothing better to do with her time. Not that he was complaining. He was just trying to piece the story together. He had the kind of mind, he liked to think, that in different circumstances could have solved complicated crimes.

Having Sylvia Crouch stroll by was an absolute godsend. In an ideal world, he thought as he went after her, she'd be without the baby. His jackpot would be her going all the way down to the river, stripping off and having a dip, but he'd happily settle for her dropping her drawers to take a pee. That would keep him going right through the year.

Along the way several hedges had to be negotiated and twice Howard had to jump down into the lane, sneak along behind her and find his way back into the field. Sylvia seemed to know exactly where she was going – went down to the bridge, turned left on to what had been the perimeter road and carried along it for half a mile before suddenly stopping. By the time Howard caught her up the baby was in her arms and she was rooting around under its blankets. The baby looked over her shoulder right at Howard. When it went back into its pram Sylvia was holding a package. She crossed the lane and tucked it in the hedge behind a milestone, turned the pram around and set off home.

As soon as she was out of sight Howard climbed down into the lane and tip-toed over. Picked out the package and pulled the string away. There was a folded workshirt, an old pair of moleskin trousers and some food wrapped up in newspaper. He stood and stared at them for quite a while before the penny dropped, then suddenly felt affronted. Felt a wonderful rage stir in him. And he pulled the string back round the package, put it back in the bushes and went back to his hiding place.

It was a while before anything happened – enough time for him to imagine every degenerate act the deserter and Sylvia Crouch had been getting up to – to imagine Sylvia with her skirt rucked up around her waist and the soldier pounding away on top of her. To feel the humiliation burn right into his soul.

When the stay-behind finally appeared Howard wanted to jump right out on him. There wasn't much meat on the fellow and Howard wondered what on earth Sylvia could see in him. He crept along the road as if the slightest sound might scare him away. But Howard sat tight. Watched him pick out the package. Watched him open it up. And when the stay-behind turned and set off back to the gate Howard paused before going after him, telling himself that there was no hurry – no hurry at all.

It was to their lasting regret that the Five Boys hadn't been around to see the rats being doused in paraffin and set alight. The first they heard about it was Mrs Heaney saying how she had been out at a cousin's at Duncannon when so much smoke came billowing down the valley that they had to bring her washing in.

The Boys hiked back out to Steere's farm the next morning, but there was nothing left but a patch of scorched earth with a fringe of blackened grass, and when they finally managed to track down Steere in one of his sheds and pressed him for some details, he just carried on sawing and hammering and seemed not to want to talk about rats any more.

The rats' cremation turned out to be just the first in a season of bonfires. As usual, autumn's debris had to be disposed of, as well as enough of the unbridled growth in the evacuated area for people to be able to get down the lanes, and for months it seemed as if the smell of woodsmoke and burning bracken was always in the air.

But May's was by far the largest bonfire – the one which drew the biggest audience and kept going deepest into the night – when the war, or at least Europe's part in it, came to an end. The wood was gathered in a single morning and for a few hours it stood up on the hill like some primitive monument. Fallen timber, rotten fence posts and broken furniture were all heaved up to it, as if the bigger the bonfire the quicker the dark days of the war would be erased.

At five o'clock the Reverend Bentley lit a creosote-soaked rag at the end of a stick and, like an arthritic St George, jabbed it into the straw at the base. Within minutes the wood was alive. It spat and crackled and the hills beyond shimmered in its liquid heat. Around six o'clock some crates of beer arrived. Five minutes later everyone was singing. And as he stood and stared into the raw heat Lewis felt his mother slip her arm around him and pull him towards her, which he couldn't remember her having done before.

When Howard Kent and Dexter Fadden swung an old armchair onto the fire an hour or so later it let out a tremendous roar and sent up a great rolling ball of amber sparks. The villagers were mesmerised by the fire – could feel its heat gently beat their cheeks. The Boys weren't sure that ending the war was such a good idea. Howard Kent had no doubt. He saw his little dynasty collapsing around him. In no time at all the village would be overrun with returning soldiers and their tales of heroism. And even the women secretly wondered whether this meant that the world was going to be turned on its head again.

As darkness fell the other bonfires became visible – one over the river at Bovey Tracy, another near Totnes and a couple out towards the moor. The church bells had been ringing all day in all the villages but seemed to grow stronger in the dark – to carry further. They rolled down the valley as if a dam had finally broken and all the war's unrung changes had come tumbling out.

Queen's Peal

Jem Hathersage looked as if he'd just taken a bite out of something bitter.

'It doesn't sound right without the six,' he said.

The bellringers stood in a circle and steadied the ropes which kinked and buckled above them. They hadn't been touched since '39 and the first round that night had brought down five fine columns of dust. Alec Bream had suggested they grease the stockheads, but no one could face the climb.

'Howard,' said Arthur Noyce. 'You're pushing on too hard.'

Howard shook his head.

'You are,' said Lester Massie. 'You work that number five any fucking harder and she'll pull you up through the belfry fucking floor.'

Howard glared at him but didn't say anything.

'Are we going again?' said Alec Bream.

'Call it,' said Lester.

'All right,' said Alec. 'And Howard, hold off a bit.'

'And quit sulking,' said Lester Massie.

Alec reached up and took a hold. '*Look to* . . .' he called out.

The other four raised their arms.

' . . . *Treble's going* . . .'

Alec tugged at his rope, which dipped a couple of inches, then flew back through his fingers, yards at a time.

' . . . *She's gone,*' he called out.

The men heaved on their ropes, one after another. A moment later the bells sounded above.

'*Two to three,*' shouted Alec. 'Lester, wake up.'

The bells roared – cascaded out into the village – and for a while the men just stood and worked the ropes.

'That's better,' said Alec. *'Four to five.'*

Lester Massie was looking at his neighbour's feet. 'Howard,' he said, and heaved on his rope. 'Where'd you get the boots?'

Howard shrugged. 'Totnes,' he said.

'Two to five,' said Alec.

Jem Hathersage looked over. 'Them aren't civvy boots,' he said.

'Two,' said Alec Bream, *'closer on your backstroke. Follow five.'*

'Them's Army Issue,' said Jem.

'One to three,' said Alec.

'I'm lost,' said Arthur Noyce.

'I told you,' said Jem Hathersage. 'We're missing the six.'

The bells turned on their frame up in the belfry like a medieval engine. The ropes wound the great wheels and the bells emptied their sound on the Boys below. They lay face-down between the joists. They were wearing their balaclavas and had their hands clamped over their ears but could feel every muscle in their bodies being pummelled – could feel their lungs having trouble taking air in.

'This is what it must have been like in the trenches,' thought Lewis.

The Boys had been prepared for the pandemonium. It was the sheer brutality of the bells threshing the air which took them by surprise. They lay on the dusty floor for what felt like an eternity with them slicing around them and their bones jangling, until one of the men below finally barked out some instruction and the bells came to rest.

The ringing stopped, but the sound took its time dispersing. The air was thick with it. Still groggy, the Boys shifted until they could squint between the floorboards at the five men below, rolling cigarettes. One was making some notes on a scrap of paper.

Lewis put his mouth up to Finn's ear. 'Which is which?' he said.

A few days earlier there had been a knock at the door and Finn's mother had got up to go and answer it. A moment or two later she had let out a terrible scream. Finn ran into the hall. Found some stranger apparently trying to strangle her and he was still trying to work out what to do when she finally managed to wrench herself free.

'Your daddy's home,' she said.

No amount of bunting or bonfires could have prepared Finn for the upheaval which followed. It was as if they had taken a lodger in. Some stranger with big boots who liked to talk and smoke and sit by the fireside. A man towards whom the whole domestic world had turned. The dinner table was suddenly crowded, the conversation seemed to keep Finn out. Bedtimes, mealtimes, even seating arrangements were all suddenly negotiable – all subject to change.

It wasn't that Finn had no recollection of the man in the armchair. It was just that the memories, when they came to him, were so fleeting they might as well have belonged to somebody else.

Finn and Lewis continued to peer between the floorboards.

'Are you sure that's mine,' said Lewis, 'with the note-book?'

'I think so,' said Finn.

Lewis looked down, as if beholding mankind from some celestial platform.

'He's almost *bald*,' he said.

The men returned to their ropes, the Boys took cover and the bombardment started up again, but within a couple of minutes the bells clashed, clattered to a standstill and the Boys could hear the men arguing about who was to blame. One of the fathers suggested having one last go, to see if they could get it right, another suggested calling it a day and having a drink, and in no time at all they were collecting their coats and jackets and heading for the door.

The lights went out and the Boys listened to the voices

retreating. Listened to the footsteps on the path. They waited another minute, then crept down the tower's stone steps and stood and brushed the dust off their jackets. Then they looked around the ringing chamber, which was still sweet with cigarette smoke, to see if their fathers had left anything interesting behind.

'They really hate Howard Kent, don't they?' said Harvey.

'Everyone hates Howard Kent,' Hector said.

Aldred found the scrap of paper which the men had been studying and held it up to the moonlight . . .

2–3	1–4	5–4	2–5	3–2
4–5	3–5	5–1	4–1	5–4
2–5	3–2	5–3	4–3	
1–3	3–4	2–4	4–5	
1–5	3–1	2–1	4–2	
1–2	5–2	2–3	5–2	

It looked like a list of coordinates – or a series of sums capable of taxing old Foghorn herself. The other Boys had a glance at it, then carried on looking around. But Aldred wanted to know why these particular numbers were so important, so he slipped the piece of paper into his pocket and vowed to try and make some sense of them later on.

The Arrival of the Bee King

There was no warning of the coming of the Bee King. No one saw a pantechnicon pull up outside Askew Cottage or any boxes being carried in. Yet, between the village retiring on the evening of Good Friday and rising the following day, he somehow managed to insinuate himself so successfully into the fabric of the village that when Mrs Heaney went by just after nine o' clock, having overslept for the first time in eleven years, she walked straight past and was picking up speed on the high street before some barely conscious cogitation ran its course, jammed her brakes on and threw her trip to the Post Office into reverse.

The cottage had been empty for over a year and Mrs Heaney had certainly heard nothing of anyone moving in, but when she retraced her steps and stood outside the cottage's bay window she had confirmation of what she'd only glimpsed a minute before. A smartly dressed fellow was busy opening a tea chest, and as she waited Mrs Heaney transferred her purse from one hand to the other so that she'd be able to wave at him when she finally caught his eye.

She must have waited in the lane for a full five minutes without him once looking up from his unpacking but when she finally gave up and went on her way she discovered that the whole village was behind with its chores. The vicarage curtains were still pulled to. The Captain's armchair was empty. The only life in the high street was the fallen plum blossom as it gently turned and shifted in the breeze.

The door to the Post Office had a habit of sticking, so Mrs Heaney threw her little shoulder against it, only to bounce back off it, and bounced off it twice more before it occurred to her that it might, in fact, be locked. She looked at her wristwatch. Tapped it. Brought it up to her ear and listened. Took a couple of steps back until the clock on the church came into view. The clock and her watch both insisted that it was ten past nine, but the state of the village seemed to contradict it and Mrs Heaney suddenly felt most peculiar, as if finding herself in a dream from which she could not wake.

She gripped the wall to steady herself. Her heart was pounding. Her vision seemed to come and go. And who knows how long that little episode might have lasted had Miss Pye not interrupted it by opening a window just below the gables and thrusting her huge chest out into the day.

She scratched the back of her neck. Squinted up the lane, then down at Mrs Heaney.

'Are you early or am I late?' she said.

None of the customers that morning knew anything about any new tenants but having heard all the speculation at the Post Office few could resist taking a more circuitous route home, to take a look. One or two managed to catch a glimpse of the fellow without actually managing to provoke any sort of response, but when Howard Kent marched up to the cottage just after lunchtime and put his nose up to the window he could clearly see him standing on a stepladder, fixing a pair of curtains to a rail at the back of the room. Howard understood what was being asked of him. He straightened his collar and glanced back down the lane. A dozen other villagers were hanging around the corner.

'Ask him if he's working for the estate,' hissed Miss Pye.

Howard had once accompanied his father on a similar mission, when, under the pretext of welcoming a young couple to the village the old man had quickly established how long the two of them had been married, where they came from and when they intended returning, as well as giving them a good idea of the sort of behaviour expected of them in the interim.

Howard wanted to prove himself to be his father's son. When the door opened, he thought, he would hold out his right hand. 'Howard Kent,' he would say, 'pleased to meet you,' obliging the newcomer to do the same. He took a deep breath, knocked and waited. 'Pleased to meet you,' he whispered. Imagined the handshake. 'Howard Kent. Very pleased to meet you indeed.'

The door seemed to have no intention of opening. Howard decided to knock again. It was only when he stepped back a few moments later to shrug his shoulders at the others that he saw the figure standing in the window, watching, and like Mrs Heaney's frustrated wave before it, felt his handshake wither and die at his side.

'Howard Kent,' he announced, trying to think on his feet. 'I would just like to . . .'

The man in the bay window cupped a hand to his ear and shook his head. Howard had to start again.

'The name's *Kent*,' he said. 'Howard *Kent*,' and this, at least, seemed to penetrate the glass.

'And I'm just calling . . . to welcome you to the village . . .' he said, then petered out.

The bridge between welcoming the stranger and extracting some personal information had somehow got washed away. Howard couldn't work out how that had happened and when he looked back at the window the man was gone. He turned to face the door and straightened his collar again, but the longer he waited the better he appreciated how the meeting was at an end.

The walk back down the lane to the other villagers was deeply uncomfortable. They were all eager to hear how he had got on. Miss Pye had closed the Post Office early.

'What's he up to?' she said.

Howard smiled to himself, as if he and the Bee King had just had a most illuminating conversation, and kept on smiling as he walked right past the assembled villagers and headed home.

His neighbours stood and watched him march down the high street.

'What do you make of that?' said Mrs Heaney.

Miss Pye folded her arms under her bosom and shook her head.

'Spurned,' she said.

The Bee King's performance the following day more than compensated for Howard's failure. The newcomer's absence in the pews had been widely noted and once the week's devotional duties were out of the way the villagers gathered in the churchyard where speculation about the fellow continued apace.

The Reverend Bentley stood and nodded by the door as the last of the congregation filed out into the sunshine and was already looking forward to his Sunday roast when a metallic clatter came down the lane and extinguished every conversation in its way.

The worshippers turned and saw the Bee King striding down the lane towards them, a metal spoon in one hand furiously rattling the saucepan in the other. He had his head held high but wasn't hanging about. He looked like a drummer who had become separated from the rest of a marching band. This, at least, was how the Reverend Bentley saw it. Miss Pye saw only a madman banging a saucepan on Easter Day. But whatever they made of him, the villagers all found themselves drawn across the graveyard to try and get a better view.

Over the years Mr Mercer had come to appreciate how a congregation liked something a little uplifting to help them to their feet and accompany them to the door, and as they left the church this morning Aldred pumped out Mr Mercer's gallant attempt at 'For all the saints, who from their labours rest'. When the organist lifted his fingers from the final chord the echoes multiplied in the rafters until they were soaked up by the stone. He pushed the stops back in, got to his feet and took Aldred's shoulder, but when they opened the back door found their way blocked by the self-same worshippers they'd just cleared from the pews.

Aldred ploughed down the path with a determination that had old Mr Mercer gasping and tottering from side to side. A strange noise came rattling through the trees – which, to Aldred's ears, sounded like a poor imitation of Mrs Fog's bell first thing in the morning, but seemed to be just as effective at pulling people in.

By the time the Bee King stopped rattling his pan half the village were in the lane beside him and the rest were hanging over the wall. Such a crowd might have been expected to elicit some sort of explanation, but the Bee King was so wrapped up in his own quiet incantation he seemed almost oblivious to them. He spoke as if trying to calm a frightened animal and stared up into the branches of a tree. One by one the villagers followed his gaze. But it was only when one old man grew frustrated and called out, 'What's he *looking* at?' that the Reverend Bentley, who was down at the front, said, 'Bees, Mr Pearce. He's got a swarm of bees.'

This news got a mixed reception. Most of the villagers were intrigued and tried to get a better view. One or two hastily left the scene. Miss Pye announced that she was about to faint, which certainly animated the Captain, who had come out to see what all the fuss was about and would have liked nothing better than to have Miss Pye land on top of him, but by the time he was anywhere near her the postmistress had been propped up against the wall by Miss Minter and was having her face fanned with her hat.

Mr Mercer arrived at the side gate to find both his wife and his Bath chair missing – had no choice but to despatch his assistant to try and track them down. Aldred set off with only the best intentions. He knew very well how little Mr Mercer liked being on his feet. But when every man, woman and child was gawping up at a tree he found it hard not to stop and have a look himself.

The swarm hung there like a great dollop of molten toffee. A few bees still fizzed about it, but the general impression was of a single, breathing thing. It looked almost hairy – as if it had been dropped in the dirt. Was about a foot thick at the top, tapering to a rounded tip a couple of feet below and was clustered around a wishbone in the tree's branches, pulling the bough down towards the ground with its weight.

Snagged on the branches, the swarm reminded Aldred of his mother's knitting when it was rolled up and tucked down the side of an armchair. But there was something deadly about it, something worrying in the way it bubbled and festered, as if it was brewing up some evil intent. The whole village stared up at it, enraptured, including Mrs Mercer, who leant against her husband's Bath chair. Aldred had never seen such serenity on her face and when the Bee King turned and whispered something to her she nodded almost unconsciously, as if there was more of her up in the tree than there was on the ground.

Aldred pushed his way through the crowd until the bees were directly above him and when the Bee King turned and handed him his pan and spoon he accepted them with the same composure he employed around the church – which threatened to slip when he noticed that the Bee King had been striking the pan not with a spoon but a key of a similar vintage to his own.

The Bee King took Mr Mercer's Bath chair from his wife and pushed it forward. Picked Mr Mercer's walking stick from the seat and lifted it, handle-first up into the tree. Hooked the branch where the swarm had settled and drew it down. The bees' wings glinted as they emerged from the blossom. The whole bundle shifted and glistened in the sun. Then, when the branch was at its very limit, the Bee King checked the Bath chair's position, gave the branch a firm cuff with the heel of his hand and the swarm fell into the Bath chair with about as much fuss as a packet of tea being emptied into a caddy. A shower of blossom followed, like a blessing.

A collective gasp came up from the congregation. In fact, the fall seemed to provoke more excitement among the villagers than it did the bees, a few of whom flitted over their new quarters but, generally speaking, seemed not the least bit perturbed. The Bee King removed his jacket and placed it over the bees in the Bath chair. Then he took hold of its handles, backed out of the crowd and departed, leaving everyone standing around in silence, as if they had just witnessed a miracle.

Mrs Mercer and Aldred helped Mr Mercer home between them, one doing her best to explain how she had come to give his Bath chair to a complete stranger and the other trying to explain how he had come to leave him hanging on the gate. The organist was deeply disgruntled, but didn't have enough breath in him to complain and they were almost home, with him wheezing and spluttering, when it dawned on Aldred what the swarm of bees had reminded him of – it looked just like he'd always imagined Mr Mercer's bad lung to be.

There was no attribute more important to the Five Boys than bravery and nothing seized upon with quite as much relish as the apparent lack of it. But so much of their time together was spent pretending to be brave when they were actually frightened it was hard to know how brave or cowardly they really were, and as he sat in his bedroom on that Sunday afternoon Aldred wished only that he had enough courage to rattle the key in the saucepan and see if any bees appeared.

He had given the key a thorough examination. Its handle was more ornate than his own but its bit and shaft were much the same. The longer he looked at it the more he was tempted to keep it – saw in it the beginnings of a bunch of keys capable of opening every lock and gate that Fate might put in his way – but within a couple of hours he was carrying the key and pan round to the Bee King's cottage, due in part to a fear that any magic in their owner's hands might be a curse in anyone else's and in part to the fact that it would give him the opportunity to see if the fellow had any more bee tricks up his sleeve.

He knocked at the door. Waited a minute, then knocked again. He shielded his eyes up against the window. The room was empty, except for a couple of tea chests with books and other, smaller boxes piled beside them and some others, sitting unopened by a wall. A few odds and ends were laid out on a table including a piece of equipment which looked like some sort of electrical lamp, and Aldred was twisting his head to try and get a better look at it when he saw someone walk past the window in the garden at the back.

He picked up the pan and key and slipped down the side of the cottage, but by the time he got to the garden gate the Bee King had disappeared. Aldred might have entered the garden a little faster if it hadn't been for all the bee-hives on the lawn. They had louvred sides, were about the same size as a doll's house (without the windows) and raised off the ground on wooden legs, but Aldred had no way of knowing whether the bees were home.

'Hello,' he said and was ready to turn and run when the Bee King popped up among the hives.

'I've got your pan,' said Aldred and held it up, but the Bee King just stared at him.

'And your key,' said Aldred, and held that up in the other hand.

The Bee King looked like a giant who had just been interrupted whilst terrorising a village. Aldred was trying to keep an eye on all the bee-houses in case their inhabitants suddenly decided to leap out at him. The Bee King had still not said a word.

'I'll put them on the path,' said Aldred and did so, then began to sidle back towards the gate.

'Come here,' the Bee King said, and beckoned Aldred towards him.

Aldred took a breath, then stepped tentatively onto the lawn. Either he'd managed to tap some new resources of bravery or was just doing as he was told, but as he approached the hives he could feel his whole body tingle with anticipated stings. He tip-toed between them, until he reached the Bee King, who placed a hand on his shoulder and looked deep into his eyes. Then, just as Mr Mercer pushed down on him on Sunday mornings, the Bee King pushed down, and kept on pushing until he sank between the hives.

The Bee King crouched down next to him.

'Listen,' he said.

Aldred listened but could hear nothing except his own fearful breathing. Then listened harder and managed to pick out a low hum coming through the hive's white wall. The Bee King's face was just a few inches away. He asked Aldred what he reckoned that sound was. Aldred thought hard but couldn't come up with anything.

The Bee King put his lips to Aldred's ear.

'*The honey factory,*' he said.

The two of them crouched there, listening, for a moment. Then the Bee King took Aldred's hand, opened out the fingers and pressed it gently against the hive. After a while, Aldred sensed some tiny vibration, like a natural engine. He could feel it quietly rumbling against his hand, and was imagining the hundreds of factory workers inside when the Bee King raised his fist in the air and brought it down hard onto the roof of the hive.

Aldred jumped. Striking a hive seemed like just about the last thing you'd want to do when you were standing right next to it. But to his amazement no bee-tornado came spinning out to envelop them and he didn't have to go screaming down the lane. All that happened was that the hive's low hum rose in a growl of irritation, then died back down.

The Bee King looked at Aldred. 'The roar of the hive,' he said.

Aldred nodded.

'If the roar rises and falls like that, the bees are happy,' the Bee King said. 'But if they roar and keep on roaring there's something up with them.'

176

Aldred nodded again.

'And do you know what the bees are saying when they roar and keep on roaring?' the Bee King asked.

Aldred shook his head.

The Bee King threw his hands up to the heavens.

'The queen is dead,' he wailed.

Pugfoist

At first, the village found it hard to generate much affection for the Bee King. Indeed, they found it hard to cultivate any sort of relationship with a man so determined to have nothing to do with them. He had made his feelings towards uninvited callers clear from the outset and on those rare occasions when he was seen out and about in the village it soon became apparent that he was not one to loiter needlessly in the street.

The Captain was varnishing a three-decker's masthead on the Tuesday when he saw the Bee King coming down the lane. He was wearing an old tweed suit, patched at the cuffs and elbows, with a basket in his hand. The Captain kicked off his sleeping bag and hurried over to the window but, having got to his post, couldn't quite bring himself to raise his arm. It wasn't the fear of hostility that stopped him or the humiliation of being ignored. He could just tell by the way the fellow was moving that there was no getting in his way.

Even Miss Pye, who considered herself peerless when it came to interfering in other people's business, privately conceded that she couldn't recall coming up against such unresponsive stuff. From the moment he walked through the door of the Post Office she did her best to crack him; tried every trick in the book – softening him up with a barrage of idle chatter regarding the weather and the state of her guttering, then trying to catch him off guard with quick-fire questions about his job, his retirement from it, whether he had any family in Devon . . . any family at all. None of which got the merest peep out of him. It was, she told Mrs Heaney, like banging your head against a brick wall, and that just because the man had a way with bees wasn't to say he had the first idea about communicating with the rest of humanity.

But right from the start the Bee King's relations with the village's children were nothing like as frosty as those with its elders, and when Aldred approached him to ask if he might make a second visit and bring the other Boys along, the Bee King agreed, on the understanding that they arrive promptly at two o'clock. So, on the Saturday afternoon all five Boys waited by the war memorial, with Hector and Finn claiming that some fellow with a few bees was not worth getting all excited about and Lewis insisting that they'd be hard pressed to find a better way of spending a Saturday than in the company of thousands of bees, capable of stinging or swarming at any time.

Harvey was wondering aloud how many stings it might take to kill a man and what sort of twitching agonies such a death might entail when the hand on the church clock juddered into the perpendicular and, after a moment's contemplation, sent out two solid chimes into the day, whereupon the Boys set off, with Aldred, Lewis and Harvey racing up the hill and Finn and Hector doing their best to lag behind.

When the Bee King opened the door it was the Boys' first chance to have a good look at him. He wasn't especially tall or broad, but certainly had a presence about him, as if it would take a train to knock him down, and as he didn't seem in any great hurry to start up a conversation Aldred took matters into his own hands and introduced the other boys. As each one's name was called out he felt the bee-keeper's eyes sweep up and down him, as if, even at this late stage, they might be found wanting and turned away. Then, just when the Boys were beginning to feel quite self-conscious and wonder how much more scrutiny they could stand, the Bee King waved them in, led them down the hall, through the living room, still cluttered with tea chests, through the kitchen, which was practically bare, and out into the garden where the hives sat whitely and brightly in a tidy horseshoe, like tiny hotels looking out over a bay.

Having heard all about Aldred's visit the previous Sunday,

179

Harvey and Hector went straight over to a hive and stood to attention, ready to crouch and listen to the bees. But the Bee King ushered all five of them down to the bottom of the garden and through the open door of the shed, followed them in, dragged an old blanket from a shelf and laid it over the threshold, so that when he stepped back out and closed the door and slid the bolt across, the Boys were effectively sealed inside.

He strode back up to the cottage and the Boys peered through the window after him.

'Where's he off to?' said Heck.

'He didn't put me in here last time,' Aldred said.

The Boys had been in plenty of sheds over the years and this one was not much different from the others, being generally airless and packed with tools and other odds and ends, but with the sweet pungency of honey mixed in with the smell of creosote. While they waited, the Boys occupied themselves by looking for a jar which might contain something poisonous and by speculating on the possible uses of various long-bladed knives. An old Golden Syrup tin, like the one they had dropped on the fire in the allotments, had a label stuck to it, which said, 'Frow's Mixture'. The one next to it rattled rather curiously when it was shaken but had a lid that didn't want to come off. The more they looked the more bee-keeping equipment they discovered. A large metal drum with a winding handle poking out of it was tucked under a bench and a set of chrome tubs and sieves were stacked beside it which were as vast and shiny as the double-handled pans and geysers in the kitchen at the back of the village hall.

The longer they waited the stuffier the shed was getting and soon the Boys had the uncomfortable feeling that they were breathing in the same hot air they had just breathed out. Lewis became more and more agitated, especially when Hector began to wonder aloud what would happen if the shed caught fire. So when the Bee King finally reappeared there was considerable relief. At least, the Boys *assumed* that it was the Bee King, for the man was shrouded by a veil which hung from the brim of an old straw boater and was tucked under the collar of his jacket. He was utterly cob-webbed. The turn-ups of his trousers were stuffed into his boots and every other cuff and opening was securely but-toned up. Only his hands were bare. In one he carried what looked like an old paint-burner and in the other a miniature crowbar.

He crept between the hives in a ghostly fashion, stopped in front of the shed window and looked in at the Boys, but the veil, which was like the muslin their mothers used when making jam, meant they couldn't tell who he was staring at. He flipped the lid back on his burner. Slid a hand into a jacket pocket and brought out what appeared to be a chunk of stale bread. He held it up, so that the Boys could see it.

'Pugfoist,' he said.

He pulled a box of Swan Vestas out of a trouser pocket. Gave it a rattle. Pushed its small drawer open; nipped a match between finger and thumb. Struck it on the side of the box and once its flame had flared and settled, held it under the lump of fungus until it glowed and began to smoke. Then dropped it in the can and clamped the lid back down on it.

' . . . to subdue the bees,' he said.

He squeezed the small bellows at the back of the canister and the smoke at the spout went from a trickle to a thick, grey plume. Then he turned and carried his can of smoke and his little crowbar over to the nearest hive.

The Boys were perfectly insulated in their shed and some distance from the action, but when the Bee King pumped some smoke into the slit at the bottom of the hive there was no mistaking the sudden intensification of sound. It was like an engine revving. The Bee King placed the smoker on the ground, positioned his feet and lifted the hive roof off. Beneath it was a folded blanket, similar to the one he had used to block up the shed door. He laid this on the grass, took up his smoker and, after a couple of preparatory squeezes, pumped an inch or two of mist across the exposed top storey. He stood back and let the smoke sink between the bars, then moved back in and began to dismantle the hive, one floor at a time.

If the bees which enveloped their master were of the sub-dued variety the Boys could only imagine what sort of mood they would have been in without the smoke, for as soon as the hive was opened up the air was thick with them, they rat-tled off the shed window and gathered in great clumps on the Bee King's jacket and veil. The cottage, visible a minute earlier, was instantly obscured by a gauze of bees. And yet the Bee King seemed to have found his element and moved among them with absolute ease.

As he prised the hive's stacked boxes apart with his tiny crowbar each one gave a sharp creak of dissent, until he had worked his way right down to the basement, and the shell of the hive was piled up on the lawn to his right and the inner boxes were piled up to his left. When he opened that last box he seemed to concentrate his efforts, tapping and tinkering like a mechanic under the bonnet of a motor car. He squeezed some more smoke across its surface, peeled away a thin metal cover, dug his little lever into the box's perimeter and released one end of a long rectangular strip. Got his fingers and thumbs under each end, gently lifted it and brought out a living block of bees.

He examined one side, then the other and took it over to the Boys in their observation shed.

'First of all,' he said, lifting the bees up to the window, 'we must learn how to read the frame.'

He asked the Boys what they thought they should be look-ing for, but they were too busy watching the bees as they knitted and fretted – feeling the same peculiar combination of fascination and revulsion stir in them as the day they saw the naked ladies in the magazine.

'Brood and food,' the Bee King said.

He brushed his hand across the bees as if clearing the froth

182

off a glass of ginger beer. Some bees moved aside, some took flight, some clung to his fingers. But the comb was revealed, the colour of cinder toffee and punched full of hexagonal holes. The surface undulated, like a saturated sponge, and here and there it was stained a darker brown, as if it had been singed by the heat of the hive.

'The queen lays her eggs,' the Bee King said, spreading his fingers across the middle of the frame, 'to keep the hive in workers.' He pointed to the corners of the frame. 'The workers put away their stores for a rainy day.'

For such a quiet man the Bee King was being unusually forthcoming.

'We do some maintenance as we go,' he said. 'And if we come across the queen, all well and good. But as long as she keeps laying and the workers keep foraging then the hive is happy.'

He lowered the comb and for a moment the sun managed to penetrate his veil.

'And what do the bees store away that we're so fond of?' he said.

Harvey piped up before he could stop himself.

'Honey,' he called out from the shed.

The Bee King jabbed a blackened finger at him.

'Exactly,' he said.

In all his years under Miss Fog's formidable tuition Harvey had never been so quick off the mark and, almost in spite of himself, he felt a smile spread across his face – felt his whole body prickle with pride.

'Honey,' he whispered again.

The Bank of England

The Boys had always found life to be a slow and exhausting business. When they weren't lumbering up and down the lanes in mud-heavy boots they were slumped by the war memorial – impossible to wake first thing in the morning and hard to budge last thing at night – but from their first encounter with the bees they sensed a momentous change in them, as if a yoke were being lifted from their shoulders or a layer of darkness stripped away.

This transformation was no more apparent than in Harvey. His early rising and newfound sunny disposition baffled his parents and was, frankly, enough of a worry without the rest of the village reporting back every time he and the other Boys were seen filing into the Bee King's place. Things came to a head one Tuesday evening when he got up and put on his jacket without so much as a by-your-leave, and his father was still calling after him when he heard the front door slam shut.

Maggie and Arthur Noyce sat by the fire and a bitter silence slowly enveloped them. Arthur turned on the wireless, but the reception kept coming and going and when his wife said, not for the first time, that Harvey had been just fine when it was just the two of them, Arthur finally snapped and stormed out of the house, slamming the front door behind him, just as his son had done ten minutes before.

The streets were silent except for Arthur's footsteps and the odd word that spilled out of him as he continued to argue with his wife. He marched up the hill at quite a pace, but whatever propelled him suddenly gave out about twenty yards short of Askew Cottage. He stopped. Looked over both shoulders. And when he set off again he crept forward on the tips of his toes.

A seam of amber light burned between the curtains, as if they contained something hot, something molten. Arthur could hear children's voices but couldn't make out what they were saying, so he slipped down the side of the house and ducked through the garden gate. The smell of the damp earth and the foliage seemed to calm him. He tucked himself away behind a bush and realised that he had become someone more likely to have an explanation demanded of them than the person demanding one.

He crept over to the window on all fours, but it was just as heavily curtained as the one around the front, so he sat on the ground with his back against the cottage and let the voices wash over him. It was the idea of his son being happy in the house behind him and the miserable atmosphere in his own that troubled him. And as time passed he thought less and less about the Boys and the Bee King – thought less and less, in fact, about anything at all – and sank into a pleasant, almost non-existence in which he was almost no one, almost nowhere in the night.

He might have sat there for as little as twenty minutes or the best part of an hour, but suddenly came to, feeling cold and uncomfortable and wanting to be back home in front of his own fire. He crept over to the gate, slipped back down the alleyway and was passing the window when a great roar of laughter erupted inside. And all his anger suddenly boiled back up in him and before he knew it he was hammering at the door.

The laughter stopped. Arthur pictured the children listening. A light went on in the hall. He could hear footsteps – a bolt clatter back – then the Bee King was standing before him, like a gatekeeper to a whole cottageful of heat and light.

'Mr Noyce,' said the Bee King.

Arthur was having trouble remembering what he wanted to say to the fellow and for a while the two men just stood there looking at one another.

'We'll not be long,' said the Bee King.

Arthur was half-inclined to be happy with that.

'I want to see my son,' he managed to say.

The bee-keeper stared at him for a moment – nodded – then turned and went back down the hallway. There were some whispered words in the living room and as Arthur waited two other boys stepped out into the hall to have a look at him. One held a piece of toast between his finger and thumb – took an elegant bite out of it. Then Harvey came sauntering down the hall, with the Bee King not far beh

He must have been drinking milk. The tiny hairs on his upper lip were dashed white with it.

'What is it?' said Harvey.

Arthur couldn't understand how such cold words could spring from such a tender, milky mouth.

'Your mother,' he said. 'She's worried.'

Harvey waited to see if his father had anything else to say. Apparently, he didn't.

'Go home,' he said. 'I won't be long.'

The door closed in Arthur's face. He stared at it for a second. Then he turned and headed home. The words were still ringing in him. It was as if, somehow, he had become the son and his son the father. He wondered how that might possibly have happened and how he could even begin to explain it to his wife.

If it had been allowed, the Boys would have opened up the hives on every visit, but the Bee King was quite insistent that the bees should not be too frequently disturbed, and in order to distract them one night he pulled out an old slide projector from one of his tea chests and showed the Boys how to set it up.

Half an hour later the lights were dimmed, the Bee King slid a rack into the projector and the first slide appeared on the living-room wall. It was of a man with a huge beard of bees hanging off his chin – a wild-looking fellow with both hands clamped on his thighs, taking the strain of what the

Bee King assured the Boys was many thousands of living, breathing bees.

The Boys sat and stared at the bee beard.

'Is it heavy?' said Aldred.

'About eleven or twelve pounds,' the Bee King said.

Harvey wanted to know what kind of weight that was and when the Bee King told him its rough equivalent in bags of sugar the Boys began to appreciate just how heavy (and sweet) a beard it was. Why the fellow had wanted to coax so many bees onto his chin in the first place and how he had achieved it were secrets the Bee King was not prepared to divulge, but of all the slides they saw that night and at all the subsequent slide-shows it was by far the most popular.

The next slide was one of the dullest. A couple of straw baskets sat on the ground in an orchard – about the same size as lobster pots. The only thing that could have been said in their favour was that they looked like the sort of baskets from which snakes have been known to be charmed. They were called *skeps*, the Bee King said, and were old-fashioned bee-houses, which didn't make them any more interesting but helped explain, in Aldred's mind at least, why the swarm the Bee King knocked out of the tree in the graveyard had been so at home in Mr Mercer's Bath chair.

These slide-shows soon developed their own little ritual in which the Boys would set up the projector, whilst the Bee King took his boxes of slides off to a corner and worked his way through them, picking each one out and holding it up to the light, like tiny frames from a beeless hive.

The whole collection must have consisted of several hundred slides, and could roughly be divided between the more general ones of hives and bee-keeping equipment and the close-ups of bees carrying out their various tasks. In one, a bee stood on its own small patch of comb with several other bees gathered around it. The bee in the middle was slightly blurred, as if it was vigorously moving. A black dotted line had been superimposed over it in a figure of eight.

'What do you think this is?' said the Bee King.

'Is it a map?' said Aldred.

'That's right,' the Bee King said. 'A bee will fly for miles in search of nectar, and use the sun as a compass. When it gets home it performs the *waggle dance* to show the other bees where the nectar is.'

Some of the slides had cracks across the corner and one or two were ridged with the contours of vast fingerprints, but every row of pupae bulged in their cells in an orderly fashion and even the man with the bee beard seemed to pose as if taking part in some scientific experiment. In one slide, three bees lined up alongside one another. A wooden ruler had been placed to their right, as if they were about to race along it. These three bees, the Bee King told the Boys, were the only variety in any hive: the *queen*, the *worker* and the *drone*.

The Boys were rather put out when they heard the workers were actually female, and further disturbed when the Bee King described how the drones treated the hive like a gentlemen's club, only to be ejected when the autumn came around. What worried the Boys was the fact that they had begun to treat the Bee King's cottage like their own little clubhouse. Here was a place, after all, where their presence was not merely tolerated but positively welcomed and their opinions given the sort of consideration they never received at home.

But the only time the Bee King's hospitality threatened to waver was when Lewis spotted a child among the hives in one of the slides. He was all dressed up like a junior beekeeper.

'Who's the little boy?' said Lewis.

He went over to the wall, as if he might climb right in beside him, and turned to face the projector.

The sunlit hives washed right over him. He shielded his eyes from the light.

'Who's the little boy?' he said again.

But the Bee King didn't answer – just pulled the rack back out and carried on and that particular slide was never seen again.

The heat of the projector filled the room with its own stifling climate. Its shaft of light picked out each dancing speck of dust. But just as the Bee King took care not to trouble the bees too often, every slide-show had at least one intermission to ensure the bright white bulb deep in the projector didn't overheat and it was during these intervals that the Boys heard their first bee stories, which, had they come from any-one but the Bee King, might have been suspected of embel-lishment.

The governor of the Bank of England, apparently, had a hive on the bank's roof in the heart of the City, so that the prudent bees stored away their honey just as their master stored away the gold in the vaults below.

Honey was good for coughs and burns and fevers. Royal jelly and propolis had between them more medicine than you'd find in any doctor's black bag. Even a bee's sting, apparently, would ease an arthritic joint – a fact which Aldred told himself he must remember to pass on to the Reverend Bentley.

Striking a pan with a metal key or spoon, as the Bee King had demonstrated soon after his arrival, was known as 'tang-ing', a traditional way of rounding up a swarm, which alert-ed the neighbours to the fact that their master was after them, and sent out calming vibrations which encouraged the bees to settle in a tree.

Pugfoist was just a weird old word for puffball, which could be sliced and fried like any mushroom, or dried and used to smoke the bees.

There seemed to be no end to the bee world's quirks and peculiarities and it was the Bee King's opinion that this, along with the meditative nature of bee-keeping, tended to attract the more solitary type. But one profession, he said, seemed to find bees particularly irresistible. He slid the rack into the projector and the sepulchral figure of a monk bent over an open hive was cast against the wall.

'Men of God,' said the Bee King. 'Monks . . . vicars . . . methodist ministers – all are drawn inexorably to the harem in the hive.'

Casting Aspersions

The villagers had always made full use of Nature's bounty – trapped rabbits, shot rooks and pigeons and stripped the hedgerows bare. But no matter how profound the war's privations, mushrooms and their close relations were always left well alone. Every fungal bloom was considered to be a danger, as if evil itself was slowly spewing up from the earth, and whenever the Five Boys went near them it was only to kick them into oblivion.

But the Bee King seemed to know almost as much about the dank world of mushrooms as he did about the sticky world of bees and on several occasions was spotted rooting at the roadside or foraging in the corner of some field.

One Wednesday lunchtime Howard Kent crept into the woods just above the village, to eat a little bread and cheese as a preliminary to getting his head down for half an hour. He sat and ate but sleep somehow failed to find him. He felt, in fact, peculiarly wide awake. He ate a little more to see if that might help – it didn't – and was becoming quite frustrated when he glanced over his shoulder and found the Bee King standing not twenty feet away.

'Mr Kent,' the Bee King called out. 'I'd like to ask a favour.'

Howard was used to being the one doing any spying and was not at all happy with things getting switched about. The Bee King strolled over to Howard, with a little trug in his hand.

'Can I borrow your knife?' he said.

The idea took a while getting through to Howard. He stared at his penknife. Its blade was still streaked with cheese.

'I suppose so,' he said.

The Bee King picked something out of his trug which looked, to Howard, more like a pickled egg than a mushroom and held it up between finger and thumb.

'*Lycoperdon pedicellatum*,' he said.

He took Howard's knife and cut into the puffball. The two halves parted in the palm of his hand. Its insides were as wet and brown as chewed tobacco.

The Bee King nodded. 'Sometimes you just have a hunch,' he said and threw the rotten mushroom into the nearest bush.

Howard held his hand out, but the Bee King seemed to be in no hurry to give the penknife back.

'It's a fine knife,' he said. 'Where did you get it?'

'Totnes,' said Howard Kent.

The Bee King had another look at it, folded the blade back into the handle and returned it to Howard. Then he took up his trug and slipped back into the trees.

By early June the Boys were released from the garden shed and would have been out among the bees a good deal sooner if they had only come up with the right attire. Aldred took along his old gas mask to one of their weekday meetings and pulled it over his balaclava, producing what appeared to be an airtight fit, but the Bee King demonstrated the ease with which a bee's sting could penetrate the knit of the wool. Heck was all for using heavy sacking. Finn twice turned up with his mother's sieves and colanders but could never quite work out what to do with them. It was Lewis who suggested using the cottage's net curtains and by their next visit the Bee King had got out his Singer and sewn them into shape. The Boys cut out cardboard brims for their caps to keep the bees away from their faces and from that point on, as long as they wore long trousers, they were more or less at liberty to go where they pleased.

They followed the Bee King from one hive to another like trainees accompanying a consultant on his rounds. Were so proud of their home-made veils that they took to wearing them around the village, which caused a bit of a stir. Lizzie Hathersage thought they looked like child brides and there was widespread concern at the idea of a grown man even owning a sewing machine, let alone knowing how to operate it. When news of the villagers' hostility got back to the Bee King he decided that the veils should only be worn around the garden, and after every subsequent session they were hung up in the kitchen beside his own straw boater, which went some way to placating the Boys.

Safely festooned beneath their veils, the Boys were free to observe the hives at the height of that summer's foraging – to watch the bees arrive, with their hind legs loaded with bright spots of pollen, and waddle into the shadows, whilst the bees ahead of them took flight again. One Saturday afternoon, having stripped a hive of all its supers, the Bee King drew the Boys' attention to twenty or thirty bees clinging to the side of the brood box with their backsides in the air. These bees, he told the Boys, were sending out a pheromone to guide back any bees disorientated by all the disruption. The bees seemed to have such a vocabulary of dancing and wiggling and special scents that Aldred sometimes wondered if he would be able to remember them all. But if there was any aspect of the bees' behaviour the Boys didn't understand they were expected to ask for an explanation, and soon they found that the Bee King's answers only confirmed what they had more or less worked out for themselves.

It wasn't long before they were allowed to handle the frames and shown how to turn them so that any uncapped honey didn't come pouring out. Hector was holding up a frame one day and studying the dimpled quilt which covered the pupae when the Bee King reached in, scratched away at the comb's surface and dragged out a small white worm between his fingernails.

'Wax moth,' he said. 'Not welcome,' and rubbed it away between his finger and thumb.

193

The Bee King was surprisingly nimble-fingered. Could nip a bee by its wings and turn it upside down, with its little legs wriggling, and point out its antennae, proboscis, sting and wax glands.

The ends of the Bee King's fingers were stained black, and Hector asked if it was the bees that caused it.

The Bee King shook his head and looked at them. 'They're printer's fingers,' he said. 'Stained for life.'

He once sneezed into his handkerchief, and as he was putting it back in his pocket a bewildered bee crept out of the folds and flew away. The Boys watched, open-mouthed. There might have been a quite rational explanation. The whole thing might have been some elaborate trick. But as far as the Boys were concerned the Bee King was able to sneeze bees into being and had his own small colony living inside him.

In the evenings they would sometimes sit out in the garden and listen to the steady hum of the bees' industry and breathe in the honey in full flow. The Boys learnt how the different sounds from the hive denoted different moods, different activities, and that each worker, far from being a mere gatherer of nectar or builder of comb, carried out a whole host of duties at various points in her short life – a nursemaid to the larvae, a sentry to keep out robber bees, a carpet-sweeper to keep the hive tidy, a punkah-wallah when it got too hot.

According to the Bee King, people used the hive as a model for whatever system or philosophy they happened to favour. A monarchist would see it as the epitome of royal patronage, a communist as the embodiment of the individual's willingness to devote himself to the state. But very few of these people, the Bee King said, had ever been anywhere near an apiary – wouldn't know one bee from another – and only an experienced bee-keeper could tell you whether the queen actually gave the orders or was just a prisoner in her own castle, carrying out the colony's commands.

When Lewis asked the Bee King what *he* made of the hive he said that, if anything, he preferred to see it as a numbers machine and the bees not as tiny bankers or foundry workers but as cogs in a vast arithmetical mill. 'Each frame is a living abacus,' he said. 'Eggs are constantly added and subtracted.' The colony was continually carrying out its own checks and balances. If a hive grew too crowded the queen swarmed, dividing the colony, to continue her arithmetic somewhere else.

The business of the hive, the Bee King said, was that of conversion: wax into comb . . . nectar into honey . . . eggs into larvae . . . pupae into bees. The colony's only concern was its own continuity. If they lost their queen the workers would take an ordinary egg, feed it regally and rear an heir to the throne. But whatever system one imagined operating in it, whatever philosophy one imagined motivated it, the hive was an entity in itself. To deal in individual bees was to miss the point. Left alone, the hive would regulate itself quite happily. Whatever questions arose were constantly answered, its problems constantly solved.

Whenever Lewis Bream raised his hand in Mrs Fog's classroom he was either bursting to go to the toilet or just plain stumped at what was on the board. He was not, by any stretch of the imagination, what Mrs Fog considered to be one of her brighter pupils, and when she saw his hand go up one afternoon during that summer of bees, with him in no evident hurry to leave his seat, she naturally assumed that she was about to be called upon to go back over the problem she had just set.

'Would you say . . .' Lewis said, then stopped and decided to come at it another way. 'Are you a monarchist, Miss, or a communist?'

Mrs Fog's blood ran cold. Her ears burned; her faculties failed her. The fact that such bile should come spouting out of a boy who was, ordinarily, little more than mute, only doubled its impact. It was as if Lewis Bream, one of the most timid, unexceptional children ever to stare up at her, had climbed onto his desk, yanked down his trousers and proceeded to toy violently with himself.

She was torn between fetching her cane and shaking the boy by the shoulders, but managed to recover herself, grab him by the ear and drag him over to Dunce's Corner, if only to give herself some time to come up with a more appropriate punishment. For the rest of the day she was badly flustered, and kept snapping her chalk on the board and losing her place in her usually seamless delivery. Lewis, meanwhile, stared into his little corner with all the dignity of a saint and when the end of the day came around, with Mrs Fog still no clearer and Lewis still not the least bit contrite, all she could think to do was write a note and send the burden of determining his punishment home with him.

Lewis spent the afternoon in Dunce's Corner, the note said, *after casting political aspersions on his teacher.*

As she tidied the classroom, her words kept coming back to her – not least the way she had referred to herself in the third person, as if this alone might provide her with some badly-needed perspective on the afternoon's events.

Back home, the note went back and forth between Lewis's parents, succeeding in confusing and upsetting them almost as much as Lewis had confused and upset Mrs Fog. Neither wanted a conversation with their son about politics, neither knew for certain what 'aspersions' were and in the end Lewis was summoned by his father, given a general dressing-down and sent to his room, where he lay on his bed and listened to the summer's evening going on beyond the curtains.

He could hear the birds fussing in the gutters and the mumble of the wireless coming up through the floor. He closed his eyes – he wasn't sure how long for – but was vaguely aware of the evening's shadows filling the lanes and when he heard his mother talking to a neighbour in the front garden he got up from his bed and opened the window a couple of inches to hear what she had to say.

She was at her wits' end, apparently. The end of her tether. She had a son with a head full of bees. Who talked earnestly about all sorts of nonsense. Who had even begun to *walk* in a peculiar way. And now, to cap it all, he had somehow managed to get that rock of a woman, that beacon of reason, Mrs Fog, in a flap.

The more she talked, the more she seemed to upset herself. Seemed to have not the least inclination to stop. She began to ramble. Started ranting – slurring. But ploughed on, getting louder and louder, until every last house in the street knew all her troubles and any remaining sense rolled back and forth, like a bottle on the deck of a pitching ship.

Lewis lay on his bed, wondering how much longer she could keep it up, when he heard a terrible shriek followed by the sound of splintering wood. There was a period of blessed silence, and Lewis pulled back the curtain to find his mother with one arm round Mrs Heaney's shoulder and her foot caught in the broken bars of the garden gate, like a rabbit in a trap.

A Cuckoo in the Nest

The intruder came at the Bee King's garden by an uncon-
ventional route, negotiating the beans, sweet peas and
chrysanthemums of the allotments, where the bees had been
foraging only hours before.

He stopped at the fence, up to his knees in stinging nettles,
and surveyed the cottage's silhouette – a solid block of stone,
with the Bee King sleeping somewhere in it and the moon
high above its chimney pots – then fed a leg through the
fence, found his footing and eased the rest of him after it.

He inched along the wall of the shed until he felt the lawn
firm beneath his feet then went straight over to the nearest
hive. Stooped beside it. Listened. Nothing but a low, per-
functory hum. Checked over both shoulders. Whispered a
few words, as if at confessional. Took a deep breath to steady
himself. Then raised his hand and brought it down hard on
to the hive.

The bees stirred. Roared up like an engine, but just as
quickly died away. The intruder looked at the hive.
Muttered a few more words to himself, shifted position.
Leant against the hive, embraced it and began to rock it from
side to side.

He was still shaking it when the bees burst out into the garden. Within seconds the night was flushed with them. And
their excitement spread from hive to hive like a contagion,
rattling all the other bees into action, until the apiary was
madness manifest.

He got to his feet, made for the gate, but wasn't halfway
there before the first wave of bees was on him. He stumbled
on for another yard or two before he fell. And as each bee
landed and unloaded its sting, it released a joyful pheromone,

which spoke profoundly to all the other bees. So that in a matter of seconds the intruder had a shawl of bees on him. Then a blanket. Then was utterly enthralled by them.

Marjory Pye couldn't think who to turn to. She'd contemplated running down the hill to Lillian Minter's and jumping on a train to go and stay with her sister, Flo. What got in the way was the fact that she couldn't muster the courage to open the lavatory door, in case the demon that had kept her cowering there since three in the morning came stumbling after her, waving its bandaged hands in the air.

She'd never considered the vicarage to be much of a sanctuary but it was one of the few houses visible through the hole in the lavatory door. The fellow in it, after all, was meant to have the whole weight of the church behind him.

She'd spent half the night cooped up in that wooden hut with nothing but a handful of chocolate limes she found in her overcoat pocket to keep some sugar in her blood. Had perched on the lavatory seat with her foot jammed against the door, and got up every five or ten minutes and peeked through the spy-hole to see if the coast was clear, but no matter how many times she looked it was never quite clear enough.

The day eventually broke, but with none of the fanfares with which daybreaks are often credited. It was, in Miss Pye's opinion, an almost painful procedure, in which the dead of night was slowly superseded by the dead of day. There was too much cloud for the sun to make any kind of entrance and there was not much birdsong to be heard, but when her path to the vicarage was finally bathed in a pale grey light she told herself that she simply *refused* to spend the rest of her life in an outside lavatory, pulled her coat around her and charged out into the day.

When the Reverend Bentley opened his front door he looked about as dishevelled to Miss Pye as she did to him. His quilted dressing gown might have cut quite a dash on a different fellow, but as far as Miss Pye was concerned he looked as if he had just jumped out of a window and brought the curtains along with him. She couldn't help noticing the couple of inches of rumpled long john tucked into his stockings and the fact that he wasn't wearing any slippers, but could hardly berate a man for his lack of decorum when she'd just hauled him out of his bed, and she'd bundled past him and was halfway down the hallway before he'd finished asking if there was anything wrong.

There were tears before and tears after, with great waves of emotion in between. But through all the upheaval, and the handkerchief clamped to her face, Miss Pye finally got around to articulating what it was she'd seen stalking the streets of the village and had kept her locked in her outside lav for hours on end.

'It was . . . a *mummy*,' she said, and buried her face back in her handkerchief.

She sobbed deeply for a while and when she finally managed to pull her hands down from her face it was only to thrust them out before her.

'Coming down the road,' she whimpered, 'with his arms out . . .'

She shuddered.

'. . . like mummies do,' she said.

She told the reverend how she had woken in the middle of the night with a bit of an 'upset' and had decided that a visit to the WC might set her straight. How she had crept downstairs, got her coat, tramped out into the garden and locked the door behind her, only to spend the next five minutes watching the moths flit about her lamp. She had given up, she said, and was about to open the door when, out of nothing but modesty's habit, she peeped through the spy-hole and beheld a mummy limping down the lane.

The reverend shifted in his armchair.

'And what was he up to?' he asked.

Miss Pye stared out of the reverend's bay window.

'Walking,' she said, as if she could still see him. 'Walking about as if he owned the place.'

The reverend nodded. Picked a speck of lint from his sleeve and examined it. 'And did you happen to see where he was headed?' he said.

Miss Pye raised an arm and pointed it feebly towards the window. Her finger followed the mummy's journey around the vicarage walls, step by monstrous step, until the Reverend Bentley himself swung into her sights and a look of even greater horror filled her face.

'Good God,' she said and started choking. 'The graveyard . . . He must have been going back to his *tomb*.'

As she wept, the reverend considered his options. He was well aware that he was meant to be a comfort to his parishioners rather than the cause of their distress, but there was simply no knowing into whose parlour the woman might next be spilling her tears.

'Miss Pye,' he said, 'I have a confidence I should like to share with you.'

She looked up at him from behind her crumpled handkerchief.

It was possible, the reverend informed her, that a man in his position might make a behind-the-scenes representation.

Miss Pye wanted to know what a 'representation' was.

'A *representation*,' he went on, 'which would put an end to these little . . . walkabouts.'

There was a moment's baffled silence.

'How?' she said. 'How can you do that?' Her face suddenly slackened. 'You *know* him?' she said. 'You *know* the *mummy*?'

The Reverend Bentley nodded, which only conjured up in Miss Pye's mind a vision of the vicar and the mummy, side by side, at the bar of the Malsters' Arms.

'But you must promise,' the reverend insisted, 'not to mention this incident to a soul. Or we'll have the whole village in a state.'

Whatever state the village threatened to get itself into was,

Miss Pye felt, never going to amount to more than a fraction of the mortal terror she had recently endured, and nothing would have given her more satisfaction than having some of her horror spread about the place. Besides, secret-keeping went against everything she stood for. Her village Post Office was the clearing house for every scrap of tittle-tattle worth the name. How on earth was she meant to keep a mummy to herself? It was enough to make a woman burst.

She looked up. The reverend's eyes were on her.

'No more mummies?' she insisted.

'You have my word,' he said.

Over the years the reverend had noticed that, when a troubled parishioner was offered a way out of an apparently inextricable predicament, they would often experience, at the very brink of release, an irresistible urge to turn and remind themselves of the torment which was about to draw to a close. So it was with Miss Pye. As the Reverend Bentley escorted her to the front door she stopped and looked him in the eye.

'The mummy . . .' she said, before the words snagged on her emotions. 'He had flies buzzing all around him.'

The reverend rested a hand on her shoulder and gently encouraged her towards the door. 'I know,' he said. 'I know.'

The Reverend Bentley had managed to keep a great tide of pain at bay by solemnly promising to return his attention to it just as soon as his caller was out of the way, and as he crept back up to his bedroom it suddenly took him at his word. A nauseous heat flooded through his body. He felt feverish, pestilent. The teaks and mahoganies of the bannisters and the hall's grand panelling were a jungle, and by the time he slumped onto his bed and peeled away his socks and long johns he was halfway towards delirium.

His hips, usually as skinny as a monkey's, looked as if they'd been packed with marbles. His knees were so tautly bloated they were almost elephantine. The flesh around both wrists was solid and senseless and his ankles looked like old Mrs Mornay's, which spilled over the tops of her shoes.

When he held the palm of one hand over his misshapen shoulder he could feel the heat coming off all the stings which were buried there. He had been invaded – hardly recognised himself. And during that first malarial morning there were times when it was possible for him to observe his own unfamiliar body and witness some of its sensations without being wholly involved in them. Then all at once the cadaver was returned to him, the pains and rages re-erupted and all the nerves and senses crackled back to life; agonies which could last for minutes or even hours – certainly long enough for him to imagine that they might have no end.

When Aldred had first mentioned the curative property of bee stings he had dismissed it, but the idea must have taken root for, a week or two later, the reverend turned up what appeared to be confirmation in a book from the library by a fellow called Lippincott. If he had known how much pain he would have to endure from the bee stings in the hope of relieving some of the pain of his arthritis he might have thought twice, but planning his raid on the hives the previous evening his only worry had been how to expose his joints for the bees' attention whilst protecting the rest of him.

He considered cutting holes in an old pair of overalls, but the only pair he could find were so baggy that they would have filled up with bees in no time at all. He thought he might scoop up a couple of pints in a jug and administer them in the privacy of his own backyard, but the possible hitches in this and, indeed, every other scheme easily outnumbered the points in their favour and vexation was setting in when he had a rush of blood to the head.

He found a couple of old bedsheets in the linen cupboard and began ripping them into strips. Took off his trousers and wound them round his legs. Did the same with his arms and torso, taking care to leave a slight crack in the binding at his hips and knees and wrists. For a man who had trouble with his knife and fork, all the tearing and the fiddling with the scissors and safety pins was a fuss he could have done without. His only comfort came from the fact that he had had the foresight to go to the lavatory before he began.

The whole venture was almost scuppered at the very last minute when he realised that he had made no provision to protect his eyes. He sat in his armchair, bandaged up to his neck, cursing, as the temperature slowly rose. Salvation finally arrived in the form of a pair of spectacles which had belonged to his mother and, once they were bound up in the bandages, created two windows to hide behind. They reduced everything to a blur, which was something of a blessing, but obliged him to walk with his arms out in front of him.

As soon as the first few dozen stings were in him his regrets came thick and fast.

'That's enough,' he said. 'Enough.'

But the bees wouldn't stop and when he fell to the ground he was convinced he would never get up again.

At the Memorial

Considering how rarely the Bee King was to be found around the village and the speed with which he usually moved, Aldred was a little surprised to come across him standing by the church noticeboard, studying a poster for an auction of agricultural equipment.

'Badly set,' said the Bee King, without turning. 'Badly printed. Some people take no pride in their work.'

Aldred stared at the poster and nodded as if he understood what the Bee King was talking about. Then he led him over the road and showed him the bullet-holes in the war memorial. Told him all about the Focke Wulf coming up the valley and how he and the evacuee had had to jump into a ditch.

For a while they just stood and looked at the memorial. Aldred asked the Bee King if he had ever visited Cleopatra's Needle. The Bee King said that he had, many years ago, which Aldred found absolutely staggering, and said that if *he*'d ever visited Cleopatra's Needle he'd be going around telling everyone in sight. He privately wondered what the chances were of the Bee King's visit having coincided with that of his father. It was quite possible, he thought, that the two of them could have stood side by side before that great monument, just as he and the Bee King now stood before the war memorial.

He watched the clouds creep by behind the tip of the obelisk and asked the Bee King if he happened to notice any names on the Needle.

'What sort of names?' said the Bee King.

'Well, the men who drowned in the Bay of Biscay,' said Aldred. But the only thing the Bee King remembered seeing on the actual monument was hieroglyphics.

Aldred withdrew into a deep meditation, until the Bee King asked if he knew what hieroglyphics were. He had to admit that he didn't. Hieroglyphics, the Bee King told him, were an ancient language – a way of writing using pictures instead of words. Aldred wanted to know what sort of pictures they were talking about and the Bee King said he seemed to remember there being a couple of lions on the Needle somewhere, as well as several honeybees.

Neither spoke for a minute, but when the Bee King noticed Aldred looking at the tablet at the base of the war memorial he asked if he'd known any of the men whose names were cut into the stone. Aldred bent down. There were two lists – one for each of the two great wars – and he placed his finger on the more recent one. Drew it down, over the names' bevelled edges, until it came to rest on the words 'Bernard Crouch'.

'Is that your father?' the Bee King asked him.

Aldred nodded.

He said he used to think that the bones of the men on the memorial were actually buried beneath it. But that he now knew that not to be the case. And when the Bee King asked where his father was buried Aldred explained how he had died defending the pyramids and that he now had his own tomb among them, somewhere down Egypt way.

On the Road to Calvary

The man from the ministry was hunched right over his steering wheel. When he wasn't staring out through the windscreen he was glancing down at the map on the passenger seat. Getting lost in the lanes around Duncannon should have been one eventuality he could have foreseen, but with each baffling mile he became more and more frantic and after each gear-change his finger returned to the map's lanes and contours with less and less certainty.

The blood-red arterial roads were far behind him and even the yellow B-roads had trickled away. The maze of lanes in which he'd got himself tangled was so faintly marked, so insipidly coloured, they barely seemed to exist at all. A single signpost would have given him a hook on which to hang some hope. But if there had been road signs he'd be dozing back at his desk in Whitehall instead of driving ever deeper into the wilderness.

The hedges continued to narrow around him and the lanes began to incorporate such uncompromising bends and fearful gradients that the next time he found himself in first gear he decided to stay there and kept his finger glued to the map, even though that finger was now as thoroughly disorientated as the rest of him.

Miss Minter was picking wild garlic from the hedgerow when the car came lurching down the lane. It pulled up and the occupant wound down the window. He looked deeply agitated and lifted his hat to reveal a bald head, covered with a sheen of sweat.

'I've lost my bearings,' he said. 'You wouldn't happen to know a Platt's farm, would you?'

'Well now,' said Miss Minter. She wasn't quite sure how to

break the news to him. 'I'm afraid Mr Platt died a month or two ago.'

'I'm aware of that,' he said, which made Miss Minter wonder what a bald little man was doing calling in at the homes of dead farmers.

She had a good look at the fellow and thought she detected, beneath all the upset and anxiety, the same arrogance as the type who were always getting themselves lost just before the Americans arrived.

'Are you from the ministry?' she said.

The man from the ministry's mouth dropped open. He nodded.

'You've still not replaced my letter box,' Miss Minter said.

He tried to wince with genuine regret. 'Different department, I'm afraid,' he said.

Miss Minter kept her eyes on him. 'And I don't think that rat-catcher ever got paid for all his poisoning,' she said.

The man from the ministry hadn't a clue what the mad old trout was talking about, but did his best to look even more contrite.

'Different department again,' he said.

By the time he pulled up in Platt's farmyard it was well past mid-afternoon. He hadn't had a bite to eat since breakfast and, at this rate, wouldn't eat again until he got to Plymouth that night, so to be met by a man whose face was so profoundly involved in a meat pie and whose shirt bulged out between his waistcoat and trousers like an unmade bed, stirred up in him all sorts of resentment before he'd even turned the engine off. The man with the pie heaved himself off the bonnet of his own motor, ambled over and laid a proprietorial arm across the roof of the man from the ministry's car. He peered inside. Looked at the dashboard, the upholstery, the fittings and finally the driver, as if he was about to make him an offer.

'I believe we said two o'clock,' he said.

'I do apologise,' said the man from the ministry. 'I lost my way.'

The man with the pie straightened up, tossed the crust into the bushes and brushed the crumbs from his hands. 'Well, it gets me out of the office,' he said.

The man from the ministry dragged his briefcase off the floor and emerged, backside-first, into the yard. The air was fresh – excruciatingly so – and when he stretched he could feel his drenched shirt drag across his back. He asked his companion to lead the way.

'The executor called us in for a valuation,' said the pie-man, as they stepped between the dried cowpats. 'We've got the sale on Thursday week.'

When he reached the barn he paused and let the man from the ministry catch him up.

'Personally,' he said, 'I reckon someone dropped a file down the back of a cabinet up at your place.'

'It has been known,' the man from the ministry said.

One of the hinges on the barn door was broken and it took both men all their strength to heave it back. The sunlight flooded in as if a curtain was being opened and illuminated several hundred signposts, all lying on their side.

'Hell's teeth,' said the man from the ministry.

'Yes, indeed,' said the other man.

It was like the site of some terrible slaughter – an elephants' graveyard. The signpost nearest them still had a clump of dried red earth attached to its base. The sign at the other end read,

HARBERTONFORD $3\frac{1}{2}$ m
DITTISHAM 5 m

and pointedly assuredly up at the roof.

The man from the ministry shook his head as he gazed across the fallen signposts. 'You found no paperwork,' he said.

'No, sir,' said the auctioneer. 'You neither?'

'Not a jot,' he said.

He had a momentary vision of someone trying to locate every last junction from which these signs had been uprooted – saw the nightmare of that afternoon's journey multiplied a thousand times.

'How are the locals coping without them?' he said.

'I shouldn't think they mind a bit,' said the auctioneer.

The man from the ministry took a few tentative steps into the barn. Some of the posts were rotten. Some of the signs had been removed and stacked against a wall like roof tiles.

'I think Mr Platt must have used some of the timber for fencing,' said the auctioneer. 'You probably passed some on your way in.'

This seemed to settle things with the man from the ministry. The auctioneer was standing a yard or two behind him but could see him slowly nod his head.

When he turned there was a look of resolution on his face. 'Do you think you could get rid of them?' he said.

'I'm sure of it,' said Jessie Braintree.

'We wouldn't want to see them turning up,' he said.

'Of course not,' Jessie Braintree said.

Dexter Fadden was only too happy to work out of doors after nightfall. He regularly removed fish which were under strict instructions not to leave the river and was forever pouncing upon the animals along its banks. On certain evenings in particular public houses he could be found negotiating the sale and exchange of some of those creatures unfortunate enough to have crossed his path – the Morleigh Arms on a Monday night could be as ripe as a menagerie – and, like most men round about, he kept an open mind when it came to offers of unusual but well-paid work.

Raybe's pig had first fired up his enterprising spirit and his commissions since had included all manner of surreptitious removal and delivery, but none was quite as strange or, frankly, strangely sinister as that offered him by Jessie Braintree, the auctioneer. It took him all of Tuesday to hack the signs off and most of Wednesday just to stack the posts. By the time he'd finished the blisters on the heels of both hands were as thick and white as raw potato. It was, he thought, an odd sort of butchery, hacking away the names of all those villages which were so familiar, but he kept it up and the floor of the barn slowly emptied until all that was left was a covering of sawdust, like a circus ring.

Jessie showed up in his van on the Wednesday evening and helped Dexter load the dismembered signs. The posts, Jessie said, would be taken care of by a third party, and when Dexter dropped him off at his house Jessie handed him an envelope, told him to be careful and sent him on his way with a slap on the back of the van.

Dexter found the field down by Bow Bridge where he was to dump them without any problem and left the van's engine running so that the headlights lit the scene. Most of the smaller signs were wooden, with the names chiselled into them, but some of the bigger ones were cast iron, weighed a ton and made a terrible clanking sound when they went into the hole. Dexter couldn't help but think of the effort that must have gone into those signs' creation, and as he carried each load from the van and threw it into the pit it rubbed him up the wrong way to be showing someone's work such scant respect.

Jessie had told him to be sure to shovel at least a couple of foot of earth over the signs – had said that he'd be round to fill the hole in the following morning but didn't want anybody finding them in between. Dexter was getting enough money to understand the consequences of not doing the job properly, but as he dug his shovel into the mound of earth, threw it into the darkness and heard it clatter over the signs, he had a terrible feeling in his stomach, as if he was somehow burying the villages along with their names.

He'd once heard a story about a gardener who kept putting name-tags next to his plants and vegetables, only to find them gone the following day. The plants weren't touched but their names went missing. This went on for months and nearly drove him round the bend. Years later, when a chimney was being swept in a derelict cottage nearby, all the missing tags came tumbling down into the grate, with a jackdaw's nest on top.

Dexter wasn't sure what the moral of the story was. He wasn't even sure why it had come to mind. But he couldn't help thinking that, at some point, perhaps in hundreds of years' time, somebody was going to come across all these road signs and wonder what on earth had been going on.

Samson's Lion

By the time the Bee King added cake-baking to their curriculum the Boys' defection was just about complete. As far as they were concerned, the food heaped on their plates at home in the evening was only going to take up space better filled with butterfly buns and macaroons.

It seemed their mothers had long been neglecting their confectionery duties. They might produce the occasional stiff, grey pie or brick-like fruit loaf, but these hadn't a chance against the Bee King's incredible strudels, and the longer the Boys spent in his company the more keenly they felt their years of neglect.

By mid-summer, mealtimes hung heavy with resentment. The Boys pushed their food around their plate and looked forward to the chimes of wooden spoons in mixing bowls. But just as the Bee King had gradually introduced them to the business of bee-keeping he now slowly revealed to them the mysteries of baking a cake. Showed them how to sieve the flour to lighten the mixture, how to fold egg whites into a meringue, how to sink the blade of a knife into a sponge to see if it was ready – how to clamp a hot tray with a tea towel without burning your hand. And as they learnt, the Boys unwittingly began to collaborate. Whilst one was rolling out the pastry another would be greasing the scalloped moulds of the baking tray. They cracked eggs, measured milk and pressed out pie lids until they were dusted from head to toe in flour and began to appreciate all the brushing and crimping necessary for their pastries to look properly bronzed and ornamented when they were finally turned out onto the wire racks.

After their first few sessions the Boys took their cakes out into the garden, but so many inquisitive bees came up from the hives that it became a necessary custom for them to eat indoors, then retire to the garden with their mugs of milk, just as gentlemen retire after dinner to drink port and smoke cigars. One evening, the Boys were lounging on the back steps and congratulating each other on a particularly successful Genoa cake when Hector noticed a bee buzzing around the Bee King, as if carrying out some reconnaissance, before finally landing on his cheek and locking on to a fleck of icing sugar at the corner of his mouth.

The Bee King didn't seem the least bit bothered – just let the bee work away at the sugar and continued what he was saying when it took off again. He took a sip of his tea. That bee, he told the Boys, would now be back at her hive telling her fellow-workers all about her little discovery.

'And how does she tell them where to look?' he asked the Boys.

'The waggle dance,' said Hector.

The Bee King nodded, and within a minute a dozen bees were circling his head, like tiny planets around their sun.

That particular incident reminded the Bee King of the story of Plato, who apparently had a bee land on his mouth when he was a baby, bestowing on him his gift for sweet talk later on in life. Several other poets and philosophers allegedly found their vocation under similar circumstances.

The Bee King seemed to know every last bit of bee lore and the Boys couldn't help but notice just how much of it seemed to be tied up with death. Bees were regarded either as death's harbinger or a talisman against it. If there was a death in a bee-keeper's family each hive had to be told and shrouded in black for the period of mourning or the bees would abandon the apiary, prompting Lewis to say that, despite the white hives and veils, a bee's favourite colour was probably black – and cited the dark insides of the hive, the black of the funerals and the black pram he imagined the baby Plato in when the bee kissed him on his lips.

If the most frequently requested slide was of the man straining under the weight of a bee beard, by far the most popular bee story was that of Samson, another strongman, who had lived in biblical times. The weather seemed to have been a good deal warmer back then – Aldred always pictured Samson strolling through the olive groves in nothing but his sandals and swimming trunks – and if the story's particulars tended to vary with each telling, it was due to the Boys' insatiable appetite for detail as much as the Bee King's tendency to digress. The bare bones of the story, at least, were always much the same . . .

Samson was walking down a country road one day, minding his own business, when a lion leapt out and blocked his path. The lion evidently hadn't heard of Samson's strongman reputation or his deadly temper, and was such a trouble-maker that it went out of its way to pick a fight with him.

Samson was happy to oblige – thought a little exercise would do him good. So he and the lion began scrapping and wrestling and stirring up a great cloud of dust. The fight must have lasted for several hours, with man and lion trading blow for blow, but when the dust finally settled the lion lay flat on its back, as dead as a doornail, which was a lesson to bullies of all shapes and sizes about biting off more than they could chew.

Samson dragged the dead lion to the side of the road, brushed himself down and continued his journey, as if this sort of thing happened to him all the time. He was away for a few weeks, but the next time he went down that same road he kept an eye out for the lion's carcass. And when he came across it he found it inhabited by a colony of bees and that the lion's ribcage, which had been picked clean by the vultures, was now packed with honeycomb.

He was a little peckish and, not being frightened by a few bees, helped himself to some of their honey. Then he went on his way again and forgot all about the lion and the bees until, a few weeks later, when he found himself in the company of his sworn

enemies, the Philistines, who were fanatical gamblers, and he
bet them some clothes and a few sheets that they couldn't tell
him where 'meat came forth from the eater' and 'sweetness came
forth from the strong'.

It was always a big disappointment when the Philistines
managed to solve the riddle, and even though Samson went
on to have further adventures, including having his hair
shorn off, his eyes put out and pulling a temple of Philistines
down around his ears, as soon as the bees and the lion's carcass were out of the way the Boys' attention began to wane.

All five Boys were very fond of the story, but Aldred in particular seemed to take it to heart. Riddles, he saw, were like
locks and keys. The right combination of words turned the
chambers and opened doors. And whilst he knew that the
answer lay with the bees in the lion, he was convinced that
another, more complicated riddle was tucked away somewhere.

One Wednesday evening, as they waited for an apple
turnover to cool, he asked the Bee King if he would write the
riddles out for him, and where he might find them in the
Bible, and later that evening he took the key from its hiding
place and slipped in through the back door. He lit a candle
and as he crept past the organ, shielded it with his fingers,
imagining the three flames the Ecclesiastical Insurance
Company was always warning him about. He climbed the
steps up to the pulpit. The Bible sat on the lectern, as if the
whole church had been built around it. He held his candle
up, unclipped the big brass clasps and began hauling the
pages over.

He managed to track down Judges without too much trouble, and the Bee King's coordinates led him straight to the
passage with Samson in. As usual, some of the Bible's words
were in the wrong order and others were too old-fashioned
to make any sense, but Aldred persevered.

Vengeance, it seemed, abounded. Samson smote his enemies hip and thigh, and once used the jawbone of an ass to 'slew a thousand men therewith'. Other slewings and smitings were recorded and Aldred noticed how they were frequently preceded by Samson calling on the Spirit of the Lord to come mightily upon him. He found the passage with the Philistines and the riddles but the jumbled syntax and the ancient words kept getting in the way, and no matter how many different ways he came at it, the hidden riddle refused to reveal itself.

He shut the Bible and crept back down the pulpit stairs. Blew out the candle and slipped into the night. Walked right round the church and was returning the key to its hiding place, with his hand deep in the wall of the porch, when he saw a light go on in an upstairs window at the vicarage and the Reverend Bentley come limping in. Now, even if he'd not wanted to watch the little show unfolding before him Aldred would have found it difficult to get away. So he flattened himself against the porch wall and watched and told himself that he'd go home just as soon as the opportunity arose.

The Reverend Bentley slipped off his dressing gown, sat on the edge of his bed and stared at the floor for a couple of minutes. When he looked up Aldred was sure that he'd been spotted, but the reverend gazed right through him, then turned, reached out to a bedside table and picked up a small porcelain pot. He removed the lid, dipped his fingers in it, pulled up the leg of his long johns and began rubbing whatever lotion or potion it contained into his knee. He rubbed some into his hips and wrists, some into his shoulders and ankles. Then he put the lid back on the pot and stretched out on the bed.

He lay so still that Aldred thought he must be praying. Either that or he was the kind of person who could fall asleep at the drop of a hat. He watched, mystified, for several minutes. Thought he must just have witnessed some sort of holy self-anointment, with frankincense or myrrh. But Aldred was lying in his own bed an hour or so later and entering something like his own state of spiritual grace when the revelation eventually came to him.

He had been contemplating the Spirit of the Lord coming upon Samson prior to him smiting his enemies, and had tried to imagine what form such a Spirit might take. And in that moment the key turned – the riddle was revealed and answered. The bees were the lion's Spirit. They gave the lion its roar.

The Waggle Dance

The Reverend Bentley did his best to keep his bee stings secret. He pulled his shirt cuffs down over his wrists, preached in his slippers, and the only thing anyone noticed was a faint whiff of antiseptic in his wake.

For the best part of a week his body was just a sack of pain. When the swelling finally subsided the thousand agonies gave way to one all-consuming itch. On the Thursday, he found that he could get in and out of bed without groaning. Three days later he found he could touch his toes. He went over and stood before the mirror. Touched his toes again.

'Good heavens,' he said.

He started taking a stroll up the hill before breakfast and, if he was feeling up to it, would sometimes have a bit of a canter on the way back down. The next time he was in Totnes he bought a pair of plimsolls and got into the habit of rising early every other day, pulling on his old cricket trousers and heading off on a half-hour run.

On a couple of occasions he bumped into the Bee King, who he naturally assumed was out mushrooming. The second time they met the reverend asked if he was having any luck, but the Bee King just nodded and strolled right past him. The reverend couldn't help but notice that the canvas bag he was carrying rattled as if it was full of chisels, and that the fellow was covered in dust.

Phyllis Massie was at the sink peeling potatoes one afternoon when someone started hammering at the door. She went down the hall, wiping her hands on her pinny – couldn't decide whether to take it off or leave it on – and opened the door to find Marjory Pye doubled up on her doorstep, trying to catch her breath.

'Phyllis,' she said, her chest heaving. 'You'd better come along.'

Considering her size, Marjory Pye could fairly motor. Phyllis did her best to keep up with her, but was plagued by visions of a son tangled up in a harvester and a husband gored by a bull.

The Captain had been the first to see the Five Boys dancing. Had watched them assemble by the war memorial, like boy scouts preparing for a five-mile hike. They hopped from one foot to the other and talked with great excitement until the Bee King arrived, climbed up onto the base of the memorial, made a brief, inaudible announcement, then climbed back down.

The Boys spread out in a circle and the Bee King stepped into the middle. He took Lewis by the hand, the two of them stood and positioned their feet. Then they set off together, stride by measured stride.

When Mrs Heaney left the Post Office a couple of minutes later the first thing she saw was Lewis Bream skipping. Then she saw the Bee King and the other Boys watching and clapping along. For a while she just stood there, wondering what they were up to, and by the time Marjory Pye popped her head out of the Post Office the Boys were all stamping and clapping as the Bee King guided Hector Massie through a couple of turns.

Mrs Heaney glanced over at Marjory Pye. 'What do you make of that?' she said. Then Marjory was off, galloping up the road towards the Massies', clutching her cardigan to her chest.

Mrs Heaney put her basket down to enjoy the entertainment. It seemed the Boys were learning the steps to two quite different routines, one of which tracked back and forth along a circle's circumference, whilst the other was more like a figure-of-eight. The Bee King led each boy through each of the sequences until they had enough confidence to carry on alone, and soon all five of them were hopping and jigging about like little morris men.

When Marjory Pye returned with Phyllis some of the Boys had taken off their jerkins and the Bee King had them knotted round his shoulders, like an umpire at a cricket match. Hector was shuffling along like a puffer-train and for a while the Bee King shuffled along beside him. When he was happy that he'd got the right idea he gave him a little pat and sent him on his way.

Phyllis Massie was dumbstruck. All she saw was her son wiggling his hips and strutting up and down the place like Carmen Miranda and the old man rubbing his hands with glee.

Miss Pye was right beside her. Saw her tilt her head back on her shoulders and let out a terrible howl.

The dancing and clapping sputtered to a halt. The spell was broken. The Boys looked over to see what all the fuss was about. Hector's mother just stood there in her pinny. It was Aldred who finally spoke.

'It's all right, Mrs,' he said. 'We're just learning to *waggle*.'

'Like the bees,' said Lewis Bream.

Phyllis rocked on her heels for a second, like a skittle, then suddenly threw herself into the fray. Grabbed her son by the arm and began dragging him away, keeping an eye on the Bee King the whole time, as if he might try to snatch him back.

'*Evil*,' she whispered, as she retreated. 'You *evil* man.'

The other Boys watched as Hector and his mother disappeared round the corner. The whole thing left a bitter taste in their mouths. For a while they just stood and looked at each other. Then they shrugged and started dancing again.

That evening Phyllis Massie and some of the other women carved out their own little circuit around the village's lanes and alleys, calling at every door and telling the whole sordid story – the bucking, the bottom-wiggling, the bare-backed dancing and how the Bee King had picked up each boy in turn and carried him on his knee.

Once they were party to the facts everyone agreed that the only option was to stop the Boys ever seeing the fellow again. And the next morning the parents took the Boys aside and told them, in no uncertain terms, that their friendship with the bee-keeper was at an end. The Boys seemed to accept the decision with surprising equanimity and within days the village had returned to something like its old order. But beneath their triumphalism the Boys' mothers and fathers had the nagging sense of a victory too easily gained.

Extraction

The Boys hung from the fence and watched the Bee King in silence. Watched him strip the hives, stack the supers, put the roofs back on the brood boxes and carry the frames into the shed. And when he pulled the door to they slipped through the fence, gathered at the window and stood there looking in on him as he'd looked in on them a matter of weeks before.

He took down a long knife, dipped it in a bucket of hot water and sliced the caps off the honeycomb. Loaded the frames into a metal drum and began cranking it up. Wound the handle so hard he seemed to summon up every flicker of a bee's wing that had gone into the honey's creation and the Boys began to fear that the shed would take off, with their beloved Bee King inside.

The next day they watched him filter the honey, then bottle it. Watched him clean the steel tanks and stack the empty boxes away. The hives had lost half their height. The shed was full of honey. Then the Bee King walked up through the garden and disappeared into the house.

It was six months since Steere had ploughed the rats up. Since then he'd fixed most of his fences, relaid the walls, trimmed his hedges and just about got his house back on its feet. He'd cleared the ditch at the bottom of the old meadow, let it drain for the best part of a month and was out on his tractor, with two-thirds of it turned already and his dinner clearly in sight.

Working a couple of acres would have been a full day's work before the tractor's arrival, but nowadays any man who could drive and keep a straight line was capable of covering five times that amount, without taking a step. When old man Pearce had pulled up on his Massey-Harris in '37 the whole village came out to have a look. The children patted its wheels and the older men circled it. The thing was a spotless monster. Looked as if it belonged in a laboratory rather than out among the elements.

'Good God, man,' said Steere to Pearce. 'You're going to have to be a mechanic on top of everything else.'

He'd got his own Allis Chalmers a couple of years later. During the war every farmer was encouraged to mechanise. But Steere still found it a tremendous novelty to be sitting up off the ground and working the levers instead of staring up some horse's behind.

The ploughshare turned the earth in four unbroken ridges, which came up raw and sodden, like Christmas pud. But when, about an hour before he was due to finish, he felt it snag on something, he heard a 'Whoa' instinctively come up out of him, even though there wasn't a horse in sight.

It wasn't the blade-busting 'clack' of a boulder. The front wheels never threatened to leave the ground. But there was something down there and once he stopped, Steere turned and looked over his shoulder and let the clutch back out, nice and slow. He crept forward an inch or two and saw some string or twine go taut between the blades. And as he let the clutch out a little more, the body came up out of the ground. Heavy, with its head slumped to one side, and the string tangled round its neck and hands bringing it up into a sitting position, like one of the Captain's ships being pulled into place.

The Bee King Takes His Leave

The sky was thick with stars and the lanes were empty when the Bee King stepped out of his house. The only sound, apart from his footsteps, was the Gladstone bag in his right hand, which gently jangled, like a milkman's crate. He went along the top road, turned down Gant's Lane by Mrs Heaney's, but when he reached Lewis's cottage he slowed down, looked up at the windows and dragged his feet, so that the loose stones caught beneath them and made a grinding, rattling sound.

At the bottom of the lane he turned right and headed towards the high street. When he passed the Crouches' house he slowed down and dragged his feet again then carried on, turning right just below the Captain's cottage and heading up towards the church.

He crossed the road, turned into Far Bank and followed the lane around the back of the graveyard, past the Massies' and the Noyces', then headed back into town. The whole walk took no more than five minutes but was carried out with all the formality of a sacred ritual, and its figure-of-eight managed to incorporate each of the Five Boys' houses, like the Stations of the Cross.

As he went by, the Five Boys stirred beneath their blankets. Slipped from their beds, found their dressing gowns and slippers and tip-toed across the bedroom floor. Eased open the windows, hung from gables, climbed down drainpipes and softly dropped to the ground.

The Bee King was waiting by the war memorial and when all five boys were finally gathered in he set off up the hill, with the sky still hours from daylight, and the boys padding along behind.

The river was flat and wide and silent and looked no more than ankle-deep. The Bee King's oars barely broke the surface, yet the trees and meadows crept steadily by and the banks unfolded down either side. The sky was locked onto the river. The land had slipped its moorings and headed back towards the moors. The water was polished with moonlight. Every clank of the rowlocks carried across it. Every whispered word.

The river unravelled. An occasional cottage stole by among the foliage, as grey as a gravestone. The Boys huddled on the boat's cross-pieces and the Bee King rowed them effortlessly out on the tide. Three miles down, the banks receded and the river became as wide as a lake and as he rowed the Bee King told the Boys how, in Egypt, the bee-keepers stacked their hives on barges and followed the seasons up and down the mighty Nile, travelling by night and releasing the bees in the morning to feed on all the blossoms along the riverside.

The Boys dozed. Dittisham went by, dark and silent. Dartmouth was tiered and terraced along its own valleys and creeks. The town came right down to the water. The river narrowed where the last of the ferries crossed it, then opened out into the sea.

The sky showed the first traces of daylight and the smell of salt water stirred the Boys. The world was waking. The water began to lift and fall beneath them. And as the Bee King finally began to work the oars the sun rose over the bay.

Lester Massie was dreaming that he was bellringing – was ringing the bells when he was just a boy. But even as he dreamed he slowly tumbled towards consciousness. And as he came up through sleep's last fathoms the one thought which accompanied him was just how badly that bell of his was being rung.

His wife's half of the bed was empty. The sheets were all in a heap. He got up, pulled on his trousers and went down the stairs. Found the front door wide open – called out but got no reply.

The sun was up; the day had gone ahead without him. Was already well on its way. The whole village seemed to be milling around the war memorial, with just that one terrible bell carrying on.

As he headed towards the crowd he saw Sylvia Crouch sitting on a doorstep. She lifted her face from her hands. Her cheeks were wet with tears.

'What's the matter?' he said.

'Oh, Lester,' she said. 'The Boys are gone.'

Half the day went by in panicked agitation. Lester Massie cycled out along the Totnes road, peering over the walls and calling in at the houses. Alec Bream went down to Miss Minter's, then on to Duncannon to see if there was any sign of them there. Jem Hathersage went round all the Boys' hiding places and made himself hoarse calling out their names. Every path and track leading out of the village was followed until those following them couldn't remember what they hoped to find.

Arthur Noyce found himself down by the river and knocked on the door of the boathouse. Old Tom stood on his doorstep, as bewildered as ever.

'Is his boat there?' he said and tried to look down the side of his boathouse.

'Whose boat?' said Arthur Noyce.

'The chap who keeps the bees,' said Tom.

It took over an hour for Arthur to round up the other fathers. The Reverend Bentley and the Captain had been checking the allotments and volunteered to join the search party; Howard Kent insisted on doing so. When they gathered by the boathouse there were seven of them in all but by the time they managed to commandeer a couple of rowing boats and push them out onto the river it was already late afternoon.

Jem and Lester took an oar apiece in one boat whilst Howard rowed the other on his own. The tide was turning against them and they struggled down the river for twenty minutes before Alec Bream suggested that each boat stick to one bank – a suggestion which the others pretended to have been so obvious as not to have been worth mentioning – but found it difficult to see more than twenty feet into the woods, and for an hour ploughed on without a single reason to raise their hopes.

Howard Kent loathed the woods. He loathed the river. He had never been to Africa but this was how he imagined it to be. The mad chatter in the trees; the sudden bristle in the branches. The untold procreation going on in the dark.

From its perch high up on a leafless branch a heron cast itself forward, lurched over the river and settled in a tree on the other side.

'This isn't England,' thought Howard. 'This isn't England at all.'

Goodnight, Children

It was a long hard climb from the beach to the cliff-top. The Bee King headed off up a path which zig-zagged precariously between rocks and boulders, the Boys followed, and when they reached the top they sat and looked out over the water in their dressing gowns like convalescents at some mountain retreat.

For the rest of the morning the Boys played tag in and out of the gorse bushes and by midday lay asleep on the grass, dreaming of boats and rivers and Egyptian bees. When they woke the Bee King was sitting among them and they propped themselves up on their elbows and watched him open his Gladstone bag. There must have been a couple of dozen jars of honey in it – gold-lidded and pristine, like the haul from a bank robbery. He picked a couple out, unscrewed their lids and placed them on the grass. Broke some bread and handed it out. Then they all sat around, dunking their crusts in the honey, bringing them streaming up to their mouths and lifting the jars to look in at the crumbs suspended there.

In the late afternoon they did some waggle-dancing, listened to a few stories and sang a song or two. But when the sun began to head towards Start Point they crept into the bunker and began to settle themselves in for the night. The Boys had never been inside a pillbox. Outside, its walls had weathered, like the rocks around it, but inside it was cool and dry. For a while the Boys kept watch at the narrow windows and picked off imaginary Germans, but as the light faded they faded with it and slowly slumped to the floor. The Bee King had fired up a paraffin burner, and the Boys kicked off their slippers and warmed their feet at it.

229

All six had their own wall to rest against and the Boys were gazing at the burner's flame and growing drowsy when the Bee King reached into his bag and produced a Golden Syrup tin. It was exactly the same as the one they'd sent flying over the roofs of the village and the ones they'd seen in the Bee King's shed. He lifted it up to his ear and gave it a rattle. Then he brought it into the light of the burner and the Boys shuffled forward to have a look.

'What do you see?' said the Bee King.

The Boys stared at the label.

'Is it a lion?' said Harvey.

The Bee King nodded.

'Is it Samson's lion?' said Aldred.

The Bee King nodded again and the Boys suddenly saw that the speckled cloud hovering above the lion was the colony of bees they'd heard so much about.

A horseshoe of tiny words was printed beneath it and as the Bee King inched his finger across them the Boys read them out.

'*Out of the strong came forth sweetness,*' they said.

The Bee King took a coin from his trouser pocket, slid it under the lid and prised it open. The Boys squeezed forward. He reached in with his finger and thumb.

'*Perpetua,*' he said, holding it up, then offered it to Aldred. He dipped his fingers back into the tin.

'*Campanile,*' he said and presented it to Finn.

Basalt, Onyx and *Stygian Black* were handed out to Hector, Lewis and Harvey. Then the Bee King put the tin away, put his hands together and rested his cheek against them.

'Sleep,' he said.

A Door into the Mountain

All the men took turns at rowing, each doing his best to out-row the one before. But after a couple of hours they were spending most of the time bent over the oars, trying to catch their breath, as the tide gently pushed them back to where they'd just come from.

The air was hot and ripe under the trees. They kept getting tangled in the roots and branches, and when the stifling heat became unbearable they rowed back out into the open water and all the midges and mosquitoes accompanied them. For the first few hours they called out from one boat to the other, if only to confirm that they had nothing to report, but by the time they were halfway down the river hardly a word was spoken and they all just stared at the woods as they crept by.

They pulled in at every shack and hamlet along the way without a scrap of encouragement, and as the sea began to loom in their minds the men became more and more desperate. Who was to say, said Alec Bream, that the boat they were after hadn't gone *up*stream, and that with every stroke they weren't putting another yard between themselves and their boys? Arthur said that Old Tom had been quite insistent that the bee-keeper always set out downriver, but as Jem Hathersage pointed out, Old Tom would sometimes have difficulty telling you what year it was.

They had no luck until they were all the way down at Dartmouth and the ferryman confirmed seeing a boat full of boys go by, first thing. He couldn't say whether they headed east or west when they reached the sea, but the fact that he'd seen them at all was enough to raise everyone's spirits and put some power back into the oars.

231

When they crossed the bar they headed east and followed Kingswear's jagged coastline, investigating every inlet, and the sun was almost down before it occurred to them that one boat should have gone west, by which time all they could do was blame one another for the oversight.

No moon rose and soon they were having trouble seeing where they were going – could hardly make out the waves breaking on the shore – and decided to land for the night. They had no food or drink. They just pulled their jackets around them and lay down on the pebbles. Then tossed and turned until first light.

Within the hour they were back out on the water, then heading west past the river's mouth. They heaved away, half-asleep and hungry. The Captain couldn't stop thinking of all that water beneath him and how little timber was keeping the two of them apart. Then Lester Massie suddenly got to his feet and threatened to tip the boat over.

'There,' he said and pointed to a boat, abandoned on a stretch of sand.

They rowed in with the waves. Dragged their boats up onto the pebbles and gathered round the abandoned boat. There were no discarded slippers, no dressing gowns. They tried to imagine their boys and the Bee King sitting in it. Howard Kent stepped forward, picked up an oar tucked under the gunwales. Brought the handle up to his nose and took a long, deep sniff. He turned triumphantly to the other men.

'Honey,' he said.

It was Jem Hathersage who found the path. He set off up it and all the others went scrambling after him. It seemed to have no end. But they kept on, from rock to rock, kicking the dust up into each other's faces and sweating and cursing, until they finally stumbled out into the sky.

They stood panting and looked around. The place was deserted – just rock and gorse and the cold blue bay behind and far below. The sun was up now and Alec Bream had a sudden, sickening feeling that it had brought into being an evil, lamentable day. There was something wrong, he thought. He turned to Lester, but Lester was pointing again.

'What's that?' he said.

One by one, the men picked out the hexagonal pillbox tucked into the hillside, and Lester was already on his way towards it when he saw the smoke seeping from the slits in its sides.

'God, no,' he said.

Then all the men were running towards the pillbox. Lester got there first but couldn't find a way in. Ran round the bunker, screaming. The rock was solid – was sealed shut. He put his face up to one of the windows but fell back, choking on the thick, sweet smoke.

It was Jem Hathersage who finally found the door round the back, among the bushes. He barged in, waving the smoke away with his hands. Found the Boys, slumped in a circle around the Bee King's burner. All five of them in their gas masks, with a frying pan in the middle.

One of the Boys lifted a fork from the pan, with a blackened lump speared to the end of it, and with the other hand pulled the gas mask away from his chin.

'Pugfoist,' he said.

The Five Boys sat on the grass with their gas masks pushed back on their foreheads and their fathers coughing and spluttering by their side. The Boys seemed perfectly happy. Seemed to be quite enjoying themselves.

Lewis still had the fork in his hand. He took an ostentatious bite of the mushroom, then offered it to Harvey but Jem Hathersage had been watching them and suddenly couldn't contain himself.

'Christ Almighty,' he said and snatched the fork from him. 'You're like a bunch of fucking girls.'

The other men turned and looked but Jem wasn't the least bit bothered. In fact, he was feeling better than he'd felt in days and was beginning to wonder how much better he might feel if he was to give the boys a good hiding and beat the bee-keeper right out of them.

The Reverend Bentley was shielding his eyes and looking over towards the gorse bushes.

'There he is,' he said.

The men turned and found the Bee King standing in the distance, watching.

'What the hell's he up to?' said Lester Massie.

The Bee King didn't move for a while. Then slowly brought his hands up to his mouth.

'Mr *Kent*,' he called out. 'I'd like a word.'

Howard was suddenly conspicuous among his peers. He looked at the others and shrugged his shoulders.

'About that boy,' the Bee King shouted. 'That boy Steere found in his field.'

The Bee King now had Howard's undivided attention. All the blood seemed to drain from his face. And as the others watched, he began to walk towards the Bee King.

'Who do you answer to, Mr Kent?' the Bee King called out.

Then Howard was running.

'Whose laws do you obey?' the Bee King said.

Howard raced across the grass but the Bee King just stood and waited. Just stood stock-still, as Howard charged towards him – until he finally arrived and threw himself at him and the two of them flew back into the gorse.

The Bee King seemed to crumple in Howard's embrace. His coat seemed to suddenly empty. Then the gorse was gone and the sea flashed far below.

Howard fell. Hit the rock-face twice. Heard something snap. Slid, flailing until he managed to grab a hold of the rock. Hung there.

'Help,' he screamed.

His left arm dangled off him – wasn't working. His feet were scrambling about. When he looked around to try and find a way out he saw that the whole slab of rock had been worked and chiselled, like one vast headstone – was covered with words.

'Help,' he screamed again.

A figure appeared high above him and Howard called out to him. But the Bee King just stood and watched him tiring on the stone.

'That boy,' the Bee King said. 'He had a father.'

Howard could feel his strength failing. He looked at his hand and saw how his fingers clung to the rim of the letter 'O'. He glanced to his right and saw 'THOU SHALT DO NO MURDER' stretching away.

His fingers slowly betrayed him. The sound of the waves swept up from below. The other commandments began to slip beneath his fingers. Then he fell, and this time fell all the way.

Telling the Bees

Jessie Braintree's first impression when he stepped into Howard Kent's cottage was that the contents weren't likely to raise more than a couple of quid. The sunken sofa and the ancient dresser were barely standing, and all the rugs had paths worn through them from Howard's daily routine.

Jessie went round all four rooms, making notes on the back of an envelope – turning the key on the wardrobe door, with some trepidation, and lifting the mattress on the old brass bed. He went out on the landing, opened his stepladder and popped his head up into the loft. Didn't expect to find anything but a few old rags, but when he turned his torch on, saw a great glittering stash of treasure packed between the joists.

Miss Minter's hinges and handles were there, along with Steere's window latches. The letter boxes of Duncannon were piled up next to a stack of collection plates. It gave Jessie Braintree such a shock he nearly lost his footing – could easily have fallen and broken his neck. But as he told his wife that night just before they put the light out,

'It was amazing – like a regular Aladdin's cave.'

The day after the Boys returned to the village Aldred woke early. He dressed, crept out of the house and left his mother sleeping. Went and stood beside the war memorial. The Captain's house and the church seemed almost unfamiliar – seemed nowhere near as solid as they had done a few days before.

He walked up the hill to Askew Cottage, slipped down the alley and into the garden. The hives were all still there, the bees still went about their business, but the cottage was as quiet as the grave. Aldred crept over to the first hive the Bee

King had introduced him to and bent beside it. Listened to all the tiny cogs turning inside.

'Howard dead,' he whispered. 'The Bee King's gone.'

He stayed and listened for a while, then went over to the next hive. Told them the news. And by the time he reached the last one it seemed to Aldred that the apiary was almost silent – almost still.

He sat on the steps. Took his handkerchief from his jacket pocket and picked out the tiny charm the Bee King had given him in the pillbox two nights before. It looked like something from a broken typewriter – a small metal tablet, smooth on one side, with a single letter on the other, reversed, standing proud of it.

'Perpetua,' he said out loud.

He placed it against his tongue. The metal was cold and he could taste the ink's bitter residue. Then he put it on the back of his hand and pressed down hard, until he could feel the metal dig into the nerves and bones. When he pulled it away it left a distinct indentation, faintly inked, of the letter 'A'.

The Reverend Bentley met the coffin at the church gates and led it slowly back up the path.

'*I am the resurrection and the life, saith the Lord,*' he said. '*He that believeth in me, though he were dead, yet shall he live . . .*'

The same four men carried Howard Kent on their shoulders as the day of the pig memorial. The rest of the village came shuffling along behind. A solitary bell tolled high above them and slowly drew the mourners in.

They carried the coffin into the church and laid it on the trestles. The Reverend Bentley climbed the steps to his pulpit and the mourners filed into the pews. When everyone was settled the reverend read a couple of psalms – one about how 'man walketh in a vain shadow' and another all about destruction and 'children of men' – then Aldred pumped out Mr Mercer's rendition of 'The Lord is my shepherd' and the congregation groaned along.

The reverend cleared his throat. It was his belief, he said, that when we depart this world we each deserve a moment's consideration, no matter what sort of life we have led. Then he said a few words in which he sought to draw attention to some of Howard's finer qualities, without dwelling too long on all the rest.

After one or two prayers, the coffin was lifted back onto the pall-bearers' shoulders and the reverend led it out into the sun. And once the church was empty Aldred helped Mr Mercer to his feet and they joined the stragglers making their way over to Howard's grave which was newly dug, with a clean, white headstone and a mound of earth at a respectful distance, waiting to go back in.

The hole itself was considerably deeper than Aldred had imagined and when the reverend nodded and the coffin was lowered into it he had to stand on his tip-toes to see where it ended up.

'Man that is born of a woman hath but a short time to live,' the reverend said, 'and is full of misery . . .'

The villagers stood and stared into the pit. The reverend's words were unrelenting and some of the mourners were beginning to wonder how many more were still to come, when the sky suddenly darkened and the bees came sweeping in.

They poured over the graveyard in one great wave. A bristling cloud, which rolled and turned above the treetops as if stirred by an Almighty hand.

An awful drone sawed through the air. An insect heat descended. And the graveyard rattled with a million wings.

As the villagers watched the bees began to settle – began to gather in the trees around the grave – until every inch of bark was coated and every branch was draped with them.

The sky was crystal clear. The drone receded. The bees shimmered on the trees. Nobody dared move – nobody except Will Henderson, the undertaker, who leant over to the reverend.

'*Forasmuch as* . . .' he whispered.

The Reverend Bentley turned and stared blankly at him.

'*Forasmuch as* . . .' Will Henderson whispered again.

The reverend seemed to come to his senses. Lifted his book and tried to find his place.

'*Forasmuch as it hath pleased Almighty God,*' he said, '*of his great mercy to take unto himself the soul of our dear brother here departed we therefore commit his body to the ground* . . .'

Aldred stood with Mr Mercer's hand on his shoulder. He looked down and managed to find a clod of earth not far from his foot. He got his toe behind it and nudged it forward. Heard it strike the coffin. Saw it spill across its lid.

The bees let out a great roar and rose up in a rapture. The sun was obscured again. Then the bees rolled and turned above the grave, drew themselves together and swept off down the lane.

Acknowledgements

Peter and Cathy Kiddle were my unpaid rural consultants on this book – an inexhaustible source of local knowledge and hospitality. Their home became my West Country HQ.

A one-day bee-keeping workshop by Cathy Maund in the mid-90s first alerted me to the potential in the beehive. More recently, Stephen Kelly let me accompany him on his rounds, resisted my ignorance with grace and ultimately encouraged me in my own tentative efforts at keeping bees.

Charlie Bellingham, Len Collict, Jean Hadley, Stanbury Hocking, Jean Parnell, Robert Tucker, Bert Ward and Pam Wills were all generous, informative and hugely entertaining. My conversations with them were the highlight of the writing of this book.

Bill Sanders, Marion Huang and Carol Stevens know a thing or two about bell-ringing. Any sense of authenticity in that department is to their credit, any flaws or inconsistencies are mine.

Thanks to the staff of the library and sound archive at the Imperial War Museum, to George Lovell for his religious instruction and Charles Boyle at Faber for his endless patience.

Most of all, heartfelt thanks to Derek Johns, Jon Riley and Cath Laing who, over the years, have given me more support, good advice and guidance than any writer has a right to expect.

M.J.